HARD HART

THE HARTY BOYS, BOOK 1

WHITLEY COX

ISBN: 978-1-989081-10-5

For Laura Malo and Janna Gisler.
Two badass chicks I am honored to know.

CHAPTER ONE

"COME ON!" Krista Matthews screeched as she hammered her palms on the steering wheel of her dark green 1993 Toyota Tercel. "Start, you motherfucker. Starrrrrrrt!"

She turned the ignition off and then on again, but the car did nothing besides groan and sputter and trick her into thinking it was going to start.

Fuck!

The clock on the dash told her she was going to be late. She glanced up at the elderly man coming out of the house in front of her. Nearly bent double, poor Mr. Geller was nearly ninety, and he still refused to use a walker.

Said his cane was just fine, even though the way he hobbled down the wet gravel driveway toward her said he should probably be in a wheelchair, not just using a walker. He lifted his cane and tapped on her window, rain dripping down over the hood of his forest-green rain jacket.

"Mornin', Constable. Battery?" he asked with a smile.

Krista blew the dark red curls off her forehead and nodded. "I think so."

"You need me to jump you?"

Oh, Mr. Geller, if only you were a few decades younger and not married to Mrs. Geller, I'd be all over that.

The twinkle in his soft gray eyes said he was fully aware of his innuendo.

Rolling her eyes with an amused chuckle, she nodded.

He toddled over to his beat-up old Ford. Within seconds, he had pulled it up in front of her car and was popping the hood. She did the same with her vehicle and watched as he deftly hooked up his truck to her car. He craned his head around her hood and gave her a drippy-faced nod.

Praying, with eyes shut and crossed fingers, Krista turned the key one more time.

Thank the elderly landlord, it worked. The car was alive.

It was alive!

Mr. Geller slammed her hood shut moments later and gave her a wave, telling her to *git* as he knew she was probably already late for work. She waved back at him with a big, thankful smile and was on her way up the driveway toward the station.

Fifteen minutes late for work, soaking wet from the run from her car to the police station, and with an earache that seemed to be a direct result of that nasty wind that had picked up overnight, Krista poured herself a cup of coffee in the breakroom at six fifteen in the morning. She prayed her partner and mentor had called in sick.

No such luck.

Today was not her day for luck.

She smelled him before she saw him. Heard him before she felt him. That disgusting body spray he seemed to bathe in. And the laugh that managed to make all the other women at the detachment swoon. To Krista, he just sounded like a creepy clown getting ready to peel off her face. It didn't seem to matter how many times she turned him down, declined his advances or politely but firmly told him no; he still thought he could wear her down and she'd sleep with him or, at the very least, grab a drink.

Like it was some rite of passage to have sex with your superior when you became a cop, or at least a female cop. She knew that it wasn't. He was making shit up. Using every lame reason in his arsenal to get into another rookie's pants. But so far, nothing had worked. No man had been in Krista's pants in quite some time, and no way in hell was she ending her dry spell with Myles Slade, king of the douchebags.

Three of them had started at the detachment around the same time, all of them women. Only Krista was left on Myles's list of women to vanquish. To cajole and coerce into his bed. So it made sense why he was so interested in her. She was the last one. He needed to get her into bed to complete the hat-trick.

Barf!

Both Wendy and Marlise hadn't gone into too much detail about their time with Myles; in fact, neither of them wanted to talk about it at all. They just shrugged it off. Said it was a night after drinks at the bar and that the man held their futures, their careers, in the palm of his hand, including making their rookie lives a complete nightmare. It was just easier to put up, shut up and move on.

The man made Krista sick. He literally made her head hurt and gut churn the moment he walked into a room. And it was as though he had some sixth sense about where she was, because Myles always managed to put himself between her and a doorway. Managed to position himself between her and escape.

"Ready to go?" he asked with a disgusting purr to his voice, coming up behind her, popping her personal space bubble with his body.

With flared nostrils, a grunt of disdain and rolled shoulders, she turned away from him. He'd only been in the room for half a second, and already he had her feeling uncomfortable and claustrophobic. She hated that he'd manipulated his way into being her trainer. She missed Janice.

"Yep," she piped, determined not to let him see her flinch. He always got mad when he thought she was deliberately avoiding him, and then enraged when she'd turn him down. Only instead of taking the hint that she wasn't interested, he'd press on as though she were simply playing hard to get and treating it all like a game. While in reality, where Krista lived, it was anything but a game.

He'd gone so far as to request to train her, and since he seemed to have the staff sergeant wrapped around his finger, Myles got away with pretty much anything, and Krista was stuck with the predator as a mentor.

"All right." Myles rubbed his hands together, a maniacal gleam in his eye. "Well, move it. We want to get a move on. We're going to go patrol the highway later today. Set up a roadblock for a bit and maybe a speed trap. Write some citations." He went to smack her butt, but at the last second, Staff Sergeant Wicks walked by, so he let his hand travel past her hip and land on the table.

"Everything okay in here?" the staff sergeant asked, wandering into the small staff kitchen.

"Everything's just peachy, *sir*," Myles said with a serpentine smile. "Matthews and I are on highway patrol today. Friday at four o'clock on a weekend is sure to nab us a few speeders." Myles was all grins. It didn't help that he looked like one might expect a serial killer to look. And not like the type of serial killer that hides in a dark alley or storm drain and uses a machete to hack their victims into tiny bite-size pieces.

No.

Myles Slade was the kind of serial killer that was handsome. His smile was almost too big and too perfect for his face, and his features were masculine and sharp. Tall and blond with square shoulders and a round face. It was easy to see why several the women at the precinct fawned over him. And his cheeks held that forever rosy glow, liked he'd just come in from the cold outdoors.

But none of that mattered when you looked into his eyes. They were the eyes of a predator. The eyes of the devil. So brown they were almost black. You couldn't see the pupil—ever. Not even in a dim room or under a lamp could you find the pupil. It ceased to exist. More often than not, Krista found herself turning away from his stare, avoiding eye contact at any cost, because the longer she held his gaze, the more it felt as though Lucifer himself was staring back at her. Soulless, vacuous holes—demon eyes.

"Good, good." Wicks chuckled. His eyes briefly flicked to Myles, and Krista almost missed it, but there was a hint of what looked almost like unease there before he masked it with a big smile. "All right, well, be safe out there." And with a nod and smile so fake not even the coffee maker was believing it, he left the room.

———

"Is this everything for you?" the teenybopper with overdone eye makeup behind the checkout asked. "You managed to find everything you were looking for okay?"

Brock Hart grunted, nodded and tossed cash onto the counter and then, without even waiting for the receipt, headed out the door to his big black pickup truck. Why was he so angry about a burned-out headlight? It happened to everyone, and yet for some reason, the inconvenience of it had him seeing red.

Though if you asked those closest to Brock, they'd all say the man only seemed to see the world in various shades of red. And not the rose-colored glasses kind of red. More like the "I hate the world and everyone in it" kind of red.

He pulled out of the parking lot and gunned it onto the road, hitting the highway in no time, where he really let the rage inside flow. Weaving in and out of traffic like a Formula One driver.

Horsepower and metal his to command. The windshield wipers were on full bore and the roads were slick from the sudden rainstorm. They still had a week or so left of summer, but fall seemed to be rearing its ugly head early.

He noticed the speed trap up ahead easily enough. Enough cars had flashed their lights as a warning, so with another grumble, his big size thirteens applied pressure to the brake before he tossed on the cruise control.

Snorting, he shook his head. She was right out in plain sight, way, way up ahead, radar gun pointed directly at oncoming traffic. Anyone coming toward her would see her and have time to slow down before she got a read on their speed. Heavy rain and gray sky be damned, she was easy to spot.

Must be a noob.

She stood on the side of the road with her hip cocked and the radar gun pointed directly at his truck.

Better luck next time, sweetheart.

Then she waved him over.

What the fuck.

He glanced behind him. She couldn't be waving him over. He was going the speed limit. Had been for the last eight seconds. But when he looked back, she snagged his eye and pointed at him. Directly at him, ordering him to pull over.

What the fuck. He'd never been pulled over before.

He slowed down and pulled over, bringing his window down in the process, ready to educate her on her error, when he came face to face with sex in a uniform. All dark red hair tucked up into a nononsense bun and the most piercing blue eyes he'd ever seen. And the body, holy jeez, if she looked half as good out of her uniform as she did in it, any man privileged enough to take her to bed wouldn't last long.

Where the fuck were these thoughts coming from?

"Good afternoon, sir. License and registration, please." Her voice was like smooth chocolate, but there was also a slight tremor to it.

Did he make her nervous? Was this her first ticket? Was he going to pop her ticket cherry? He handed her his license and then dug the registration out of the glove compartment.

"Do you have any idea how fast you were going ... *Mr. Hart?*" she asked, the shake still in her voice and now in her hands as she continued to avert her eyes and read over his information.

"In fact, I do. I had the cruise control on."

Her head snapped up from the registration, and her perfect little mouth widened. "You did? How fast did you have it set at?"

"The speed limit ... of course."

She grabbed the radar gun out from under her arm and studied it intently, as if it were a piece of scripture and she was trying to quickly commit it to memory. Brock raised his eyebrows patiently, getting a kick out of how clearly flustered this little champion for justice was getting.

She appeared cold. Water dripped off the brim of her hat and tips of her lashes, and her cheeks burned a bright pink. He remembered cold, wet nights out in the field on missions. All was well until his underwear got wet. Once his drawers weren't dry then he was a more miserable fucker than normal.

She narrowed her eyes and looked back up at him. "I'll be right back." Then she stalked off toward her patrol car, his license and registration still in her hand.

All part of the scare tactic. Make 'em sweat.

Brock knew the drill.

Not that he'd ever been pulled over before, despite his need for speed, but he'd been in the passenger seat enough times with friends who were pulled over to know she was going to take her sweet-ass time coming back.

She hoped to come back to a truck where a frazzled driver waited. Ready to confess that he had indeed been speeding, had jaywalked yesterday and may or may not have a dead body in the back of the cab.

But Brock Hart was no ordinary man.

No ordinary driver.

It took more than being pulled over for speeding and waiting for a cop—a hot cop no less—to rattle his nerves. So instead he simply watched the headlights of the oncoming traffic and the rain bead down the passenger window in meandering rivers.

To his surprise, she didn't make him wait. Within three minutes, she was swaying her saucy little hips back to the truck, a smug smirk on those sensuous lips.

She glanced down at his license and then back up at him. Yeah, he didn't look at all like his picture. His buzz cut had grown out a bit, he had what his mother called "a permanent five o'clock shadow" on his jaw, and his face had filled out a bit. That picture felt like a lifetime ago. Taken just days after he'd returned from his final mission overseas. The only thing that would never change were his green eyes.

She squinted at him and then back down at his driver's license again. "You may not have been speeding, Mr. Hart. It would appear I mistook you for the car behind you, but your headlight is out and that's a"—she began filling out the citation on her citation pad —"sixty-dollar fine." She licked her lips and swallowed a few times.

He smiled, a real rarity for him, but for some reason this woman pulled it from him. "All right, but just so you know, generally, a blown headlight usually results in a verbal warning, at the very most a written warning."

Her head jerked, and she nearly dropped her pen. "You a cop?"

He shook his head and shrugged. "No. But I know how it goes." He enjoyed the dash of red that raced across her face. "Plus, I'm heading home right now to go change it." He grabbed it off the passenger seat and held it up. "This is the new light right here. And if you issue me the ticket, I can just dispute it in court once it's fixed."

She looked like she was about to puke. "Did you keep your receipt?"

"Yes."

A big ol' lie.

She puffed up her chest, pushing her breasts toward him, and he couldn't stop himself. As hard as he tried to keep his eyes on her face, he let them fall to the name plate on her chest for just a second, *Constable K. Matthews*. She caught him looking and made a noise in her throat, which forced his eyes to fly back up to hers. Her jaw was clenched firm, and the flush that had been snaking its way up her neck and cheeks now worked its way into her hairline. The woman was the color of a poppy.

"Listen, don't tell me how to do my job. Yes, a warning is typical, but if I want to issue you a fine, I will."

He liked her fire.

He bit the inside of his cheek. He was determined not to smirk if it killed him. "Sorry, officer."

She huffed, a little bit of wind appearing to have re-entered her sails. Her blue eyes glowed in an oncoming headlight. "Just get out of here ... and it's *constable*." The last part was whispered so low he could hardly hear her. She handed him back his information and, without looking back, headed toward her car.

Brock shifted in his seat, the half-chub in his pants twitching uncomfortably against the zipper of his jeans.

Well, that was weird.

For some strange reason, as he pulled back out into traffic, he felt lighter, less angry. The red in his vision was less scarlet and more of a burnt orange, kind of like Constable Matthews's hair ...

CHAPTER TWO

"ANOTHER BEER?" Mickey asked.

Brock nodded.

"So, how's your mum?"

Mindlessly shelling a peanut, Brock tossed the husk onto the bar in front of him before popping the nut into his mouth and nodded. "Good, good."

"Maisie's been meaning to call her. Misses their stitch and bitch since she broke her wrist."

Brock grunted. "How's her wrist?"

Mickey's light-blue eyes twinkled. "Hasn't slowed her down much. She's still in the garden every day, still cooking. Only thing she can't do is stitch, and it's killing her. Had plans to make each of the grandkids a quilt for Christmas. Doesn't look like that's going to be happening."

Brock snorted and nodded for the umpteenth time when Mickey slid a fresh draft in front of him.

"Tequila, please," came a strong, feminine voice beside him.

Brock glanced up from where he'd been studying the condensation on his beer glass, only to see a mass of red curls plop down beside him, followed by the sweetest, most beautiful smell. Honey-suckle, maybe? He really had no idea. He only knew that he liked it.

Mickey poured an ounce of tequila, placed a lime wedge on top and set a shaker of salt with the drink in front of the mystery redhead. She did the ritual of salt, shot and lime before wiping the back of her wrist across her mouth and asking for another.

Brock lifted one eyebrow at Mickey. But the Santa Claus-looking bartender-slash-surrogate father just snorted, smirked, shrugged and poured the lady another.

"Hope you're not driving, sweetheart," Mickey said as he brought up a bowl of limes and placed them in front of her.

She tossed back the second shot and shook her head. "No. I'm a cop. Wouldn't dream of it. I'll cab or walk if I have to."

That voice.

She's a cop.

Same one?

Couldn't be.

Brock glanced next to him, but all he saw was curls. Had the cop's hair been the same color? He couldn't remember. That wasn't something he normally paid attention to. He knew she was a redhead. A hot redhead. But was this the same cop? There had to be other redheaded cops on The West Shore. But then what was she doing here in Fern Valley? The West Shore was a good twenty minutes from here.

Finally, after what felt like ages of inconspicuous glancing at the woman next to him, waiting for her to move her hair or turn her head slightly, she reached her pale, slender hand up and tucked a wavy strand behind her ear.

It was her.

"Another one, please," she said, lifting her head at Mickey.

Brock chuckled to himself. Had the little copper had a rough day? Only sorority girls and people looking to forget their day slammed tequila the way Constable—shit, what was her last name again?—was.

"Rough day?" he asked.

She grunted as she licked the salt off the back of her hand. "You could say that." She downed the shot and popped the lime into her mouth before turning to face him. And damn if those bright blue eyes didn't double in size from surprise. She sucked the lime into her mouth by accident and began to choke.

Stifling yet another smile and the urge to laugh, Brock swung his arm out and began pounding her on the back with his palm. "Y'all right, *constable?* Gonna live?"

Squeezing her eyes shut, she coughed the lime into her hand, reached for the tall glass of water Mickey had placed in front of her after shot number two and chugged it, all the while glaring at him over the rim as she drained the water.

"What on earth are you doing here?" she asked, coming up for air and once again wiping the back of her wrist across her mouth.

"Same as you."

The corner of her sexy little mouth lifted. "Drowning your sorrows?"

"You have sorrows?"

She let out an exhausted sigh and nodded.

"You should probably eat something if you're going to continue slamming back the drinks the way you are," he said.

"Yeah?" She sneered. Brock wasn't normally the kind of guy interested in chit-chat, but for some reason he wanted to know more about this lively little cop, despite the fact that the vibe she was throwing his way said "leave me the fuck alone." "You going to buy me dinner?"

"I can," he said smoothly. "After all, it's the least I can do after you let me off with a warning this afternoon ... *Constable ...* "

"Matthews."

Right.

"Constable Matthews."

She squinted at him. "Thanks ... uh ... "

"You don't remember my name, do you, constable?" He chuckled again, grabbing a menu and pushing it in front of her. "Pick something. I'm buying."

She rolled those striking blue eyes and opened the menu. "Deluxe burger with bacon, mushrooms and extra pickle."

Brock caught Mickey's eye and held up two fingers. The bartender nodded.

"Do you remember my name?" Brock probed again, scooting his barstool just a tad closer to hers.

"I pulled over *a lot* of people today. Issued *a lot* of citations. I can't remember everyone's name."

"Brock Hart. And you're Constable K. Matthews. What does the K stand for? *Kantakerous?*" His chest and shoulders bobbed at his own mirth and, as hard she was trying to fight it, because that was obvious, a bubble of a laugh leaped from her throat.

"Krista," she whispered, raising her eyebrow and nodding at the bartender when he asked if she wanted another shot.

"You live around here?" he asked, rolling her name around in his head and deciding it suited her.

She nodded. "You?"

"You live around *here?*" he asked in surprise, ignoring her question. "Doesn't a cop's salary pay well enough for you to live ... I don't know, *not* around here?"

She lifted one slender shoulder and shrugged, thanking the bartender when he placed another shot in front of her. "I grew up in a small town. On a dirt road, out in the middle of nowhere. This is home to me. I'm not used to the big-city life. I like peace and quiet. I like the idea of having bears and deer in my backyard. Plus, I'm a rookie. I make peanuts."

"Bears?"

She nodded. "They used to raid our apple trees all the time."

"Do you rent some property around here?"

"I rent a basement suite in a big house on a chunk of land a few kilometers or so down the road."

Mickey ambled over and plopped two big, beautiful greasy burgers in front of them, the plates piled a mile high with thick, wedge-cut fries. Krista's eyes went wide, and he smiled to himself at her childish glee. The burgers were awesome. She had a right to be impressed.

Brock reached forward and took a bite of a still-steaming fry. "Eat up, otherwise you won't be able to walk home given how much tequila you've just slammed back."

She shot him a surly glare but dove in anyway. "And I plan on having more."

The bar was located pretty much out in the middle of nowhere in a municipality known as Fern Valley, which was part of the Greater Victoria area. Not far, but at the same time far enough from the prestigious and comely homes on Prospect Lake. This part of town wasn't exactly where doctors and lawyers were buying their 1.2 million-dollar homes. It was more where rednecks parked their double-wides and drove their pickups into the bushes for burial when they stopped working. But that suited Brock just fine. He liked his solitude and the quiet. And the seedy dive bar located in the middle of the middle of nowhere was half his. He'd co-bought it with Mickey when the old guy retired, and Brock served as a silent partner. He checked in and handled the business side while Mickey managed the staff and tended bar. It was a biker bar, a redneck bar, but it was home, and Brock liked it.

He watched in the mirror behind the bar as Krista chewed her food slowly, a small, sexy smile on her face. She closed her eyes and hummed softly. Jordy in the kitchen always made a killer burger. Brock's taste buds were just as happy as Krista's. And fuck what he would give to be that burger right now, rolling around on her tongue and in her hot little mouth.

"So, *Brock Hart,* if that's your real name?" she finally asked on a swallow. "Where do *you* live?"

A smile jogged on his lips as he methodically chewed his fries. "Around here," he finally said. "Walking distance."

"Stumbling distance?" She snickered, digging into her own fries. "'Cause that's what we'd do, stumble there. Or at least me. That tequila's hit me hard. Good call on the food."

Brock didn't say anything. He simply studied her face. She had a tiny bit of mustard at the corner of her mouth that he wanted to wipe, lick, or suck off for her. Preference on the latter.

"You want to get out of here?" he finally asked.

"I ... uh ... "

He lifted one shoulder cavalierly and then shoveled fries into his mouth before taking a healthy sip of his beer to wash it all down.

She eyed him curiously before nodding at Mickey for yet another shot. "I had an awful day," she said quietly. "I'm drinking to forget."

"Did you have to stand out in the rain and issue tickets all day?" he asked, his volume matching hers. He drained his beer and lifted an eyebrow at Mickey for another.

She nodded but then shook her head. "I didn't issue any citations. And then there was a fatal accident on the highway we had to deal with."

"I'm sorry," he said. "Those are never easy."

She shook her head again. "No, they're not."

It seemed like she was avoiding his gaze on purpose now, swirling her last remaining fry around and around in a big puddle of ketchup until it was limp and covered in red. "I don't want to be a traffic cop," she finally managed to whisper. "I didn't want to be out there. Besides you, I pulled over two little old ladies and didn't have the heart to cite them."

He snorted. "Yeah, my dad was a cop, said it was tough when

he'd have to pull over a car for speeding only to find a wrinkled little blue hair behind the wheel. For the most part, they drive slow as fuck, but then once in a while you get an eighty-five-year-old Mario Andretti with a medical alert bracelet, going sixty in a school zone."

To Brock's surprise and delight—which also surprised him—she burst out laughing, nodded and then slammed back the shot in front of her. Damn, she was cute. And she smelled incredible.

He nodded, signaled Mickey and told him to put everything on his "tab."

Krista finally finished that last fry and drained the water glass in front of her. She let out a loud and satisfying *ah* before lifting her head and batting her lashes at him.

"You look different from the picture on your license," she said. "I like your hair longer. And your face has filled out."

His skin prickled. He hoped to God she didn't ask anything personal. Brock never got personal.

She leaned forward so their faces were only six inches apart. Her breath smelled of tequila and ketchup, but it was quickly over-powered by the most divine scent—floral and sweet with a hint of spice. It wrapped around him and he had to force himself not to shut his eyes and inhale deeply.

"Hmm?" he hummed, wondering what she was looking at.

She blinked those diamond blues at him and smiled coyly. "You have beautiful green eyes. And the scruff beard is hot, definitely better than the clean-shaved look of your picture."

She'd remembered that much about him? Was she coming on to him? Was she always this forward, or was the tequila making her brazen? Either way he didn't care. She was hot as fuck, and if she said the word, he'd have her home and clawing up his back before the clock struck twelve.

"You owe me, you know," she said with only a slight slur to her words.

He decided to play along. "I do, do I? I bought you a burger and covered your tab. I'd say we're square for whatever it is you think I *owe* you."

With a sultry little lip bite and a head shake that tousled those untameable curls of hers, she said, "Nuh-uh."

"Nuh-uh?"

"I let you off with a warning. And we both know you *were* speeding right up until you saw me. You tossed on the brakes at the perfect moment."

Well, she had him there.

"So I owe you then?"

She nodded.

"I'm not sure you should be drinking anymore, and I'm not a fan of dessert. How do you propose I *owe* you ... *constable*?"

Her pink tongue darted out between her lips and ran seductively along the seam. "Stumbling distance?"

A growl built at the back of his throat. He hadn't gotten laid in ages, and this little sprite had him sporting a half-chub since earlier in the day. Did she have her handcuffs with her still? Maybe an officer's hat?

Sliding off the barstool, he slung his leather jacket on and held out his hand. "We'll be there in less than ten."

She was all grins as she hopped off the barstool. Did she not have a coat? It was freaking cold outside. All she seemed to have was a worn and weathered gray hoodie. The woman needed a coat.

She followed him to the door, which he held open for her. The wind hit them both in the face like a wet slap, and she immediately shivered, pulling her hood up and shielding her face her hand.

Brock grabbed her other hand again and pulled her along, only to stop when they were shielded from the wind. He pulled off his leather jacket and held it out for her with nothing but a grunt. She slipped her slender arms into it and then, without a word, he grabbed her hand again and pulled her into the night and the wicked autumn weather.

———

IT WAS like something out of a movie. He unlocked the door to his house, revealing nothing scary or remarkable, just your run-of-the-mill dark and cold foyer, with a shoe rack, a coat hook, and a bowl for keys. Then, before Krista knew it, he was on her. His hands in her hair, his warm, hard, delicious body pressing up against hers. Their lips and tongues danced and dueled as they furiously fought to relieve one another of clothes. It was their first kiss. They hadn't said a word, or more like *he* hadn't said a word on the ten-minute jog through the rain. It'd just been a series of grunts as he let her know which house was his and fished his keys out of the massive leather jacket she was wearing.

But maybe that's the way it was supposed to go. No pleasantries, no mindless chit-chat or get-to-know-you bullshit. Because she didn't really care who this Brock guy was at the moment. All she cared about was that he was promising to help her forget her shitty day with orgasms, and that was good enough for Krista.

At least for tonight.

Moaning from how good he tasted, from the ferocity of his kiss, she leaped up and wrapped her legs around his hips. With a moan of his own, he stalked up the stairs and down the hall to the bedroom. His tongue held power, thrusting in and out of her mouth, swirling and diving with such animalistic force, such primitive need, that all she wanted to do was bite him, every hard inch of him. Bite his lips, bite his chin, bite his pecs, bite his abs, bite his ass.

He tossed her onto his bed and then quickly started to strip, so she did the same. He'd already relieved her of his jacket and her hoodie on their way from the door to his room, so all that was left was her blue T-shirt, jeans, and underwear. She was down to her panties and bra in seconds, and when she glanced back up, there he stood. Godlike, but so very, very real. Not just a beautiful figment of her inebriated imagination. Big, hard, toned and so goddamn gorgeous all she could do was stare. The rain had ebbed on their jog over, the fierce wind pushing away the dark bulbous clouds. So now the moon was out, high and bright and peeking in through the blinds at them like a dirty voyeur. Its bright light cast his body and face into menacing shadows, forcing harsh angles to be chiseled even sharper, but they only made him look all the more handsome. Fearsome and mysterious. His square jaw was set into a determined scowl, and even in the moonlight she could tell his eyes were the fiercest emerald green she'd ever seen.

She reached for him. "Help me end my day right," she purred. Hoping it sounded as sexy out loud as it did in her head.

His grin was salacious. Then slowly, ever so slowly, as though he thought he might crush her, he lowered his body down onto hers. But his mouth wasn't nearly as gentle. He plundered her. Took and took with his lips, teeth and tongue. Stole the air from her lungs and demanded moans from the back of her throat. Was he trying to make her come just from his kisses? Because with the way things were going, that wasn't entirely off the table.

He tasted like beer, but she probably tasted like cheap tequila, and in the end, it didn't matter. They both knew what this was. It was hot, sweaty, need-driven, make-each-other-feel-good drunk sex with a stranger. The fact that there was beer on his breath as his tongue massaged hers into passive submission only spurred her on, made her want him, made her want his body and this night even more. She wrapped her legs around his waist and bucked up into him, feeling the granite hard length of him press into her pelvis. She ached to touch it, to feel him in her palm, to watch his face as she brought him pleasure.

But she hardly had time to finish that thought before his mouth left hers and began traveling down her body. His hands roamed and unlatched the front clasp of her bra, allowing her breasts to spill out. Warm, wet kisses were dropped along her chest and nipples, her ribcage, her belly button, her mound, and then lower. His fingers made deft work of removing her panties.

"No, no!" she protested, having had enough one-night stands in her day to know that oral sex was not always expected in this sort of situation. It was a bump-uglies, scratch-an-itch kind of situation, right?

But he just grunted and flicked out his tongue, hitting her clit in just the right spot, which caused her leg to jerk and practically knee him in the skull. He chuckled diabolically but didn't lift his head or stop his delicious torment. Instead he spread her wide with his big fingers and dove in deeper. Lips, tongue, nose and fingers all brought her insane pleasure, coaxing and thrusting, lapping and kissing. She was wild for him, wild for an orgasm, but as he continued and the tequila seeped deeper into her body, she knew she'd only be able to manage one climax for the night, so it had to be a good one.

"Oh God … " she moaned, grinding up into his face. She caressed her breasts, tugging on her hard, achy nipples. Unlike earlier, when she was chilled to the bone, now she was scorching hot. Her hands moved down her body to rest on top of his head. His hair was soft. A bit of a longer buzz cut, but he pulled it off. It tickled her inner thighs as his head continued to bob up and down, his mouth doing despicably wonderful things. In drunken curiosity, she continued to explore his head, traced the outer shell of his ear with her fingers, felt the muscles of his forehead and brow pinched in complete and utter concentration. Damn, even a blind woman would know this man was sexy.

His teeth grazed her inner thigh. He nipped gently, making her squeak. All the while, his fingers continued to plunge, coaxing the orgasm from her until she was within an inch of her sanity, her head thrashing wildly on the bed, pleas for more spilling from her lips.

"Fuck me!" she demanded, knowing she wasn't going to last much longer but also knowing she wanted more than just his head buried between her legs. She wanted all of him buried there.

He gave one final sweep up between her folds with that masterful tongue of his and then reared up like a proud lion ready to pounce; his big, muscular arms bulged with the weight of him on either side of her head.

"Are you drunk?" she asked, not quite wondering why she felt the need to inquire about his sobriety, but somehow feeling it was pertinent information at the moment. The moment where the head of his cock was getting ready to impale her.

"Yes," he said gruffly, the strain and frustration of not being inside her evident in his tone. "But no beer goggles. I'd fuck you sober, too." And then she wasn't allowed to talk anymore. His mouth found hers again as he sank balls-deep inside.

He was a big, feral force within her, pushing her body to the edge, only to churn his hips just right and pull her back before she tumbled over the ledge, riding that paper-thin line for what felt like forever. Her nails raked down his thick, hard back. She relished the way he shivered when she squeezed his flexing butt cheeks. The man was pure muscle, rock beneath her fingertips. Brock the Rock. His teeth fell to her neck and shoulders. He began to bite and lick. His lips found her nipple; he suckled, bit, and she lost it.

The climax raced through her. She clenched around him, savoring every charge and quivering on every draw as he slid his thick length across her sensitive channel. She was lost to the sensation of it all, lost to his passion, lost to the way he made her feel.

Guttural moans filled her ear as he found his own release, clamping down hard onto her swollen and needy breast, flicking the bud with his tongue as his hips continued to thrust and punish.

He was heavy on top of her, not frighteningly so, which was

surprising, given his size. But as the euphoria of her climax slowly dissolved, she realized that she was tired and wanted nothing more than to go pee and then curl up into bed.

Reading her mind, Brock pulled out, helped her to her feet and pointed to the bathroom. A man of few words but a multitude of talents elsewhere.

When she came back out, he had gotten her a glass of water and pulled the sheets and duvet down. She didn't even bother looking for her underwear. She just drained her glass, wiped the back of her wrist across her mouth and snuggled into his pillow. She was asleep almost instantly to the scrumptious smell of him, his warm body inches from hers across the bed.

———

THE NEXT MORNING, Krista woke to the sound of a bear, or perhaps a dragon, roaring in her ear while a big, thick, hairy tree trunk lay draped across her stomach and beer-scented wind ruffled the hair on the back of her neck. Afraid to open her eyes, she grimaced as the memories of last night came flooding back.

She knew what she'd done.

Knew where she was.

She'd gone home with Brock. They'd had incredible sex and then subsequently passed out. But she just wasn't ready to see it. To see the reality of her sad, drunken choice.

Who was a fan of the walk of shame?

No one.

It was called the walk of *shame* for a reason.

The words "for shame" screamed at her in her mind, competing with the headache.

She'd done it once or twice before, the walk of shame, and it was always embarrassing. At least this time she had worn running shoes and not strappy hooker shoes. Slowly, quietly, she pried open her eyes, only to come face-to-face with the man who'd rocked her world and then some just a few hours earlier. His eyes were closed and his mouth partially open, giving him almost a childlike look. Devastatingly handsome, and now rugged too with a five o'clock shadow of sexy scruff. And it was the first time he didn't look on edge or high alert. The lines in his forehead had relaxed, and his eyebrows were no longer pinched. He was at ease, at peace.

She studied his face a little bit longer; small white scars dotted his chin along the left side, most likely where stitches or staples had been at one point, while another, redder scar in the shape of a sickle and about the size of a raisin ran up into his right eyebrow. How old was he? It was hard to tell. She glanced down at his arm as it draped across her belly. Soft, dark hair covered freckles, while a big, calloused hand gripped her ribs.

He made a noise as if he was about to wake up, and she braced herself for the awkward morning chit-chat. Instead he just rolled over, leaving her devoid of his touch and, for some strange reason, melancholy because of the loss. But she took her opening and silently slid out of bed, tracked down her clothes and then, like a stealthy ninja, left his house, hoping to God that it wasn't pouring rain outside.

CHAPTER THREE

5 weeks later ...

ON NASTY DAYS, which were in abundance in November, it was a blessing that the police station had an in-house gym, a place where cops could go and work out before or after shift with top-notch machines and equipment without ever having to leave the comfort of work. So when she couldn't get a run in because Mother Nature was having a temper tantrum and thrashing the wind and rain around Fern Valley, Krista headed to work a few hours early and hit the gym. Started the day off right, with a clear head. Got the endorphins pumping.

It was four thirty in the morning, and the station gym was dead quiet. She'd woken up feeling queasy, but rather than think too hard about it, Krista just chalked it up to the idea of having to work with Myles all day. That was enough to make anyone nauseous. So instead, she went about her morning routine at home, ignoring her roiling stomach, and pounded back her raspberry and spinach smoothie as she made her way out the door. A run always made her feel better. A run would set her day right before she had to deal with Myles.

But when she stepped onto the treadmill and started to run, she couldn't. Her boobs hurt. Like crazy hurt. An average C-cup and accustomed to wearing pretty tight sports bras for exercise, the girls were not normally an issue. But today running was absolute torture. And her stomach was not feeling better at all. Could almond milk go bad?

Without giving it too much thought, she hopped onto the elliptical instead, only that made her boobs hurt too, and it also made her want to barf.

What was going on?

Not wanting to completely waste her morning, she lifted a few weights and did some squats, but every movement had her seeing spots. And whenever she'd lift her arms over her head, she felt like she was going to pass out.

Was she getting the flu?

Praying that this wasn't an omen for a shitty day to come, she gave up and hit the showers, deciding instead to run out and grab a bite. Even though the thought of food made her ill, she had to eat before work.

A hangry cop was a scary cop.

She was just leaving the locker room to head to her car when Myles blocked her path.

"Hey, Matthews, ready to go?" He grinned, winking like he was God's gift to women and she should be grateful he was her mentor.

"I guess." She shrugged. "I'm going to run and grab some food and then I'll be back." And before he could insinuate himself into her errand, she reached for the nearest door, opened it and stepped inside.

Fuck, it was a bloody broom closet!

Perusing the produce section of the grocery store ten minutes later, the bin of bright green limes on sale quickly brought her thoughts to Brock. She'd been thinking about him a lot over the weeks. And yet, she deliberately avoided going back to that bar, so much so that when she went for a run or drove anywhere, she took the long way. Just in case he was in the area, she avoided both his house—because now she knew where he lived—and the bar. And he hadn't bothered to get in touch with her, either, so apparently, they were both of the understanding that it had been one night of drunken fun, with no strings and no expectations. So then why was she kind of disappointed that he hadn't called?

Maybe because you didn't give him your number and then snuck out the following morning, you dummy!

With time to kill before her shift, she continued to wander aimlessly around the grocery store. But nothing looked good. Nothing even remotely made her salivate or caused her stomach to rumble. In fact, everything, even the roasted red pepper soup in a tetra-pack, which she pretty much lived off, sounded disgusting. But if she headed back to the station, she'd have to see Myles, so instead she strolled up and down the aisles until she found herself in the tampon section.

Did she need any?

She couldn't remember.

Her period was never regular, and she wasn't on the pill; she just got it when she got it. She'd tried going on the pill, but the hormones had made her crazy and gain weight. She'd always used condoms with boyfriends. A calendar flashed into her head and she began to do the math.

When was her last period?

How long had it been?

Was she late?

She felt off.

Out of sorts.

Was that PMS?

Was that why she felt sick and her boobs hurt? Her boobs had never hurt before when she was PMSing.

A gasp took her breath away when the calendar finally synced in her brain and she realized she hadn't had her period since before that night with Brock. *Well* before that night with Brock. Had they used protection? They had to have, right? But she couldn't remember. They—particularly her—had been incredibly drunk and so caught up in the moment, in the passion.

Holy crap.

Locating the pregnancy test section, she grabbed a box off the shelf and read the back as her heart raced inside her chest and her sweaty hands slid across the shiny cardboard of the box. It fell to the floor with a thunderous *thunk*, or at least it was thunderous to Krista. Now the whole store probably knew what she was doing, what she was thinking. She looked around. The aisle was thankfully empty, so hastily, she grabbed two boxes of different brands, a chocolate bar and a box of tampons—wishful thinking—and headed to the checkout.

It felt as if she were wandering around with two hot bricks in each of her coat pockets as she made her way to her car, having stupidly refused a plastic bag.

Could she wait until her shift was over to take the test at home?

Twelve hours was a long time to wait.

Should she go back to the bar and find Brock so they could take the test together?

Was she being a hypochondriac, fretting about nothing?

Probably.

But a baby wasn't nothing. A baby was a huge something. A huge something with tiny feet and tiny hands that altered your life forever.

A million thoughts ran through her mind as she drove back to the station, the paranoia setting in and feeling like a bowling ball in her belly. Meanwhile something *else, someone* else could be growing in there, too.

She had to know.

Krista couldn't go an entire shift, half a bloody day not knowing if there was a human inside her. At least then, if she knew, she would know.

Brilliant logic, Krista. You receive your invitation from Mensa yet?

Once back at the station, she locked herself in a bathroom stall in the women's locker room.

The instructions said to pee on the stick midstream and then wait three to five minutes.

The longest goddamn three minutes of her life.

Six minutes later, she walked out of the bathroom stall, her heart beating rapidly inside her chest.

What was she going to do?

The word *screwup* was on repeat in her head as she splashed cold water on her face and stared into the mirror. She looked sickly. Did morning sickness happen that fast?

"All I wanted to do was prove myself," she said to the woman staring back at her. "Prove that I'm not a screwup and that I can … that I *am* a good cop." Her throat grew tight from the fight to keep her emotions in check.

No. Not now. She wasn't going to cry now. She had a job to do. A job she was good at. She'd cry later when she was alone.

A banging on the bathroom door made her jump. "Come on, Matthews. Wipe and get a move on."

God, Myles was a disgusting pig.

She bit the inside of her cheek until the pain replaced the ache in her throat, then she threw her shoulders back and pushed open the bathroom door.

"Ready to go?" Myles asked, skipping up behind her and winding up to try to slap her butt again.

Only this time, with ninja reflexes and fire in her belly, she turned around and faced him square on, baring her teeth like a mother bear. "Don't you dare touch me!"

"Whoa," he said, rearing back and putting his hands up in fake surrender. All the while a sinister smile that said he wasn't apologetic at all danced across his face like The Joker or Jack from *The Shining*. "Jesus Christ, Matthews, what crawled up your ass and died today? You on the rag or something?"

Sexist prick.

Yes, because the moment a woman asserts herself and tells you to back the fuck off, she has her period.

Fuck. She did not need this right now.

"Just leave me alone, Slade," she said quietly, venom in her tone but no longer in her heart. She had bigger fish to fry, bigger, more important, more life-altering things on her mind than that sexist pig.

He rolled his eyes and just flashed that same big, creepy, wily, wolfish grin, one that showed his canines like he was some kind of mangy, starving, would-chew-off-his-own-leg-if-he-had-to-but-would-rather-chew-off-yours hyena. "We've got a call on another domestic. You ready?"

She nodded, swallowed and pushed everything into the back of her mind for later. "In a minute. I just have to grab my badge."

———

KRISTA'S GUT was still in knots as she pulled into the parking lot of the bar later that night. The domestic assault they'd been called out on early that morning had been disturbing, and in the last few weeks, she'd been to some doozies. But this particular one had been worse than ever and forced her to focus intently on her gag reflex to suppress the hell out of it, while wrangling in every ounce of self-control and training she had.

If it were up to her, and laws be damned, she'd have shot the bastard on sight. He'd beaten his girlfriend almost to death. He'd come home drunk after having lost his job and had taken it out on her until she'd passed out. A friend had found her the following morning and called the police. In the end, after they'd taken the victim to the hospital for her injuries, which were plentiful, they found out she'd been pregnant and the assault had caused a miscarriage. It was all Krista could do not to shed multiple tears along with her. The woman cradled her flat and bruised abdomen and wept for hours on Krista's shoulder as Krista's hand discreetly snaked down to her own stomach and hugged the inconvenient little miracle inside.

With a wince, a sigh and a stomach in tight knots, she pushed open the big, well-worn wooden door of the bar and was immediately hit with a wave of déjà vu: loud music, boisterous laughter, the clink of utensils against plates and beer steins being plunked back down on the tables. A cacophony of Friday-night fun in a country biker bar with just a tinge of underlying fear or perhaps threat percolating around the edges. She knew that if things got just the least bit out of hand, or the wrong thing was said to the wrong person, all hell would break lose in an instant, and Santa Claus behind the bar—she never did learn his name—would be bringing out his shotgun to maintain order.

But she wasn't afraid. She'd grown up in a small town. The local barkeep was her uncle, and she'd waitressed in a place very similar every summer when she'd come home from college. She could banter and joke with the best of them. And one thing that had served her well waitressing all those summers—and was continuing to do so in her new career choice—was to look past the exterior. Just because someone *looked* rough around the edges and ready for a knife fight didn't necessarily mean they were. Appearances can be deceiving, and it was better to go with your gut. Take Myles, for example. He was clean-cut and friendly, but Krista would rather spend every waking hour of the rest of her life with the bearded man in the corner wearing a leather vest half buttoned up, showing off his giant skull tattoo on his hairy chest, than an extra five minutes with Myles. To her this was normal. This was welcoming. This was home.

She took up her old perch at the bar and waited for Santa Claus to notice. When his light blue eyes finally snagged hers, his smile was heartwarming, and for just a moment, she wondered if maybe he *was* Santa, taking a break from being the ultimate Arctic overlord to hang out with the mere muggles.

"Well, aren't you a sight for sore eyes?" He chuckled, wiping down the counter and offering a grandfatherly wink. "Was starting to think it was something I said that scared you away for so long. Or did it take just this long to get over your hangover from all the tequila?" His laugh was deep and raspy like he was just getting over a cold or had smoked since he could walk. "You here to see Brock?"

She nodded sheepishly. "You, uh ... you don't know where I could find him, do you?"

Without prompting, he placed a glass of fizzy red liquid in front of her. Krista shook her head and pushed it away, the reality of the next eight months slowly settling in.

"Relax," he said softly, "it's cranberry juice and ginger ale. It'll help calm the nausea."

She squinted at him. "Nausea?"

Leaning against the bar, he cocked a hip and gave her a tilted eyebrow. "Honey, I'm a retired detective. Doesn't take a rocket scientist to add up the clues. You show up here, white as a sheet, about a month or so *after* you spent the night with Brocky. I've got five kids. Two of which were glorious accidents. I know how it works."

Her eyes went wide. "A-are you Brock's dad?"

Holy hell, did the grandfather just find out before the father? She was doing this *all* wrong! ALL WRONG!

He shook his head. "Naw, Brock's daddy's been gone for some time now. But he and I were best friends. We were on the force together. Brock helped me open up this bar after I retired. He's part owner ... *silent* owner, mind you. Doesn't much care for people or the chit-chat."

"So, where is he now? How can I find him?"

He closed his eyes for a second and then swung his big frame over to the food window after one of the cooks had hit the bell. He wandered back toward her, bringing the decadent scent of greasy french fries with him. He plopped the basket down in front of her, then reached under the counter and brought out a bottle of ketchup.

"Another thing that helped my wife. She must've eaten nearly a thousand pounds of potatoes between all five pregnancies. It's what she lived off for the first three months, only thing she could keep down. French fries and ginger ale."

Krista dove in without hesitation, ravenous from not having eaten anything all day and suddenly feeling like she might chew her own arm off if Santa didn't order her another basket posthaste.

"What's your name?" she finally asked, licking ketchup off her finger, her eyes rolling into the back of her head at how truly magnificent everything tasted.

He smiled. "My real name is Michael, but everyone calls me Mickey."

She took a sip of her cranberry and ginger ale. "Can you help me find Brock, Mickey?"

"He's on a job right now for a few weeks. So when that happens, we don't really hear much from him until he's back."

Was he a spy? A ninja? What kind of job had the man going off the grid for weeks on end? Especially in this technological day and age?

"He's in security," Mickey said, reading her mind again. "Surveillance, security, protection, intel, that kind of thing. Right now, I think he's on some kind of surveillance job, but he couldn't tell me much. Just that he'd be away for a few weeks."

She couldn't escape the shiver that suddenly wracked her body. She was going to have to keep this baby-size secret to herself for even longer.

"There's no way I can get in touch with him sooner?" she asked, almost pleaded, her pulse racing and eyes going wide when Mickey plunked another hot basket of fries in front of her. She could have kissed the man.

He just shook his head and refilled her drink. "'Fraid not. Though if you leave me your number and name, when he comes back, or on the off chance he checks in, I can let him know you're looking for him. Who knows, he could be home tomorrow. That's sometimes the way with these jobs." He placed a notepad in front of her, and she hastily scrawled down her information, loathing the idea of having to tell Brock something like this over the phone but hating the idea even more of having to tell him face-to-face.

———

It was another three weeks before she heard even the faintest of squeaks about Brock. Liking Mikey and the vibe, she'd gone back to the bar numerous times and just sat and chatted with the big, friendly bartender. Tonight was one of those nights. Krista was just getting ready to pack it in and wish Mickey a good weekend when his cell phone buzzed on the back counter.

"Looks like Brock is home," he said. "Just got in. Said he'd come by the bar tomorrow to check on things."

Krista swallowed the hard, sandpapery lump in her throat and nodded, grabbing her coat and shoving her arms into the holes. "Thanks."

———

Balancing his duffle bag, a box of pizza and a six-pack of beer in his arms, Brock pushed open the front door of his house, only to be greeted by the *chirp chirp* of his alarm. Plunking everything down on the bottom step, he quickly disengaged the alarm and toed off his shoes.

Exhaustion was an understatement about how he felt right now. That three-week stint up in northern Alberta casing a warehouse that was rumored to be doing some human sex trafficking had been brutal. Thankfully, he'd been able to drag his brother Rex along, so at least he wasn't alone and didn't have to hunt the monsters himself.

But he was glad to be home. He sniffed the air as he shut the door and listened for any peculiar sounds. Twelve years in the navy and with special ops had taught him to home in on all of his senses, always. And he was doing just that. He'd made some enemies over the years, and although most of them were either dead and buried or serving significant time in prison, one could never be too cautious.

But nothing smelled, sounded or felt suspicious, so he lugged everything upstairs and flicked on some lights. His belly grumbled at the smell of the pizza he plunked down on his leather ottoman. He glanced at the duffle bag full of dirty clothes and then again at the pizza box.

Laundry could wait.

Sloughing off his jacket like a second skin, he sank down into his big La-Z-Boy recliner, popped open a bottle of beer, flipped the television on to the news and dove into his meat lover's pizza with extra mushrooms and banana peppers.

He was four slices into his extra-large but only half into his bottle of beer when there was a knock at the door.

Grumbling at the inconvenience of being interrupted and too tired to deal with people, he flung open the door seconds later and nearly swallowed his tongue.

"Hi," she said shyly, toeing at a dead leaf on the front stoop and averting her gaze.

A grin spread across his face before he could stop it. The last two months had been spent dreaming about this woman's luscious body and whether he'd ever get to taste it again. Was she here for a booty call? She'd been a little lioness in the sack and brazen.

Did he like that?

Yeah, he did.

"Constable Matthews?" he asked, giving her a moment to compose herself.

She licked her lips. "Uh … hi," she said again. He liked that he flustered her.

One eyebrow slowly drew up his forehead in curiosity. "Hi?"

"Um … Mickey … at the bar, he told me you were back. C-can I come in?"

He moved out of the way and allowed her to enter, though even with his back pressed up against the wall, her shoulder still managed to brush his chest when she walked past him. He couldn't stop himself and inhaled as her hair swished past his nose. God, she smelled good. That scent alone had haunted him for weeks, had him waking up with a stiff cock most mornings and with nothing but his palm in the lukewarm shower to satisfy the fantasy.

She toed her gray ankle boots off but left her coat on before following him up the stairs. He led her into the living room and motioned for her to sit down on the couch opposite his La-Z-Boy. With a groan meant for a man twenty years his senior, Brock sat back down in his chair and watched as her bright blue eyes took in her surroundings, zeroing in on the pizza.

"Want a slice?" he asked, lifting up the box and holding it out to her.

She shook her head. "No, thank you."

Leaning back in his chair, he brought his beer bottle up to his lips and took a sip, amused by the odd expression on her face. She seemed so different than the other two times they'd met. The first time she'd been this cocky cop with something to prove; the second time she'd been down in the dumps and then off her face drunk. But now, now she seemed almost nervous, scared and unsure of how to behave.

He knew he was a big guy, and many had called him scary. It wasn't an opinion he chose to remedy by acting like a teddy bear. No, fear was a good thing. Fear kept people at arm's length and kept them from getting complacent and acting irresponsibly. Kept them from asking him too many questions. And yet, there was something about the little cop and the way her big blue eyes blinked at him that made him want to embrace the teddy bear side and pull her into a hug ... or tear off her clothes and carry her back to his room. Either scenario would do.

"What can I do for you, Constable Matthews?" he asked. "Beer?"

She shook her head again. "No, thank you."

He nodded again and drained his beer bottle. "You here for a booty call?"

Her eyes flashed up to his from where she'd been staring at his socked foot, propped up on the footrest of the recliner. "What? No!"

Another smile jostled his lips before he shrugged. "'Cause I wouldn't say no. But I'm guessing based on the way you scurried around my bedroom, trying to silently collect your clothes, only to duck out of my house in the early morning and then walk-of-shame your ass back to the bar to get your car, you're not interested in an encore." He pouted. "Shame. You know I would have driven you if you'd just asked."

She muttered *shit* under her breath.

He was about to open his mouth again and tease her some more when she cut him off. "Did you wear a condom the night we had sex?"

Now it was his turn to go all weird and awkward and quiet.

But it seemed like she'd finally found her voice and her spine. "Did you wear a condom?" she asked again.

Fuck!

He couldn't remember. Normally it was a no-brainer. He suited up before he fucked, but he'd had a few beers and he hadn't been with a woman in a while, let alone one who revved his engine like the little cop. Just before she'd dropped the condom bomb on him, he'd been thinking about grabbing her curly red ponytail and tilting that sexy neck up for a kiss. Her lips were pouty and plump, and he could only imagine they would feel like heaven wrapped around his cock.

But he did none of that. Instead he just stared at her, trying to remember back to their hookup and whether he'd slapped on a rubber. He couldn't remember. Couldn't remember seeing one in the trash the next day or finding a wrapper on the floor.

Fuck almighty, had he really been that careless? That irresponsible?

Brock cleared his throat. "Uh, you not on the pill?"

She shook her head.

He swallowed. "I don't remember using a condom."

She gritted her teeth before answering. "I don't remember you using one either."

Fuck. He hadn't been *that* drunk. More just *caught up in the moment*. But he'd never forgotten to use protection before. Fuck.

His mouth opened and then closed, and then opened, and then closed again. Had he blinked?

It didn't feel like he had.

His eyes hurt.

His head hurt.

His heart was threatening to beat out of his chest.

Was he having a heart attack?

His left arm wasn't in pain. That was a good sign. His eyes

focused on Krista's little feet, planted firmly on his hardwood floor. Her socks were hot pink and green with small orange cats on them. And for some bizarre reason they made him want her even more.

With a hard swallow, he finally lifted his head. "Are you ... ?"

She nodded.

"And it's ... it's mine?"

She nodded again.

"You're sure?"

"I hadn't been with anyone in a long time, and I haven't been with anyone since. Unless you believe in immaculate conception of a non-virgin, non-practicing Christian, then yes, I'm sure. I'm pregnant, and you're the father."

He ground his teeth together and let out a long, slow exhale through his nose. "We need to get married."

She gaped at him. "Uh, no we don't."

"Yes. It's the right thing to do."

She let out a petulant huff and glared at him, pushing herself out of her seat to stand in front of him. Her chest puffed up. "We are *not* getting married!" she snapped. "That is *not* the right thing to do."

"Yes, it is."

"We hardly know each other. We're not in love. We are *not* getting married." She plugged her hands on her hips and stuck one foot out. Her stare was enough to melt steel. "I only told you about the baby out of courtesy. If you're not interested in being a dad, that's totally fine. I can do it all on my own."

Heat flooded Brock's face and chest.

Did she just say *out of courtesy?*

What the fuck.

He stood up, invading her personal space until there was no more than six inches between their bodies. "Listen up, woman." Sexy blue eyes slowly lifted from his chest to his face. Her lips parted. "That's my kid you're carrying, my *family,* and I will damn well take care of it. I will damn well be a part of its life, and there isn't a damn thing you can do to stop me."

Fire ignited in those wide eyes of hers, and a flush of pink invaded her cheeks.

Oh, she was mad.

He was madder.

How dare she come here out of fucking courtesy?

"You need to move in here," he said, cutting her off. "That way I can take care of you and the baby. Be a part of the pregnancy, too. That's my family you're growing in that belly of yours, and I take that shit seriously. Family is everything to me."

Her brows furrowed, and she poked a bony little finger into his chest, pushing hard to make him back up, but not hard enough.

He didn't budge.

"Listen, you bossy jackass, I am not marrying you, and I am not moving in here. No one, and I mean *no one* tells me what do to."

The tension in his forehead was back. "Well, then, what *do* you want from me? Money? A trust fund for the baby? Name it and I'll do it. I won't be a deadbeat dad. This kid *will* have me in his life."

"Or her."

"Right. Or her. What do you want from me?"

She'd been so strong. Timid and nervous at first, but then owning her predicament and tearing off the news like a Band-Aid. But now she seemed lost again, just as fragile and nervous as when he'd opened the door to find her standing there on his doorstep: eyes bright, cheeks rosy and hair a sexy mess, caught up in the wind.

He was still angry as fuck at her. But he was also angry at himself. How could he have been so careless? So irresponsible?

That had to change now.

He glanced down at the pizza box again, picked it up and held it up to her. "Have you eaten?"

Food. Pregnant women were always starving, right?

Exhaustion stole across her face, and with a sigh of resolution she reached for a slice. "I don't know what I want," she confessed through big bites, moaning from how good it was. Brock glanced at the pizza box but was suddenly too overwhelmed with the news to eat.

She licked her lips, and without thinking or asking, he darted to the kitchen, returning a moment later with a glass of water. She took it with thanks and drained it in seconds.

"I'm coming to the next doctor's appointment," he said, watching her wipe the back of her wrist across her mouth and then continue eating the pizza. "And any other appointments. I don't want to find out the sex. We'll do a prenatal class too. I'll be in the delivery room."

She paused mid-bite. "You're a bossy fucker. Do I get a say in *any* of this?"

"Get used to it, woman." He reached for his beer bottle and drained it. Fuck, he needed something stronger. "I ain't going anywhere."

CHAPTER FOUR

Three days later, Brock found himself maneuvering his big truck down the gravel driveway to Krista's house. She wasn't expecting him. They'd agreed to meet at the ultrasound place, but he was curious to see where she lived and wanted to show her that he was all in for this baby thing. Even if she didn't want him, he wanted her to know that this kid was going to be raised with a father and not just a weekend dad.

No.

He'd be there for everything. Birth to graduation, his kid would have a dad.

Slamming his truck door, he took in the property. It was a nice piece of land, with what looked like an old barn, a small field for some goats, horses or cows at one point, but the grass had taken over and the livestock was long gone. A chicken coop stood empty and quiet off near a small plot of raised beds, and what looked to be an old pigpen with a trough and lean-to was now filled with dandelions and weeds. The land had potential, but clearly the landlords were too uncaring or perhaps too old to fulfill that potential any longer, and it was falling into disrepair.

Oh, what he would do with a piece of land like this.

Her "front" door was around back and down a couple of steps. It didn't look like she had much head room, but then again, the woman was lucky if she was five-foot-five. He ducked under the staircase leading up to the balcony above and rapped on her door.

No answer.

He knocked again, this time harder, longer and louder.

Still no answer.

Fuck.

Panic flooded him as his big palm engulfed the knob and he gave it a quick turn. If it wasn't open, he'd kick the fucker down if he had to. Her car was out front; she was home. What the fuck was going on?

But the door was open, and he let himself inside, having to duck again to get in under the doorjamb. He was about to call out for her when the sound of puking caused him to pause.

The place was small and dated but clean and cozy. He saw the door to the bathroom leading off the hallway and made his way toward it.

"Krista?" he asked softly, seeing her kneeling on the floor, hunched over the toilet, one hand bunching her hair at the nape of her neck while the other one gripped the bowl tight enough to make her knuckles white.

He was about to say something when she pitched forward and heaved again. Before he knew it, he was inside the bathroom and pushing her hand away from her hair, holding it off her face for her as both her hands clutched the bowl. He located a black hair elastic on the sink counter and quickly tied her hair up, then his hand fell to her back, where he did the only thing he could think of. He began to gently rub. His big fingers traced her delicate spine, feeling every ridge and bump, every muscle tighten as she heaved up more into the bowl.

She groaned and slumped forward, resting her forehead on the back of her hand. "What are you doing here?"

"I came to offer you a ride to the ultrasound. Figured we could go and grab lunch after and discuss this baby-raising thing a little more. Set some parenting parameters."

She twisted a bit and gave him the side-eye, only lifting her head slightly from her hand. "Parameters?"

He lifted one shoulder. "Or whatever."

Suddenly, a little tabby wandered into the bathroom, brushing affectionately against his leg before stepping into the litter box beside the toilet. It scratched a few times in the sand, then began to do its business.

"You have a cat?" he asked, weirded out by the intense eye contact the cat was making with him as it squatted.

"Penelope."

Lifting his hand from her back for a moment, he ran his fingers through his short, bristly hair. "Jesus, woman, don't you know pregnant women aren't supposed to change cat litter?"

She lifted her head up and, using her hands on the bowl, pushed herself up onto her knees. "How do you know that?"

"I've been reading."

"Reading what?"

"Parenting books."

"Who the fuck are you?" she murmured. He helped her with a hand under her elbow. He gave her some space by retreating to the narrow and dimly lit hallway.

She joined him a few moments later and followed him out to her kitchen. He went to her fridge and opened it. All it contained was half a carton of milk, a bowl of soup in a Tupperware container and three apples. Her freezer didn't prove to be much better, besides a few bags of frozen french fries.

"That's it," he said, slamming her freezer. "You're coming to live with me. Before I was willing to let you do what you wanted, but that was until I saw that you have no food and are cleaning a cat litter box. You need food."

She rolled her eyes. "I have food. I'm not coming to live with you."

He scoffed. "Not enough." His eyes glanced at the clock on her oven. "Grab your purse. Otherwise we'll be late."

Glaring at him, she did as she was told, slinking into her jacket as she pushed past him and out into the cold November day.

"Don't you lock your door?" he asked, watching her head to her car.

She rolled her eyes again and pushed past him, digging her keys out of her purse and locking it. "My landlords are always home. Besides, the door is shoddy. A raccoon could bust in if the wind was blowing from the right direction."

He grunted. "No excuse. Lock it from now on. And we definitely lock the doors at my house. Have an alarm too."

"I'm not living with you," she murmured, not letting him get ahead of her and making her way toward her car.

"You're driving with me into town, though. We'll discuss the living together thing more later."

"No," she said, opening up her car door. "I plan to go grab some groceries after the ultrasound. I've worked nights the last three days and haven't had time to go shopping."

She didn't give him a chance to respond before she started her car. Or at least attempted to start her car. But instead it just sat there and sputtered.

Not bothering to even ask, he made his way to his truck and drove it closer to her car, positioning them bumper to bumper. He popped the hood of his truck and motioned for her to do the same. With a growl he could practically hear through the car, she complied. He hooked up their batteries and instructed her to start 'er up. Seconds later, the sputter turned into a rumble, and exhaust was floating out from the back like a chimney.

He unhooked the jumper cables and shut both hoods. But before she could pull away and leave him there, he walked over to her side of the car, opened the door, leaned in, grabbed the key and shut it off.

"What the hell?" she asked, trying to push him out. Her car wasn't exactly big, and he was taking up a lot of her personal space. But that smell of hers was making it hard for him to concentrate.

Pulling her key from the ignition, he stood. "You're driving into town with me. Then we'll grab lunch and groceries. I want to make sure you're eating right. Taking care of *our* baby."

If looks could kill, he'd be six feet under.

He snickered to himself but hid his face by glancing off toward the sky and the dark clouds. Shit, more rain. Like they needed more.

He liked her stubbornness. Liked her fight and temper. It was all the cuter coming from such a tiny package.

She growled and huffed as she abandoned her car and complied, falling into step with him as he headed to his truck. Like the gentleman his mother had raised, he held open her door for her and watched her tight little ass flex as she climbed up into the cab.

"That's better," he said, slamming her door and chuckling at the glare she was giving him as he rounded the front of the truck to the driver's side. "Much better."

"I HAVE TO PEE," Krista said with a wince as she and Brock sat there in the waiting room of the ultrasound clinic.

"Isn't that a good thing?" he asked. "Means your bladder's full."

"Yes. Doesn't mean it's not uncomfortable as hell." She gave him a curious side-eye. "How'd you know?"

One bulky, leather-clad shoulder lifted half an inch. "I've been reading."

"Krista Matthews?" said a woman in blue scrubs and square frameless glasses, interrupting Krista's thoughts before she could think of a witty comeback for the man sitting next to her. Instead she just breathed a sigh of relief and pushed herself up out of the chair.

"Oh, thank God," she murmured, following the woman down the hallway to one of the rooms, her big burly shadow hot on her heels, smelling all sexy and shit.

"Just in here," the ultrasound tech said, holding open the door.

Krista and Brock followed her inside, where a bed sat under an overhead light, and beside it was a monitor, keyboard and chair. A television was perched up in the corner of the room with a blinking screen.

"On the bed, please," the technician instructed.

Brock held out his hand, and Krista gave him a dubious look.

What the heck was his hand for?

"Do you need a hand up onto the bed?" he asked.

Damn, he was being so nice it was hard to stay mad at him, despite how pushy he was behaving. Making her ride with him, insisting they grab lunch. What was he trying to do? Date her?

Not that she *needed* the assistance, she took his hand anyway and allowed him to help her hop up onto the bed.

She did as she was directed, and before too long, the tech was swirling the wand around in the goop on Krista's flat abdomen.

"We're just going to check on baby's size today," the tech said. "Make sure of your due date and that there is only one in there."

Krista's eyes went wide, and her head snapped from the technician's face to Brock's. "Do twins run in your family?" she asked, her tone edged with panic.

He simply shook his head.

She let out a long, loud sigh of relief. "Mine either."

Quietly, they both watched as the technician continued to

move the wand around her stomach. And then suddenly, a worry so startling, so frightening took over.

What if the woman couldn't find a heartbeat? What if there was no baby?

A lump harder than stone formed in Krista's throat. It may not have been planned or with someone she loved or was committed to, but that baby had already become such a fixture in her life. In her mind. It couldn't not be there.

"I-is there ... " she started, not sure she wanted to finish her question for fear of the answer.

Thump, thump, thump, thump ...

Before she knew what was happening, Brock's hand was on hers, squeezing until she wasn't sure there was any blood left in her fingers.

"And that's baby's heartbeat. Strong and steady," the technician said. She pointed to the screen perched up in the corner of the room. "And there's baby."

Brock and Krista glanced up at the television, where lo and behold, a little black and white bean-shaped thing sat twitching on the screen. You could already see the formation of eyes, head, arms and legs.

"Holy shit," Krista whispered, her eyes getting wet.

Brock squeezed her hand even tighter. "Yeah."

CHAPTER FIVE

"You feel like a burger?" Brock asked after the forty-minute ultrasound appointment that had left them both blissfully speechless and with a sleeve of black and white pictures with labels like "foot" and "hand" and "face." Even though in reality they looked like no more than blurry blobs that could just as easily have been a giraffe or platypus fetus.

Eyes glued to the pictures, Krista nodded. "Sure, whatever."

No more than a grunt. He held open the truck door for her, and she climbed in, her heart swelling and her mind spinning as she just continued to stare at the pictures.

"You tell work yet?" Brock asked, pulling out of the ultrasound clinic parking lot. "Should be switching to light duty. Desk shit."

Slowly, she peeled her eyes away from her child. "No."

"Tomorrow."

"No."

"Yes. Your job isn't a safe one, and it's not responsible for you to be continuing on with your regular cop duties. And it's not responsible of me to let you."

She narrowed her gaze. "*Let* me?"

He nodded with another grunt.

"I'll *let* work know when I'm good and ready. I haven't even been a rookie six months. Light duty would set me back."

My job is everything to me.

She had to prove to her family, to everyone back home that she wasn't the screwup they thought she was.

"Plus," she continued, "I'm fine. I'm not showing yet, and it's not like I'm a New York beat cop chasing down bad guys on a daily basis or engaging in shootouts. Some days it's nothing more than highway patrol."

He snorted, and she couldn't stop herself from snorting too. Her shitty highway patrol shift and her reaction to it had been what landed them in their current predicament. Oh yeah, highway patrol shifts were the bomb diggity.

"And we both know how much you *love* highway patrol," he jeered.

She glanced out the window. "Yes, *quite.*"

"You need to tell work," he insisted again, taking a left into the restaurant parking lot.

She grumbled at him, swiveling in her seat to show him her best irritated glare. "Just give me some time, okay?"

He seemed neither convinced by her plea nor fazed by her temper. Instead, he fixed her with a look of his own, one far more deadly than the one Krista had been attempting. "You have one week." Then he shut off the engine, opened his door, hopped out and ended the conversation.

―――――

"You NEED to move in with me," Brock said before biting into his bison burger a short while later. Since he'd *ordered* her to disclose her pregnancy at work, they hadn't said a word to each other while sitting in the restaurant waiting for their lunch. It'd been awkward as hell, but Krista wasn't about to break the silence when the man was clearly comfortable with it and she was pissed off at him. He simply sat there in his seat, looking larger than life and attracting stares and ogles from all the little snappily dressed waitresses.

"So you've said," Krista retorted dryly. "You're definitely not shy with your *opinions*." She hadn't wanted anything besides french fries, so she'd asked for a double order of poutine and was currently in cheesy, gravy, potato heaven. "And I believe I've declined the offer. I'm happy where I live."

He shook his head and used his big hand to grab the napkin off the table and wipe his mouth. "My opinions aren't wrong. And now that we've seen the baby ... " he trailed off.

She lifted one shoulder dismissively. "How does that change anything?"

"It just does," he snapped. "It's real. It's in there. My kid. And I want to be part of every moment. Before he's here and after. Plus, I saw your fridge. It's fucking empty. My kid needs food. And not just french fries."

"It's my kid, too," she said, a lot of her fight dissolving. "And I told you I'm going shopping."

Goddamn it. This he-man alpha protector thing was turning her on.

"*We're* going shopping."

"God, you're a pushy asshole," she said, taking a sip of her water.

"Yep. But responsible. And I'm responsible for that little monkey in your belly. So you'll move in with me so I can take care of both of you properly."

She exhaled. "I can take care of both of us just fine."

"And leave me out of it?"

"No. I said you're welcome to be a part of the baby's life as much as you like."

"And I'd like it to be 24-7. Plus, you *really* shouldn't be

changing the cat litter, and I'm not coming over to do it every day."
He chugged his iced tea in two swallows. "And we get a fair bit of
snow out where we are. Road is narrow and windy out toward your
place too. My place is safer."

Jesus, the man was relentless. But despite being an alpha jackass, the more he spoke, the harder a time she was having not
agreeing with him—about *some* things. The first trimester so far had
been really hard. Harder than she expected. And even though she
usually just wanted french fries, some nights she was craving home-
cooked food like a stir-fry or her mum's meatloaf. Only she didn't
have the groceries or energy to make it and instead just ate more
fries or roasted red pepper soup.

Eyeing his sexiness over the rim of her water glass, she took
another sip. She'd been denying it all day, but being around Brock,
having him take care of her, touch her hand, the small of her back,
it'd been nice. Albeit also frustrating because he was a pushy
fucker, but it'd been nice. And he certainly wasn't hard to look at.
Or smell. Would moving in with him mean they could have sex
again? Would she ever have sex again? She'd been as randy as a
bitch in heat these past few weeks—when she wasn't nauseous that
is—and her poor vibrator was on its third set of batteries since the
test had been confirmed positive. Chewing on an ice cube and
blearily remembering his head bobbing up and down between her
legs, she gave him her best negotiator face.

"Okay, let's just say, for hypothetical purposes, that I do move
in with you. I'm going to need to know a heck of a lot more about
the man I'm moving in with than I do now."

He visibly stiffened, and even though she couldn't see it, an
invisible wall came crashing down around him.

He grunted. "Okay."

"Do you have any siblings?"

He nodded. "Three younger brothers."

"And your parents?"

His jaw twitched. "Dad died when I was twelve. Mum lives across town."

Her heart clenched inside her chest. Mickey had mentioned Brock's dad was gone. Didn't mention when he'd died though. "I'm sorry about your dad."

He grunted and lifted one shoulder.

"Did you mother ever remarry?"

He shook his head.

She let out an exasperated huff. It was like pulling teeth to get the man to open up. "Look, if you want me to consider moving in with you, you're going to have to give me more. I'd prefer to get my information from the source. But I'll do a background check on you at work if I have to."

The man looked like he was going to vomit, but he shut his eyes for a moment before starting. "My mother never remarried, so when my dad died, I took on the role as father-figure to my brothers. All four of us have done a stint in the Naval Reserves. Like our dad. Dad became a cop, though, after."

"Are any of your brothers cops?"

He shook his head again. "No. We were recruited by Joint Task Force 2, and then ran special ops."

Krista's eyes went wide. Was he still doing that now?

He must have read her expression. "I retired."

She sat there in quiet contemplation for a moment. Sure, he was a bossy ass, but he didn't seem like a *bad* guy. She put away bad guys. And she wasn't getting that kind of a vibe from Brock. Pushy? Yes. Alpha? Yes. Bad? No. He was definitely one of the good guys.

She lifted her eyes to his from where she'd been staring at her plate. "So, if I move in with you, then what?"

"Then I take care of you and our baby. I'm responsible for that child."

"Are you always responsible?"

He didn't even blink. "Yes."

Did the man know how to have fun? Or had he abandoned all whimsy the day his father died, becoming the man of the house?

She studied him for a moment, all sexy and broody. Those walls of his were up, but from the way the left side of his jaw ticked, she wondered if there was perhaps a hairline crack in his fortress. Was he worried she was going to say no?

He said he wanted to take care of her and their baby. She really didn't want to do this alone. She could and she would if she had to, but she didn't want to.

She dragged her teeth over her bottom lip, suddenly wishing it wasn't so damn hot in the restaurant. "All right, let's just *say* I move in with you. We're going to need to set up some ground rules first."

Rule #1: We get to have sex again.

Rule #2: We get to have lots of sex.

Rule #3: Sex! Sex! Sex!

But instead, she took a deep breath and started, "Rule number one, you are *not* the boss of me. This alpha male, bravado thing needs to stop. I'm nobody's *pet*."

He didn't say anything. The man didn't say much. Instead, he was all devastatingly sexy smiles as he chewed his burger triumphantly. And boy did that smile make her not only want to move in with him, but also jump his bones, wear his ring and give him as many kids as he wanted.

Yeah, Krista was fucked.

———

KRISTA DIDN'T KNOW what to expect when she moved into Brock's place. Would they share a room? A bed? Meals? Condiments? She'd had roommates before, but they'd always been other women, and she wasn't sexually attracted to any of them or expecting a child with them either. This situation was an entirely new kettle of fish, and by the awkward way they danced around each other in the kitchen the first few days, it was just as new for Brock.

But in the end, it wasn't as weird as she anticipated. After the ultrasound appointment and lunch, they'd gone grocery shopping. Then he'd followed her home and pretty much insisted she start packing right then and there.

Exhausted, cranky and tired of fighting him at every turn, she acquiesced. In no time, both her car and his truck were full of stuff, plus Penelope, and she was knocking on her landlord's door, letting them know the plan. Which was she was going to continue to pay rent for a bit, in case things with her broody and grumpy new roommate went sideways.

Brock's house was a decent size and boasted several bedrooms. She had her own room, own bathroom and, after some reconfiguration of shelves, they split the fridge down the middle, sharing staples like condiments, milk and eggs.

The only thing they seemed to continuously disagree on was television shows. The man was addicted to the news or police and crime dramas, where all Krista wanted to do was abandon reality, her job and tragedy altogether when she was off the clock and watch The Food Network or Home and Garden Channel.

It quickly became a race and a battle for the remote, and Monday night was one of those nights. Krista had worked a day shift and was just getting into her "comfy pants" fresh from the shower when Brock called her for dinner.

So far, he'd been home every night and was proving to be no slouch in the kitchen, though every meal had been some kind of stir-fry. Not that she was complaining; it was better than roasted red pepper tetra pack soup and french fries.

"Smells good," she said, wandering into the kitchen.

He was just finishing plating, gave her a side-eye and grunted a response.

She couldn't get a read on the man. One minute he was all Mr.

Sensitive and holding her hair as she lost her biscuits in the toilet, and then the next he was a closed book, almost seeming angry and barely saying two words. Did he have multiple personalities? And if so, had she met them all yet?

She went to reach for her plate with what looked to be delicious beef and broccoli over wild rice, but he pulled it away at the last minute, a wickedly sexy gleam in his eye.

Oh, shit.

Not this again.

Growling, she reached for it again. But he held it out of reach and used his other hand to finish plating.

"You're an ass," she grumbled at him, throwing her hands onto her hips.

"And you're a brat."

"I'm not going to do what you think I'm going to do."

"Bullshit."

"I'm starving. Your *child* is starving."

Another sexy side-eye, followed by a snort.

He finished dishing up his plate, which was nearly twice as full as hers, and then hesitantly handed over hers. Their eyes met, and suddenly everything was a blur as they both raced out into the living room in search of the remote.

Why she hadn't hidden it earlier, she didn't know. Perhaps it was because she secretly enjoyed this ridiculous little routine where they fought over which show to watch. It was oddly comforting and normal.

"Damn it!"

"You snooze, you lose," he said smugly.

She eyed him coyly. "The *baby* really likes The Food Network."

He grunted again and made himself comfortable in his chair, switched the television to The Food Network and dove into his dinner.

She chuckled to herself.

A teddy bear with a suit of armor. That seemed to be Brock Hart. At least the little bit she knew of him anyway. Would he take off his suit of armor for her eventually?

Her eyes fell to his lap.

Would he take off his pants too?

"This is really good," she said, mopping up the last bit of sauce from the bowl with her pinky finger a short while later.

He grunted.

"Had a mini orgasm in my mouth."

He grunted again, but this time his eyes slid from the television screen to hers.

She grinned at him.

He tipped up his beer bottle and took a long, healthy swig, not bothering to remove his gaze from where it was currently searing her skin.

Her breath caught in her chest as she took in the way his thick, sexy, muscular throat undulated as he swallowed. She was mesmerized. Her nipples pebbled beneath her sweater. She hadn't bothered to put a bra back on after her shower and was instead in a T-shirt and hoodie. But combined with the sore breasts from the pregnancy, they also suddenly tingled and ached for his hands to ease their strain and heaviness.

"What's with the look?" he asked, his hand falling to Penelope, who had jumped up and made herself at home in his lap.

Lucky cat.

Krista licked her lips. "You, uh ... you seeing anyone right now?"

Those sexy, bushy, caterpillar-like eyebrows furrowed. "As in *dating?*"

She lifted one shoulder. "Dating. Sleeping with. You a free agent or contracted out?"

His chest lurched on a silent laugh. "Free agent. No time for dating." His eyes remained focused on the chef on the screen. But she could tell he was thinking. Those caterpillars pinched even closer together. "Are *you* seeing anyone right now?" he asked.

Quickly, almost *too* quickly, she shook her head. "No."

He nodded.

"Um ... " She knitted her fingers together and pulled her gaze from the side of his face.

"Um?" he mimicked.

Just ask. What's the worst that can happen? He turns you down, then things are horribly awkward from here until the kid graduates high school?

She lifted her head. His eyes were pinned on hers.

"You interested in a *beneficial* arrangement?"

A tick at the side of his mouth was his only tell. "Are you asking me if I'd like a 'friends with benefits' arrangement?"

She nodded.

"Yes."

Her mouth dropped open. "Yes?"

"Fucking you was great. I'm not fucking anyone right now. Neither are you. Doesn't look like we'll be fucking anyone else for a while." He tilted his head toward her stomach. "Might as well fuck each other." He nodded. "Seems like a reasonable solution." His gaze drifted to one of her pregnancy books on the coffee table. "Besides, that book says a pregnant woman's libido increases, and from the buzzing sound emanating from your room each night, I'm guessing you'd like the real thing by now."

Her bottom lip nearly hit the floor.

He heard her?

"Thin walls, baby."

Was the house on fire, or were those just her cheeks?

He grabbed her with scary ninja stealth and hauled her over to the couch to straddle his lap. "The night we made the baby was fun. We don't have to worry about protection. I see no downside.

We can do it for as long as it works." He rested both of their bowls on the side table before letting his hands come up and cradle her ribcage and back. She couldn't stop the sigh that escaped her from how good, how right it felt to be in his arms.

They hadn't had this much contact since that night ... and yet it didn't feel nearly as weird as she expected it to. She didn't expect it to feel this *normal*.

She licked her lips. "You're being very businesslike about all of this. Should we be drawing up a contract?"

He shrugged as his hands traveled up under her sweatshirt and his thumbs grazed her peaked nipples. "It's the practical solution to both of our problems."

She had to choke back a laugh even as her body trembled beneath his erotic touch. "And what would be *your* problem? You can't tell me *you* have trouble getting laid."

He didn't say anything but instead grunted and adjusted himself, making his arousal, his need for her very present.

"Besides," he went on, "I'd rather fuck you than watch this cooking show garbage any longer." His mouth crashed down on hers, and his tongue wasted no time waiting for permission and wedged its way into her mouth, lapping and twirling around her own.

And once again, they were frantic. What had just moments ago been a relaxing dinner between what was quickly becoming two friends and future co-parents was now a lust-filled and almost determined animalistic need to fuck. Hands roamed and peeled away at clothing as fast as their fingers could move. Leaning forward, she licked his throat and pressed a kiss to his Adam's apple before he pulled away, and she motioned to remove his shirt. Krista paused and just stared as he tossed the soft black cotton to the floor.

"Holy God." She swallowed. "Are those even real?" She poked a finger at one of his pecs. It was hard as stone. "And those? Are those real too?" Both her hands ran up his arms and gripped his biceps. Once again, boulders beneath her fingertips. She hadn't a chance to admire him, his beauty, his power, his strength when they were together last time. It'd been late, dark, and she'd been incredibly drunk and single-minded. But tonight, they were sober, the light was on, and the man in front of her was a work of art. Art that needed to be, deserved to be ogled, worshiped, appreciated.

"Everything is real." His voice was deep and thick. With brute force, he grabbed at the hem of her hoodie and pulled it over her head, bringing her T-shirt with it. His eyes flared as he drank her in, raking her body. His scan stopped on her stomach, and his chest actually shook as his hand fell to her belly, his eyes searching hers for permission. She gave it to him.

"You're sure I can't hurt the kid?" he asked softly, his fingers and palm taking up the entire span of her stomach. He was warm, and his touch soft, although calloused and worn from hard work. She felt safe in his touch, in his arms.

"I'm sure." She smiled.

"Well in that case ... " And with the flick of his wrist, he pushed her up out of the chair and off him and stood up.

Shirtless and rippling with muscles, Brock seemed even bigger, even fiercer standing in front of her. His heated gaze fell on her face and a small, barely discernible smile tugged at the corner of his mouth before he gripped her hip and spun her around, pulling the back of her body tight against his. His tongue trailed down her neck, shoulder and back up again. His teeth nipped at the shell of her ear as one hand made its way below the waist of her pajama pants and into her panties, drawing delightful little circles around her throbbing clit. She closed her eyes and leaned into him, savoring his touch, how good it felt to have his hands on her again. She pushed her backside into his growing erection and giggled when he groaned, bucking into her.

He bent her over, pulling her pajama pants and underwear down in the process. She kicked out of her pants and then stood there, her fingers kneading the soft leather of the couch as Brock's capable hands massaged and caressed her craving backside.

Was it too early to ask him to spank her? She'd have to put a pin in that and see. Because one thing for sure, Krista liked it a little rough. Liked a little pain with her pleasure.

He gripped both her hips, positioned himself behind her, and then drove home. She let out a soft grunt from the impact, but damn if it didn't feel good. She loved this position, which was ironic given how submissive it was and how in control she liked to be. But they wouldn't finish like this. This was just the beginning. She squeezed her muscles around him as he pushed into her.

She needed this.

God, how she'd needed this.

Her vibrator just wasn't cutting it these days. And now, after another taste of Brock Hart, she wasn't sure it ever would.

Lost in the moment, she reveled in the feeling of Brock deep inside her, filling her, fulfilling her. The spank came out of nowhere, startling the daylights out of her. She yelped and then fell face first into the couch, her arms flying out from under her and causing Brock to slip out.

"You okay?" he asked, helping her up.

She looked back at him and smiled. "Yes. Again."

Triumph, wicked and primal, glimmered in his green eyes. "Sorry, I should have asked first."

She shook her head. "No. I want more. Harder." She assumed the position and he was back inside her in seconds. Three hard, lightning-quick smacks had her panting and pushing into his palm, grinding her backside up to reach his pelvis. Her pussy dripped down her thighs, and her legs shook from his power.

He was having a hard time holding on. His grunts and wavering patterns said he was riding that beautiful edge between insanity and pure bliss. But she wasn't quite there, and she wanted to be on top.

"Let's ... let's change positions," she said breathlessly, motioning to stand up. "You sit on the couch, and I'll straddle you." His eyes flared lambent as she stood back up and turned to face him. His gaze settled on her breasts. He licked his lips. "Careful with these, though. They're rather tender."

He sat down on the couch. Krista's top teeth snagged her lip and bit down hard at the sight of his cock straight on. They'd had quick and dirty sex in the dark last time, so she hadn't really had a good view. But there it was standing at attention, hard, thick and eager as it rested against his belly. She climbed onto his lap and put her thighs on either side of his, rising up only to sink back down. A groan escaped them both. He brought his hands up and cupped her breasts, flicking and twisting the nipples, bringing one to his mouth and laving at it with his velvety tongue. She bobbed up and down in his lap, letting his pubic hair and pelvic bone hit her clit in just the right way.

She was close, damn close. And then Brock did something unexpected, yet again. The man was full of surprises. He gripped her by the ponytail, hauled her head back and up, then lunged at her mouth, capturing her sighs and gasps with his own.

They came together, finding their release at the same time, connected as the pleasure unfurled and ripped its way through them. Slashing and shredding everything in its path until they were limp and boneless, chests heaving.

With a ringing in her ears and a smile on her face, Krista tucked her nose against the crook of his neck and inhaled his scent. So manly, so sexy, so strong, so *Brock*.

Then, taking another risk, because tonight seemed to be a night for pushing past her comfort zone, she licked him. He was salty and tasted mildly of soap, and she wanted more. A whole hell of a lot more.

They sat there for a while in post-coital silence, allowing their breathing to return to normal. Their sweaty skin blossomed in gooseflesh as the chill of the house settled on tired, naked bodies.

"Wow," she finally breathed, breaking the silence.

He grunted in response beneath her, his fingers dancing delicate and divine trails up her back. For a bossy jackass, he certainly had a sweet side when he wanted to.

"More of that for sure."

Another grunt.

"Do you do more than just grunt? How about talk? I mean we're living together, having a kid together, and now sleeping together, might as well get to know each other," she said with a small laugh. Not even her laugh could force the virile strength of him from her body. If anything, he was growing harder. Could he go again? *Already?*

Brock cleared his throat, his face a mask of fierce alpha determination. "I fuck." Then, without an ounce of warning, he pulled her off him, shoved her back into the plush couch and was back inside her, making her eyes shut and her entire body clench around him as she forgot all her questions and thought of nothing but how good it felt, how good *he* felt on top of her. Inside her. Surrounding her.

CHAPTER SIX

Krista hadn't even been paying attention to the days or weeks or how quickly they were ticking by. One minute, it was the November long weekend and the entire police station was taking part in the annual Remembrance Day ceremony downtown, and then the next they were getting their schedules at work for the Christmas holiday season, which was only two weeks away.

Despite being *ordered* to disclose her pregnancy at work by her overbearing and bossy-ass roommate, she still hadn't. She didn't want to jeopardize her career by going on light duty too early. She knew what she was doing wasn't right, and she'd probably catch shit for it when she finally started to show and *had* to disclose her pregnancy, but for now she felt fine and needed the experience, despite how exhausted it left her each day.

On top of the pregnancy, back-to-back night shifts and the stress of being a rookie cop wore her down even more. The nausea was mostly gone, but now the hip and back pain were showing up, and that was almost worse than the puking.

Normally night shift sucked. Even on a good day, it sucked.

You'd think it'd be quiet, what with most people sleeping, but no. Ruffians and hooligans of the most despicable kind tended to be nocturnal, preying on the weak and weary as they slept. And these last two night shifts had been particularly awful.

They'd brought in a man who had not only fled from the scene after breaking and entering a woman's home and trying to force himself on her as she slept, but he was also drunk and hostile. He nearly head-butted Krista when she finally managed to cuff him as they escorted him to the SUV. After she and Myles had booked him, he attempted to trip Krista and then kneed Myles in the crotch as they hauled him through the station. For a drunk guy, he was still surprisingly agile.

It was too bloody early in the morning/late in their shift for leniency, so for once, Krista didn't begrudge the force Myles used when he tossed the douchebag into the holding cell.

"Sleep it off, motherfucker," Myles grumbled, knuckling fatigue out of his eyes.

Krista nodded, stifling a yawn but failing miserably. They were just walking out of the cell when the man started to cough, like seriously, might-hack-up-a-lung cough. Both Myles and Krista paused. She lifted one eyebrow at him, which he returned with his own skeptical smirk.

"You okay there, asshole?" Myles asked the man dry-heaving in the corner. After his initial assaults, they hadn't bothered to remove his cuffs, mostly for their own safety.

"Should we take off his cuffs?" she asked. "What if he needs to pee?"

"Smells like he's already pissed himself," Myles replied with a scoff.

"He might need some water."

Myles let out an exhausted and exasperated huff. "Fucking bleeding heart, Matthews," he murmured, getting his keys out of his pocket and walking over to the man, who was at the moment bent on his knees with his hands behind his back, his face a mere inch from the disgusting jail cell floor.

"Here, let me get those cuffs off you so you can go grab some water."

Krista had to hand it to Myles. For a jerk and a man who had nearly lost his ability to have children just an hour ago, thanks to this drunken attempted rapist, his tone wasn't entirely unpleasant. There was a hint, just a smidgen of compassion.

Maybe he did have a heart?

He walked around behind the coughing prisoner and went to unlock his cuffs. But as soon as the cuffs were off and Myles was tucking them into his belt, the prisoner leaped up from his knees and grabbed Myles around the neck, putting him in a headlock. Myles fought the guy pretty well, thrashing around and elbowing him, but the man had at *least* fifty if not seventy-five pounds on the cop, and he was also drunk and desperate.

A very dangerous combination.

Krista watched as the prisoner's hand started patting around Myles's duty belt in search of his gun. He was only inches away from grabbing it, but it was his left hand, and the way Myles was struggling, the man couldn't maintain a purchase on the weapon.

"Help, Matthews. Help me!" Myles grunted as he struggled to get out of the choke hold, his feet flying around. His fingers were near white as they tried to pry the man's arm from his neck.

Cop instinct trumping mother's instinct for just a moment caused her to fly into action and run to the aid of her partner, despite how often she'd thought about choking him out herself over the last few months. Krista wrapped an arm around the drunk's neck, applying enough pressure to cut off his air. His grip on Myles seemed to loosen, but not enough. She couldn't pry his hand from around Myles's neck, and the prisoner still hadn't managed to unholster Myles's gun, so deciding disabling him was her best bet, she tightened her grip around his neck and reached for her taser. She was just about to free it when the man's desperation for air caused him to rear back and head-butt her in the face. The elbow of his free hand came back and nailed her hard in the belly. On instinct she released him, recoiling back against the wall and cradling her abdomen as blood gushed out of her nose and stars spun behind her eyes.

"Matthews!" Myles bellowed. "Call for fucking backup!"

But she just sat there, stunned. Her head was no longer in the moment—it was in her belly, and after that elbow, she couldn't in good conscience put her baby in jeopardy again. No. Mother's instinct now trumped any instinct or training she may have received as a cop. She couldn't, she *wouldn't* risk it.

"Help!" Myles screamed, just as he managed to swat the assailant's hand away from his gun, pull out his expandable baton and start whacking the drunk over the head. Finally, the drunk let go, and Myles scrambled away, pulling his gun out and fixing it on the man.

Fury flooded the room as Myles pushed himself up to standing. He fixed his gaze on the perp before flicking it to Krista. "You'll pay for that."

Just then two more cops, Marlise and Allie, came rushing forward and into the holding cell.

"Everything okay?" Marlise asked. Her eyes roamed the scene, taking in Krista lying there on the floor covered in her own blood.

Allie rushed forward and helped Krista up. "You all right?"

Krista nodded, using her shirtsleeve to wipe up her face. "Yeah, I'm fine."

"Come on, let's go get you cleaned up before we write up the report," Allie said, fishing some tissues out of her pocket and handing them to Krista.

Myles was busy handcuffing the prisoner, who was now being held at gunpoint by Marlise.

"This isn't over," Myles said as Krista walked past him, his onyx eyes saying so much that a chill colder than any winter storm sprinted down her spine.

————

SHE WAS STUCK in court the following day, all day, and thankfully without Myles beside her. She had to lay charges and participate in the prosecution of the man who had beaten his wife to a bloody pulp, inevitably causing her to miscarry. It had been a trying day, an exhausting and emotionally draining day. More than once, Krista caught herself rubbing her stomach as they went through the gruesome details of that horrific night.

She watched as the poor woman recounted each punch, each kick, her whole body quivering with a mix of rage and overwhelming sadness and loss. Krista ached to get up from her seat and go wrap an arm around her, comfort her and tell her that it would be okay; she was free of him and could start a new life, one free of harm and heartbreak, and the doctors said she would still be able to have children. But Krista couldn't. That was not her job while in court.

Her job was to present the facts and recount her participation in what had happened that night. But what she *could* do, and what she *did* do, with cutthroat clarity and vitriol-laden eloquence, was nail the bastard to the wall with every single detail she could— every scratch, every blood drop, every sexist slur he'd muttered to her and to his wife when they'd knocked on their door that day. She painted him to be the most disgusting, deplorable excuse for a human being imaginable, because he was. She couldn't sit and wipe away the tears of his wife, but she could sit on the stand and do everything in her power to make sure he never laid on a hand on anyone ever again.

Brock had been away for the past two days for some high-profile personal security job on the mainland, so she had the house to herself. Which, despite the lack of orgasms and stir-fry when she walked through the door after work, had been nice. He was a bossy, pushy, demanding bugger and, even though they were slowly developing a friendship as the weeks ticked by, it was nice to *not* have someone cramming a pre-natal vitamin and spinach-infused smoothie down her throat every morning. A person can only eat *so* much spinach before they start a revolt.

And it was probably a good thing he didn't see her the night following the court appearance, because after a dinner of french fries and roasted red pepper soup, she lay on the couch, spooned Penelope and cried. Cried for the woman on the stand, for all women who were abused and assaulted, harassed and beaten. Cried for the baby that would never be, for her baby safely nestled in her belly and the terrible world she was bringing it into. She cried for herself and the fact that as much as she tried not to be, she was a screwup. She'd gotten knocked up on a one-night stand, nearly got her mentor killed and, in the process, could have lost the baby. She was a total screwup.

It wasn't until she was fresh out of tears and sadness that the rage finally took over. And the guilt. She's been stupid to go this long at work and not disclose her pregnancy. The woman on the stand had lost her baby because of her husband's anger, not her job as a secretary; meanwhile Krista was recklessly endangering her child every day by going to work.

Brock was right.

Damn him.

She needed to switch to light duty, needed to be responsible and think about more than just her career. It used to mean everything to her, but now, there was something bigger, something more important. She cradled her abdomen with her hands and vowed to her unborn child that tomorrow she was going to march into Staff Sergeant Wicks' office and request the change. She needed to start being responsible. She needed to start thinking about someone besides herself.

Unsure of the time, but exhausted from the day and mental toll it had taken, Krista passed out on the couch sometime between the house-flipping show and the garden renovation show only to wake up the next morning at 5 a.m. to the sound of someone coming in the front door.

Disoriented and exhausted, Krista sprang up from her spot on the couch, aware of the drool puddle beneath her chin but not caring enough about it at the moment.

"Who's there?" she called out, her eyes adjusting to the light in the living room as they scanned the area for a weapon of sorts.

"Me." Followed by a grunt and then heavy footsteps on the stairs. Seconds later, his head popped up behind the wall separating the living room from the stairs. Unable to control herself or the magnitude of emotions of the last few days, Krista leaped up off the couch and hurled herself into his arms.

———

"Oof," was all he said as his arms made their way around her.

Brock was bagged from the last few days of following around the high-profile celebrity in Vancouver, but all that vanished when a look of pure defeat and terror met him at the top of the stairs. His nose fell to her hair, and he inhaled before he knew what he was doing. Fuck, she smelled good. She always smelled good.

Felt good in his arms, too.

"You okay?" he asked. She was crying against his shirt, and the man was at a loss. He'd never really been in a relationship long enough to have to deal with the emotional roller coaster that was a woman. Sure, he'd dealt with PMS, but this seemed way more than that. And then it hit him. The baby.

Panic flooded him at the thought that Krista might have miscarried while he was away. Grabbing her by the elbows, he pushed her away from him, stepping down one stair so that they could be eye-to-eye. "Krista!" He shook her gently. "What's wrong? Is the baby okay?"

She was staring at her purple and yellow striped socks, her hair an untameable halo around her head and hanging in her face. But he saw her nod, and he exhaled. The baby was okay.

Swallowing past the hard lump of dread in his throat, he nodded with her and stepped up, leaving his bag at the top of the stairs and pulling her around and into the living room where they could sit down. "What's wrong?" That's when he noticed that her nose and around her eyes was a mottled blue and purple. What the fuck?

Her slight body trembled and breath hitched as she fought the sobs, still unable to look at him.

Moving his hands up to her shoulders, he shook her again. "I can't help you if I don't know what's wrong. Who did this to you? Is the baby okay?"

It was several agonizing seconds later before she finally lifted her head, her beautiful blue eyes glassy and red-rimmed from all the tears. "You were right," she whispered. "I need to switch to light duty."

Brock's eyes went wide, and emotions he wasn't even able to label hit him like a dam breaking. "What happened?"

Averting her gaze, she studied the floor just behind his shoulder. "There was an incident at work with a man we had in custody. He attacked Slade and then me when I tried to help. I could have lost the baby with how hard he hit me. I went to the ER after work and double-checked everything was okay, and it is. The baby is fine. And then yesterday I had to go to court for that domestic assault, the one where she did lose the baby ... " Her bottom lip jutted out, but she quickly tucked it behind her teeth to keep her composure. Her gaze shifted, and she met his eyes once again. "I'm sorry. You were right. You win. I'm going to go in today and request light duty. I don't want to endanger our baby any longer. I'm sorry I've been so stubborn." Then she crumpled against him, and the tears were back.

He carried her over to the couch and plopped her onto his lap, doing the only thing he could think of, and that was hold her.

It seemed to be enough.

———

ROUGHLY FORTY-FIVE MINUTES LATER, Brock watched Krista head to work. She'd rattled him this morning. More than any woman, possibly any *person* ever had. He'd begun to admire and enjoy her stubbornness—for the most part. It showed her strength, and damn if his woman wasn't as strong as they came. But it also pissed him off that she still hadn't switched to light duty at work. He'd thought about putting Rex on her detail and having him follow Krista while she was on shift just in case she got into any trouble. But his brother didn't know about the pregnancy yet, and he didn't want Rex to think he was some psycho stalker guy who didn't trust the woman he was currently sleeping with.

But to see her so broken, so defeated and deflated, hadn't made him feel good. He hadn't *won* anything, as she'd said, besides maybe peace of mind. Even that didn't do much to ease the turmoil and confusion roiling inside him. He wanted her and the baby safe. Their safety, their lives were his number one priority.

What had it cost her? The spark was gone from her eyes. The fight and feistiness seemed to have vanished in those two days he was gone. She'd barely been able to get herself ready for work once she'd stopped crying and all but choked back the smoothie he made her for breakfast. And it'd all been done with sullen eyes and robotic movements. Had he broken her? Had Slade? He'd never be able to forgive himself if it was the former, and Slade wouldn't be breathing much longer if it turned out to be the latter.

CHAPTER SEVEN

"You COMING to the Christmas party on Saturday, Matthews?" Myles asked, causing Krista to jump out of her skin. She was raw and exhausted from her morning cry-fest on Brock's shoulder. Not to mention embarrassed. So far, he'd seen her barf her guts out, but he hadn't seen her cry.

She'd remained strong, tough, resilient.

But she couldn't stop herself, couldn't control the flood of emotions, good and bad, that had assailed her the moment he'd walked through the door. And without even thinking, she collapsed against him and let every feeling from the last few days fall out onto his hard chest in the form of warm, salty tears.

Even though she'd slept through the night, not even having to get up to pee, she didn't feel rested at all. Her eyes hurt, her head felt full of cotton, and the realization that she was no longer going to be doing "real" cop stuff and saving the world from the bad guys hurt more than when she'd had pepper spray shot into her eyes during training at the academy. She finished filling her water bottle at the sink in the staff kitchen before turning to face Myles. His tone seemed much more civil than the last time they'd spoken. Had he forgiven her for not coming to his rescue again with that drunk guy in the holding cell?

No matter what, Myles was a manipulative bastard. He had to be working some angle. Her gaze drifted to the open door behind him. "I don't know. I haven't decided yet."

"We should go together."

She swallowed and tried to give him a small smile, but it was a struggle. The thought of dating this man, even going to a work function together, made her skin crawl. "No, thank you."

"It's going to happen, you and I," he said smugly, trying to come across as flirty and playful, but instead he was just creepy and off-putting. "And what better time than the Christmas party? A dark corner, too much rum and eggnog, mistletoe ... "

Grinding her molars together until her jaw ached, she looked him square on. "Myles," she started, "I want to apologize for the other day. I'm really very sorry that I didn't jump back in to help you. The guy knocked the wind out of me. I thought he'd broken my nose. There was so much blood." She glanced down at her feet. The man's eyes were too disconcerting to maintain contact with. Toeing at a scuff on the floor, she continued, "There's no excuse, though. I'm very sorry. I'm glad Marlise and Allie were able to get there in time. I'm glad you weren't seriously hurt. I wouldn't have been able to forgive myself. If you need to report me to Wicks, I completely understand. But it will never happen between us. I'm not interested in you that way. I don't want to date anyone I work with, especially not a superior. I'm flattered, but I'm sorry. I'm going to have to say no."

She motioned to push past him, but he stuck out an arm and stopped her, his grip on her forearm painful. Of course, she'd inherited her mother's pale skin tone and bruised like a freaking peach.

"Let go of me." She hardened her eyes, refusing to let him see her fear. He couldn't know he scared her, because if he did, he'd use that power. She swallowed again and then finally lifted her head to catch his gaze. "Please."

He released his grip, and the terror slowly began to drain from her, only to be replaced by even more when instead of leaving, he walked to the door, shut it and locked it, stalking back toward her, smirking triumphantly.

"I'm all for the chase, Matthews. But I'm getting sick and tired of this little cat-and-mouse game. You know you're the only rookie that hasn't given it up to me? I'd like to change that. Or would you prefer I tell Wicks about the other day?"

She lifted one shoulder. "I told you that you can. I deserve to be reported." Fuck, she *really* didn't want him to report her, but he had every right. She secretly hoped calling his bluff might have the reverse effect and he'd just let it go.

"I won't ... for a *price*." His free hand came up, and his index finger grazed her collarbone.

Fury and disgust ran neck and neck inside her. "You make me sick," she spat out, trying to move away from him, but he grabbed her again, this time by the bicep. "There are plenty of women here who *want* to sleep with you. Why do you have to go after the one who *doesn't*? We're supposed to be the good guys. You can't blackmail me, and I won't sleep with you to keep you quiet. Go ahead, tell whoever about what I did. I'll take my punishment."

He lifted one shoulder casually. "I want to break you. And I'll do it."

What the hell did that mean? He was in front of her and let the knuckles of his free hand graze slowly down her cheek and neck, landing on her chest. His finger circled the underside of her breast, and he grinned, his pupils dilating as he caught the scent of fear in the air. She batted his hand away and grabbed his fingers, bending them backward until he yelped, his other hand releasing its death grip on her upper arm.

"I told you not to touch me," she warned. Thankfully, between the academy and her father, Krista was no slouch when it came to self-defense. She'd taken down bigger men than him at the academy. But what she lacked was experience. Myles was a senior officer. He knew more tricks and wrist flicks than she did, and before she knew it, he had her spun around, her back to his chest and her stomach pressed hard—too hard—against the counter. She winced from the sudden pain, her brain immediately flying to the little jellybean or avocado or whatever it was now inside her. She prayed it was okay.

"Like it rough, do you? Well, I can work with that." He tore at the buttons on the front of her shirt and shoved his hand inside her now-open shirt and fondled her breasts. Squeezing just a bit too hard. His warm breath on her neck smelled faintly of coffee and whatever he'd eaten earlier that day. She struggled with all her might to get away, but instead he just pulled tighter.

"I could kill you or fuck you right now," he said, a menacing chuckle in his tone. He flipped her back around to face him, pinning her arms behind her with his free hand.

Krista tilted her head up and met his gaze. Nothing but blackness stared back at her. "You make me sick," she said with a sneer before rearing her head back and spitting in his face.

If eternal darkness could grow even darker, even bleaker and more desolate, it did so in Myles Slade's eyes. His lips curled up into a sinister smile. "I'm going to enjoy breaking you, Matthews." Then his mouth crashed down on hers, and he rammed his tongue to the back of her throat as his hands on her wrists tightened until she fought not to cry out in pain.

But she wouldn't go down without a fight. If he was going to take her right here in the work breakroom, she was going to make it as difficult for him as possible. She chomped down hard on his tongue until she tasted blood, making the man yip like a poodle and release her in the process.

"Fucking bitch!"

He lunged for her again, but Krista had managed to sprint to the door, one hand on the knob, the other on the taser firmly in her hip.

His eyes drifted down to her hand. "You wouldn't dare."

"Just try something like that again, and we'll see. I'd rather get suspended for what I did in that jail cell or go to prison for tasing a cop's dick than let that dick anywhere near me," she whispered, using every last ounce of energy she had left to keep her voice from quavering. She unlocked the door and opened it. "Stay. The. Fuck. Away. From. Me." Then she turned around and headed to the locker room to go and fix her shirt.

———

Ignoring the fact that she was supposed to be out on patrol with Myles, after finding a new shirt in her locker and splashing some cool water on her face, Krista made her way to Staff Sergeant Wicks' office. Every muscle, every bone, every fiber of her being trembled as she brought her fist up and rapped on his door.

"Enter," he barked, the shuffle of papers greeting her as she slowly opened the door.

Was his office abnormally hot and stuffy? Or were those just her nerves causing sweat to break out on the back of her neck and between her breasts? Stupid hormones.

"Matthews?" Wicks said, lifting his head. "Shouldn't you and Slade be out on patrol?"

Krista licked her lips, tossed her shoulders back and stepped inside, closing the door softly behind her. "May I speak with you, please, sir?"

He nodded at the empty chair in front of his desk.

Holding on to the back of the chair, she slid into the seat, grateful to be off her feet for a moment.

"What can I do for you, rookie?"

Right! She was a rookie. Hadn't even been on the force a year, and she was already requesting light duty and complaining about her partner. She was going to be labeled as "that" person. The whiner. The snitch. The rookie who couldn't keep her legs shut and got knocked up in the first six months of her career.

Wicks lifted one bushy salt and pepper eyebrow. "Rookie?"

"Sir, I'm pregnant."

The other eyebrow joined its twin. "Really?"

She nodded. "Yes, sir. I apologize, as I know this isn't ideal. It wasn't planned. Just a ... happy accident, if you will. But I'm here to officially request light duty even though I know I should have sooner. And I apologize. It is no longer in the best interest of me or my partner for me to continue working in the field." She exhaled. Her gaze moved from his light brown eyes to his stapler. The stapler couldn't possibly look at her with as much judgment as she was sure he was looking at her with at the moment.

He cleared his throat. "Well, congratulations, Rookie. I'll be sorry to pull you from the field. You're a good cop. Slade has nothing but good things to report about you."

He what?

Krista nearly swallowed her tongue. And she must have made a noise or a face of disbelief, because Wicks cocked his head. "You don't believe me?"

Blinking half a dozen times, she shook her head to clear out the bullshit. "I ... it's just, well, I was also coming in here to file a formal complaint about Constable Slade."

The staff sergeant's jaw visibly tightened. "Oh, really?"

Her head bobbed. "Yes. Since early on, Constable Slade has been inappropriate with me and making sexual advances. I've asked him to stop, but he doesn't seem to take no for an answer. Just earlier he cornered me and ripped open my shirt and touched me and kissed me." The back of her eyes burned with the desire not to cry. Her throat wasn't much better off as it slowly threatened to stop her speech altogether with each word she got out.

But Wicks didn't seem fazed. His jaw just tightened a little more, and his chestnut eyes darkened. "Do you have any witnesses?" he asked.

She couldn't be certain, but it almost seemed as though there might be trepidation in his voice. And what the hell did witnesses have to do with it? They took any and all sexual harassment cases seriously, whether the victim had a witness or not. Why was she any different?

She shook her head. "N-no, sir. There was no one in the lunch room just now, and all the other times we were out on patrol. I didn't think I required a *witness* in order for my claim to be taken seriously."

Fuck, now his brown eyes looked more like Myles's black ones. Dark and soulless. "I'll handle it," he clipped. "Besides, you're going on *light* duty now, rookie. You won't have to work with Constable Slade anymore. This can all be water under the bridge."

Water under the bridge?

Her mouth hung open for maybe a moment too long before she finally had to snap it shut. Was this really happening? Was he really dismissing her complaints?

Blinking a few times and resisting the urge to pinch herself, she finally found her voice. "Are you not going to deal with this, sir? I mean, I can't be the *only* female officer who has had issues with Constable Slade."

The staff sergeant let out a weighted, almost irritated sigh. "You're moving on to light duty. I don't see the issue."

Before she knew what she was doing, Krista had pushed back her chair and was standing over her superior's desk, hands on her hips, body hinged forward, glowering down at him. "That's irrelevant, *sir*. I'm making a formal complaint about Constable Slade and his inappropriate work behavior. Now if you're unwilling to handle this, then I have no problem going to HR. But I *thought* I was to come to you first?"

Well, that seemed to have knocked the cotton from his ears. Only it also seemed to have set that cotton aflame. Red flooded the older man's cheeks, and his face hardened. Slowly, purposefully so, he rose up out his chair. He was a tall man. Maybe not as tall as Brock but damn close, and even with a big wooden desk between them, he towered over her. She was forced to lift her head and tilt her neck to look him in the eye.

"I hope that wasn't a *threat ... rookie?*"

She swallowed, suddenly feeling the size of a gnat and just as easily squishable. "No, sir. Not a threat."

"Good. I didn't think so." His face softened a touch, though you could probably still shatter crystal on it. "I'll deal with Slade. No need to involve HR just yet. It'd take ages for anything to happen. I'll file your paperwork for light duty right now, and you can head on upstairs and see Mallory. She'll get you sorted out." Then, before she could say anything, even mutter a thank you, he spun around and showed her his back. "Dismissed." And that was the end of that, apparently.

Confused, frazzled, and worried about what had just happened with the staff sergeant, the incident with Slade in the break room and what would happen *now* that the word was out about her pregnancy, Krista made her way toward the offices.

"Hey!" It was Slade.

Oh, of all things holy.

"Where the fuck are you going? We have patrol." Careful not to lay a hand on her where anyone walking by might notice, he approached Krista in the narrow corridor between Wicks' office and the stairwell heading upstairs to the other offices. He stopped roughly six feet in front of her, clearly still pissed about their altercation earlier. Well, good. So was she. And hopefully the prick would be getting what was coming to him soon enough.

"I'm on light duty now. You're officially no longer my coach."

His eyes bugged out, but that didn't make them any less spooky looking. "You knocked up?"

She didn't answer him.

"Are you?"

"It's none of your business. Medically I need to go on light duty." With that she left him standing in the hallway and headed upstairs to find Mallory.

———

HE DIDN'T HAVE to hear her to know she was home. He could *feel* her presence. And not in some paranormal spirit type way. No. That shit was dumb. If ghosts existed, he was sure his dad would be haunting him every waking moment. No, the house became a home when Krista stepped inside. He could feel her warmth. Feel the change in the atmosphere. Smell that sweet and unique smell of hers, even when masked by a day's worth of work out on the streets.

Busy standing over the stove and pushing meat and veggies around in a big wok for dinner, he waited for her to come up the stairs. Only she didn't. Ordinarily, it took roughly twenty-seven seconds for her to shut the door, hang up her coat, take off her boots and ascend the stairs. And based on what the clock on the microwave said, she'd been home for nearly three minutes. What was up?

He glanced toward the staircase. A curly red ponytail was all that he saw. She was sitting on the last few steps, staring straight ahead at the front door. Turning off the element on the stove and ignoring his grumbling stomach, he headed down the stairs.

"Forget how to walk?"

She didn't say anything.

"You're not that far along yet that you need me to carry you, are you?"

Not even a shoulder shrug.

She wasn't a big person, but he certainly was, and trying to push past her small frame on the steps without stepping on her or putting his elbow into the drywall proved to be a challenge. But he made it and then crouched down in front of her in the small entryway.

He wasn't used to dealing with the rickety wooden roller coaster that was female emotions. Toss in the pregnancy hormones, and he was so far out of his comfort zone, they could have been on different continents. That roller coaster was in the dark, missing a wheel or two and in an abandoned theme park. But he was trying to show her he was in this baby rearing thing. Pregnancy and all. One hundred percent. Shoving down his instinct to say "women" and shake his head, he took a deep breath and tried to meet her eyes. "What's up?"

Slowly, she let her gaze leave the front door and fixed those brilliant blue eyes on him. "I told the staff sergeant about the baby. I'm officially on light duty."

Thank fuck.

One less thing for him to worry about. He was starting to think he was getting an ulcer from the stress of her being out in the field every day.

"Good."

She didn't seem nearly as happy as he was. Understandable. She was a tough cookie, and had the roles been reversed, he wouldn't have been happy about having to give up a job he loved. But she needed to start thinking about more than just herself.

Reaching out, he tucked a wild, wavy strand of her hair behind her ear. "What's wrong?"

She swallowed, and her eyes darted down for just half a second to her wrist before flying back up to his face. But his own gaze wasn't nearly as quick. Where the fuck did that bruise come from?

He reached for her arm, but she tugged it away. He reached again, and this time, she let him take it. "Where'd this come from?"

Her jaw clenched.

"Krista ... "

Letting out a deep, rattled breath, she started, "Slade. He cornered me in the staff room this morning. Got physical. I managed to fight him off, though."

Suddenly, there was a ringing in his ears.

Where the fuck was that coming from? Did she hear it, too? Heat flooded his face and chest, and red seemed to cloud his vision. A stroke?

No.

Fury.

He wanted to go find this Slade motherfucker and kill him. Or at the very least break every bone in his body so he couldn't lay a hand on any woman, on *his* woman again. She'd mentioned Slade in passing a few times. Called him a "tool" and a "pain in the ass," but she'd never said anything about him being a lecherous bastard, too. The fucker would pay for touching her. He'd pay dearly.

"Ow." Krista went to pull away, snapping him out of sudden blood lust. He glanced down at his hand on her wrist, his own fingerprints now where her bruise was.

Regret hit him square in the solar plexus, and he avoided her stare as he let her go, muttering, "Sorry."

"S'okay." She rubbed at the spot he'd been squeezing.

He reached for her wrist again, this time gently rubbing the pad of his thumb over her bruises, hating that he'd left his own marks. Though his wouldn't turn into bruises. Her pulse beat strong and steady beneath his fingertips. "You're okay?"

She snorted a small laugh. "Yeah, I think I'll live."

He lifted his head and waited for her to meet his gaze. "I mean about Slade."

"Oh." Her top teeth snagged her bottom lip for a moment

before she spoke again. "No and yes. I mean I handled him ... *after* he manhandled me. But I handled him. Held my own. Then I reported him to the staff sergeant at the same time I requested light duty and divulged my pregnancy. But it was weird. The staff sergeant seemed reluctant to take my complaint about Slade any further. Considered it *water under the bridge* now that I am no longer going to be his partner."

Brock pinched his brows together and glowered. "He's still a fucking predator."

She nodded, her blue eyes finally gaining their sparkle again. "I know. And I said that. I said if the staff sergeant wasn't going to do anything about it, then I would take it up with HR. That seemed to rattle his cage, and he said he'd deal with it. Though I'm not convinced."

"Neither am I," Brock muttered.

"Once Mallory got me all set up at my new desk today, I started doing some digging."

Oh fuck.

But instead of losing his shit, he didn't say anything, just lifted an eyebrow and hummed, encouraging her to continue. The last thing he needed to do was scare her out of his house by blowing up or losing his cool.

She should not be doing any digging, though. That was Chase's job.

"Figured, might as well. I have the RCMP database at my disposal. Couldn't hurt to look into Myles a bit. See if he's got a file in HR on sexual harassment and stuff."

"And?"

Fuck. What had she found?

Her mouth drooped into a frown. "Not much."

"But I think I'm going to talk to Wendy and Marlise. They both slept with Slade. I'd like to see if he was as rough and forceful with them as he was with me."

Brock really didn't like the idea of Krista digging around on Slade. If Slade found she was snooping in his past, shit could hit the fan for her. And it's not like Brock could just barge into the station and throttle a cop.

Clenching his jaw, he moved his hand to her elbow and encouraged her to stand up. She did. "Let's talk about it over dinner. The baby needs food. And I'm starving, too."

A coy smirk tugged at the corner of her mouth. He motioned for her to begin climbing the stairs.

"Another stir-fry?" she asked, heading up the steps.

He grunted, wishing their relationship was more than just roommates who fucked and that he could reach out and pinch her ass. "Kung Pao. Baby needs vegetables."

"Mmm."

"Hungry?"

She reached the top of the stairs, then lifted her shirt over her head. "Not for food. It's been a shitty day, and I'd rather forget it altogether if I can. Even just for a bit. What do you say, *roomie?*"

Brock's stomach grumbled at the same time his cock jumped to life in his jeans. "You are a horny little thing, aren't you?" He grunted, removing his black T-shirt and following her into the kitchen. Suddenly his hunger could wait. He hadn't gotten laid on the regular like this in ages and couldn't remember the last time the sex was this good, either.

She nibbled on her lip again. "When you look like that I am." Her eyes drank him down, lingering long on his abs and pecs before fixating on his biceps. She seemed to love his arms, digging her nails into his muscles whenever she came. Unlike the marks on her wrist, he loved the marks Krista left on his skin. Bite marks and nail trenches, scratches up his back. She really was a little lioness, and he loved it.

He took a few steps toward her, reaching for the button on her pants. He had her naked in seconds. Now all he had to do was get her beneath him. Her chest heaved with each breath, and he allowed his eyes to drift down her body. Her hands cradled her lower abdomen, and that's when he noticed a faint, but noticeable —because he'd put it there—bump. It was barely discernible, and to anyone else they would have just chalked it up to maybe a second cinnamon bun at lunch or something. But they both knew better. He allowed his big hand to cover hers, and for just a moment, they stood there quietly in the kitchen, her completely naked and him nearly the same, bonding over the little miracle in her belly.

She smiled up at him, linking her fingers with his. "It's official. I'm starting to show."

He grinned back, his heart rate picking up at the intimacy of her actions. It was one thing to be balls deep inside her, but the gentleness of her touch, of their linked fingers was freaking him out. He swallowed down the nerves and made sure his smile was extra big. "It's beautiful. You're beautiful."

Her eyes were glassy and full of emotions as she gazed up at him. "Who are you, Brock Hart? I can't figure you out. Bossy and demanding one minute and then sweet and saying all the right things the next." Her smile was small. "Some days I feel like I'm living with two different men."

He swallowed and tried to remain in control. Since she moved in, he'd felt like he *was* two different men, and it was freaking him the fuck out. He dropped his hand from her belly, unlinking their fingers in the process. His smile faded as well. He needed to get back to the task at hand. And that task was fucking. Fucking he could do.

She seemed to be waiting for him to answer. She cocked her head sexily to the side and nibbled on that goddamn bottom lip again. But he had no answer for her. He didn't recognize himself either. So instead he did what he could, what he wanted to do, what they both *needed* him to do. He took her. Hard.

Their bodies mashed together as he grabbed her ponytail and

pulled her toward him, devouring her mouth and forcing her lips apart. Lips roamed, teeth nipped and hands frantically peeled away the last shreds of clothing that remained on his body. She leaped up onto his hips without warning and locked her ankles around his back. His hands had a firm grip on her luscious ass, and with driving force, he bulldozed them over to the nearest wall, plastered her up against it and slammed home.

He pumped up into her with rhythmic vigor, his arms flexing with the weight of her petite frame. He dug his fingers into the plump flesh of her ass, relishing the way the globes contracted as she met him thrust for thrust as best she could.

She snagged his bottom lip between her teeth and chuckled when he gasped from the sudden snap of pain. It felt like she'd drawn blood, but he didn't care. He loved his little lion and how ferocious she could be. Her nails raked down his back, clawing at him, grappling and pulling him harder and deeper into her. He growled as he nipped her shoulder, allowing his mouth to slowly travel farther down her arm, alternating between naughty bites and sensual kisses. But then his mouth landed on the bruise. On Slade's hand print, wrapped purple and blue around her tiny, pale wrist, and he fucking lost it.

Like a rabid beast, he let out a growl that made her eyes flash open and her whole body tremble against his. He picked up speed, hammering into her even harder, claiming her, all of her. Demolishing any trace or mark that Slade may have made on her body. She would never belong to anybody but Brock ever again. Nobody else could have her.

He was seconds away from coming. Everything felt so damn good—the way her hot little pussy squeezed him like a fist, her nails digging into his biceps, and her teeth on his neck. The woman was vicious, and he loved it. He'd never felt more alive than when inside Krista. She tightened herself even more around him, tossed her head back against the wall and let go.

"Oh ... G ... od!"

He lifted his head up to watch her. Her eyes fluttered shut so she could ride out the waves of euphoria in the dark. He let his mouth fall to the crook of her neck, nipped her just below the ear, inhaled her sweet scent and joined her in her bliss.

He poured himself inside her, finding his release and letting his walls, the walls he'd so carefully built around himself, crumble down for just a second.

Their chests heaved against each other as they fought to calm their heart rates and breathing. She clung to his body like a limpet as he peppered light kisses along her collarbone and neck then gradually down her arm. His tongue swirled erotically around Slade's bruise before softly kissing it.

She ran her hands up his back and into his hair, pulling on his ears until he lifted his head to face her.

"You need to be careful," he said, his voice gravelly. "Don't go digging around Slade anymore. If he finds out, things could get ugly. Just put your head down and do your work."

The contented just-been-fucked-*thoroughly* look slid from her face. "Like a good little pregnant copper, you mean?"

He ground his molars and went on the hunt for his boxers. "Yes. You don't need to go poking your nose where it doesn't belong."

She found her shirt and pulled it over her head, not bothering with her bra. He loved it when she went braless. Hell, the woman would look unbelievable in a burlap sac.

"It is *my* job. And as long as I get all my own tasks done, if I do this on my free time, it shouldn't matter. I don't want him hurting another rookie, another *woman* if I can help it."

"Neither do I. Doesn't mean *you* need to be the one to stop him." He tugged his jeans on and watched as she slipped her underwear over her slim legs and up beneath her T-shirt. It didn't hit him until then that she was wearing one of *his* T-shirts. When had she swiped that?

She grabbed her own jeans off the floor but didn't pull them on. She usually changed into pajama pants or stretchy yoga pants when she got home. "If I can, I will." Then she stalked out of the kitchen in a huff, her wild, curly red ponytail the last thing he saw flying around the corner.

CHAPTER EIGHT

STUPID BROCK HART and his bossy-fucker ways. Why couldn't he let them both ride the waves of post-orgasmic bliss just a touch longer before he went ordering her around? She'd divulged her pregnancy, gone on light duty—what more did he want from her? She was still a bloody cop and determined to be a good one, too! Part of being a good cop was following a lead, an instinct, and like a dog with a bone, seeing if that lead went anywhere. And after the way Myles had behaved in the breakroom, tearing open her uniform and fondling her and threatening her, there was no way in hell that was his first offense.

No.

The man probably had a thick file in HR full of complaints. She just needed to find it.

After changing into pajama pants, Krista tossed on her pissed-off cop face and joined Brock for dinner in the living room. He politely changed the channel from the news to the Home and Garden channel when she walked in. A bowl of steaming veggies and chicken over rice sat on the leather ottoman waiting for her. She didn't say anything to him but simply picked up the bowl and dove in. Between skipping lunch so she could investigate Myles more and that bit of aerobics in the kitchen, she was starving.

Penelope jumped up into Brock's lap where he sat in his La-Z-Boy, and he began mindlessly petting her until an appreciative purr joined the cacophony of evening sounds. Krista watched him quietly—this bigger-than-life man, the father of her child, her room-mate who shared her bed (on occasion), a man she still knew abso-lutely nothing about. And yet, as the weeks ticked by and she saw glimpses, microscopic fragments of the person who was buried deep down and hidden behind those impenetrable walls and even more impenetrable chest, she began to feel a stirring of something deep in her belly. And she didn't think it was just gas or the possible flutterings of their little one-night-stand miracle.

Only whenever she addressed it, asked him anything about himself, brought up the big differences in his personality, he would shut down. Just like he had in the kitchen. He'd shown her such tenderness on the stairs, shown her a glimpse into the heart of Brock Hart, but when she brought it up, he shut down, shut her up and fucked her until she could barely walk. Then, when the ecstasy dissipated, he had the mask back up, the bossy-fucker mask, and he was telling her what to do. She just didn't get it. Was she really no more than a pregnant fuck buddy?

"What?" he said gruffly, not bothering to look at her but knowing she was looking at him. The mask was on, the walls were up, and any thoughts she may have had about trying to get to know him more quickly dissolved.

She hid her disappointment and flashed him a big, sexy grin. Well, at least she could have on-demand orgasms. "You wanna have a shower?"

Taking great care not to piss off Penelope, he gently placed her on a pillow and then set his empty bowl on the coffee table, standing up and heading toward the bathroom, removing his shirt as he went. "Lucky for you, woman, I can get it up more than once a day. Come on!"

She giggled as she skipped after him, peeling off her clothes and leaving them like a trail of breadcrumbs down the hallway.

She'd find out more about him tomorrow.

CHAPTER NINE

IT'D BEEN a blessing in disguise, truth be told. As much as she didn't want to go on light duty and forfeit learning as much as she could in the field as a rookie cop, Krista was thankful for the reprieve. Her hips were grateful, along with her feet, and she wasn't nearly as tired come nightfall as she had been after twelve hours of being in the field handcuffing bad guys and keeping the streets safe from evildoers. She quickly fell into an easy routine at her desk, getting her workload done in record time, and then spending the rest of her day digging into Myles's past. Unfortunately, there wasn't much there. Either the guy was clean and just now starting to act like a predatory douche, or he'd managed to slip into the RCMP database and erase his files. Krista's money was on the latter. She just had to keep digging.

As Krista slung her bag over her shoulder and turned off her computer, she yawned and then yawned again. Was there going to be a stir-fry waiting for her at home? She hoped so. Brock had been up at the crack of dawn and out the door that morning, not even bothering to poke his head into her bedroom before he left, as he'd started doing, to ask how she was feeling and if she had felt "the little monkey" kick. She missed seeing him. Missed the routine. As stoic a man as he was, he seemed to be genuinely giddy about the idea of getting to feel the baby move.

They'd spent the night before decorating the Christmas tree they'd picked up over the weekend. Apparently, in all his years of living in the house by himself, Brock had never put up a tree. He said he always just went to his mother's, so he had no decorations, not even a wreath for the door. So, at Krista's insistence, seeing as this was her first Christmas not spent in Tanner Ridge with her family, they filled the house with all the little hints of holiday cheer and festive delight that Krista had brought along with her from home.

But even after emptying her lone box marked "Christmas Crap," the house and tree still seemed sparse. So, munching on a gingerbread man and humming "Jingle Bells," she ducked out to Walmart for more random baubles and doodads. They spent a lovely evening building Santa's Christmas Village and making the little elves and town people in her Christmas village do dirty and naughty things to each other.

It almost felt like they were a normal couple, preparing for their last Christmas before baby.

But she knew better.

He made it very clear whenever he shut down that they were just two people who fucked like bunnies and just happened to be having a child together.

But that didn't stop her from making a second batch of big bulky gingerbread men, with muscly arms and pensive scowls on their faces, as she puttered away in the kitchen later that night after work. She gooped the word "BROCK" into the center of one big gingerbread man's chest, gave him gumdrop buttons and M&M eyes. And right before heading to bed, and making damn sure Brock was nowhere to be found, she picked up the confection with a frown and kissed it square on the lips.

THE FOLLOWING MORNING, with a headless gingerbread man in her hand and a full mouth, Krista parked her car behind the station. Winter sucked. Even now, working banker's hours, it was still dark when she started and finished work, wasting the day away inside concrete walls like some common prisoner.

Today, Mallory had her working in booking and processing and then possibly organizing the evidence locker. Slamming her car door and shivering from her lack of gloves, Krista paused. Eyes were on her. She felt them like a mosquito perched on her arm. A slight prickly sensation wended its way up her spine. Myles? No. He had no reason to watch her. He could see her any time he wanted, and so far, since she'd moved upstairs to the offices, she'd barely seen him at all. No, these eyes were different. They didn't feel altogether sinister, just … curious.

Spinning around and checking for anything nefarious or out of the ordinary, she surveyed the area. But there was nothing out of place. A pair of crows nattered on a power line, and a black cat sprinted across a nearby driveway. Yet despite all that, she couldn't shake the feeling that she was being watched.

Giving the area one final sweep but seeing nothing shady, she shook it off, crossed her fingers that it wasn't Myles, and headed inside.

KRISTA WAS dead on her feet and absolutely starving by the time she clocked out from the station. She had completely missed lunch, being caught up in the evidence locker with Mallory. The two had decided to reorganize and refile everything. Thankfully, they both appeared to have a touch of OCD and a penchant for alphabetization, so the system they devised together worked well.

She drove to the grocery store and trudged inside, dodging other weary patrons who were probably going to buy far more than they needed because they were shopping hungry. And once again, like earlier that day, the feeling of being watched was back, tickling the hair on her neck and putting her whole body on high alert.

She was being followed.

Someone in the grocery store was only there because Krista was. They were watching her, following her, tracking her, which couldn't have been easy given how busy the place was.

But that didn't matter. She was being spied on, stalked, and come hell or high water, she was going to find out who it was and what they wanted.

Making sure her belly was hidden beneath her heavy winter coat, Krista put her best cop face on, pulled her badge from her purse and began canvasing the place.

Up and down the aisles she roamed, no longer aware of her growling stomach but on an impromptu manhunt. She was hunting her hunter, determined to confront him and find out why she currently felt like a bug under a scope.

And then she saw him, sticking out like a sore thumb, standing by the checkout reading a fish and wildlife magazine, with his ball cap drawn down over his brow and a dark gray hoodie. He was big, like Brock big. His shoes and clothes were clean, and the Tissot watch on his wrist said that he had taste and style but wasn't pretentious. This was not some junkie or homeless man out to exact revenge because she'd made him move sleeping spots. This was a guy with a job and money, and yet he was making it his sole mission to keep tabs on her. Why?

But unlike Mr. Ball Cap, Krista was going to play it cool. It would do no good to march up to him and demand to know what he was up to. He could simply feign ignorance and claim that she was some crazy lady who thought she was being followed but wasn't.

Instead, she continued to wander up and down the aisles,

perusing and shopping, stopping to check the ingredients on a box of cereal or compare prices of salsa. Every time she turned the corner onto a new aisle, there he was, his basket loaded with miscellaneous items to make it look real, but it was the way he stopped and the way he walked that said he wasn't there to shop.

Krista had been shopping with her dad, her brother and now Brock enough times to know that men didn't wander when they shopped. They shopped like they were on a mission. And that mission was to get in and get out in as little time as possible, and then carry all twenty-seven bags into the house in one trip.

She made sure to establish a pattern of how she was roaming the aisles, a pattern that he could anticipate and follow, and once she knew he had it, she deviated and doubled back, coming up behind him, until she was close enough to smell him. He smelled good.

"Why are you following me?" she asked, just a hint of accusation in her tone, but not enough to make him think she was off her meds or something.

He spun around and gaped at her, a look of utter shock on his face. His eyes went wide. That's when she noticed that they were the same color as Brock's, and the longer she looked at him, the more she saw the similarity. This one was younger for sure, but their build was the same; big bulldozer bodies, Christmas ham hands, and dark caterpillars that bobbed and furrowed along the forehead. Only where Brock's hair was close-cut, this brother apparently preferred to shave it all off and was sporting a bald head beneath the ball cap. She remembered asking Brock his brothers' names before but couldn't for the life of her remember them at the moment. Which one was this?

"I'm not following you," he replied, managing a hangdog expression. But his glittering eyes betrayed him.

Krista rolled her eyes. "I'm not stupid. You've been following me for the last half hour. Now which brother are you, and why is Brock having me followed?"

Giant twin dimples flashed back at her, like someone had taken a nail gun to his face. "Ah, you got us." He grinned.

Us?

She blinked and shook her head, planting her hands on her hips and hating that she had to crane her neck to look up at him. "Why is your brother having me followed?"

He scratched the back of his neck and removed his hat, revealing a very round and shapely bald head. If it weren't for the dazzling smile and the soulful green eyes, one look at the man and you'd think "killing machine."

"Brock said you're having some trouble with a guy at work, so he asked us to keep an eye on you. We don't follow you while you're at work ... " He looked down the aisle and then raised his eyebrows as a man of equal size with a very bald head, but no hat, came swaying toward them. Another brother? "Well, at least not when you're not partnered with Slade."

Hmm, so Brock hadn't mentioned the baby or her switching to light duty yet.

Good.

She was already pissed at him enough for siccing his brothers on her, let alone spilling their baby beans too early.

"He's got *two* of you following me?" she asked, taking in the other bald brother, one who was apparently much better at covert operations, because she hadn't spotted him at all. "He's got you following me while I'm getting groceries?"

Brother number two stopped in front of them, only he didn't offer a smile. He simply scowled and nodded at his doppelgänger.

"Erm ... well, actually ... " the ball cap brother murmured. He glanced up the aisle and, as if on cue, like a happy little puppy but not at all the runt of the pack, another behemoth came loping toward them. Only this one had the most luscious blond, beach-bum, surfer-dude hair Krista had ever seen. And it trailed behind him like a short jet stream of gold. His giant combat boots made heavy, loud clomping sounds on the white store tiles, and a giant smile took over his whole face.

"Three of you!" she practically screeched, having to look up, way up, into all their eyes.

Brother number one stuck his hand out. "I'm Rex. That's Chase, and this shaggy mop—dude, you really need to cut your hair —is Heath."

Speechless, with anger building like a winter storm inside her, she took each of their hands, trying her hardest to crush their bones with her grip, but they all seemed to get a kick out of her attempt and chuckled amongst themselves.

"Why is he having me followed by all *three* of you?" she asked again, wanting to get her facts straight before she went and tore a strip off their older brother.

Rex rolled his eyes. "Well, he kind of actually just had *me* following you. But I told Chase and Heath what I was doing, and they were curious. They wanted to get a peek at you. Brock never introduces us to any woman he's seeing or even talks about them. So the fact that you're special enough to have protection ... well, we got curious."

The fact that he considered her someone special stirred butterflies in her belly and made her sway where she stood. Or perhaps that was the hunger, fatigue and aching hips. Either way, she had to reach out to the shelf of—oh fuck, were they seriously in the condom aisle? What were the bloody chances?— to stabilize herself. She made sure to keep her hands clear of the box of Magnums. The men simply watched her, equal parts concern and curiosity drifting across each of their handsome faces.

She took a deep breath, grounding herself before she let go of the shelf. "I appreciate your concern, boys, and your willingness to help your brother out. And I will deal with Brock later, but I assure you I'm fine. I can handle myself."

"Did you know that Myles was relocated to your detachment because of sexual harassment at *two* other detachments across the country?" piped up Chase, the one who reminded her more of Brock and wasn't overly generous with his smiles.

He and blondie shared the same midnight-blue eyes and light-colored eyebrows, but Chase was scarier looking and had scruff along his chin and cheeks, with a thin white scar running along the length of his jaw to his left ear. There was no mistaking the level of threat this man carried with him every moment of every day.

Krista's mouth hung open. "How'd you find that out?"

He lifted one shoulder, a hint of smile tugging at the corner of his lip before retreating and settling into a frown. "Don't ask questions you don't want to know the answers to."

Heath slapped his big brother on the back. "Chasey here is our resident hacker. He could hack the Pentagon if he wanted to."

"You hacked into the RCMP?" The flare in each man's eyes made her quickly bring her volume down several notches. The bald Goliath with a knitted brow was not how one would envision a hacker. Where were the glasses? The button-up shirt? The nervous blinking eyes from being out of the sunlight too long? No, this guy looked like he could snap an old growth red cedar in half and not even break a sweat.

"*Don't* ask questions you don't want to know the answers to," he repeated.

"Brock's asked us to help you and help him look into Myles Slade a bit more," Rex added, trying to defuse the situation and not draw any unwanted attention from shoppers or staff. "Right now, we know you're safe. We saw Slade go home. But we just wanted to get a peek at you." He flashed me another big smile. "You're cute and got a set of balls on you. We can see why he likes you. Don't let him get away with any shit, okay?" Then they all turned to leave.

Only Heath turned around, his nose wrinkling with his smile. "We'll see you at Christmas dinner, right?"

———

Brock's phone buzzed on his nightstand as he towel-dried his hair from the shower. He'd just gotten home from work. It'd been a long two days out in the field. A long two grungy days with no shower and nothing but his thoughts to keep him company. But now that Krista was on light duty and his brothers were keeping an eye on her, Brock didn't feel so bad about leaving her for a day or two to attend to work. Though things would certainly change when the baby arrived. He'd already talked to his boss about taking some paternity leave as well as no longer working long stretches away from home. One or two nights, tops.

He snatched his phone. It was a message from Rex.

"She caught me ... I mean us. She's pissed. Gutsy though. Cute too. Great ass."

"Fuck," Brock grumbled under his breath, tossing his towel onto the floor. "Last time he's on fucking recon."

He heard the keys in the front door and braced himself for a slam, followed by a gruff but feminine huff and stomping up the stairs. But there was none of that. Not even a sound. Was she mad? Rex said she was pissed. And Brock already knew his roomie-slash-fuck-buddy had a temper. That was one of the things he liked most about her. Well, maybe not her temper, but her grit was a huge turn on. He'd never liked the damsel in distress or the weak female who *needed* a man to save her. He liked a woman who knew how to take care of herself and get shit done. An independent force to be reckoned with. And Krista was all that and more. Plus, she was dynamite in the sack and could bake a mean gingerbread man.

Holding his breath, he waited for her to emerge in the doorway with a scowl on her face and fury in her eyes. But nothing happened. Not even a creak on the floor or a frustrated sigh. What the hell was going on?

Scratching the back of his neck at the sexy little enigma he lived with, he turned to his dresser drawer in search of boxers. The rice cooker was on, and he was defrosting some chicken. If she gave him fifteen minutes, he'd have black pepper chicken stir-fry ready for her. Perhaps feeding the beast would soften the fury and she wouldn't threaten to leave or, even worse, stop sleeping with him.

He was just tugging up his boxer briefs when a faint but discernible throat clearing caused him to release the elastic a little too early and a little too hard. "Fuck!" Determined not to buckle from the pain, he bit back a wince and instead flashed her the biggest smile he could muster, even though inside it felt like he was going to throw up. "You're home late."

She stood there, clearly exhausted, but otherwise with nary an emotion on her face. Eventually, she lifted one eyebrow. "Mhmm."

"How was work?" Maybe if he showed interest in her day, he'd throw her off and she'd forget all about his stupid brothers spying on her.

Her mouth slid into a half-smile. "Long ... and hard," she purred. "Hard to do your job when you have *other* things on your mind."

What the hell? But he had to keep his cool. Was she playing a game? What was her angle? "Oh yeah?"

She nodded. "Mhmm." Her gaze flicked to the bed. "On the bed," she demanded. "I've been thinking about this *all* day."

He climbed onto the bed. "I've been thinking about this for days."

"Have you now?"

He nodded. "Yeah." Brock pulled his boxers off again and tossed them onto the floor. "Nothing but thoughts of you, of *this* to keep me warm."

She licked her lips and reached into the pocket of her jeans. "Is that so?" The rattling sound of what could only be a pair of hand-cuffs brought Brock's attention to something other than Krista's killer breasts. They'd really started to fill out and get firm over the last month or so. And she'd become so responsive to his touch, too. Biting her nipples nearly made her come on the spot.

His eyes widened as she climbed onto the bed and straddled him. "Uh, what's the plan?"

"What does it look like?" She smiled wolfishly. Even though he hated being in any kind of submissive position, his cock leapt against the apex of her thighs. "I'm a bossy little control freak, and I plan to make you my bitch. What do you think of that?"

His Adam's apple bobbed in his throat. "I, uh ... "

Brock Hart was no one's *bitch*. Unease settled in his stomach like a lead weight, even though his cock and balls had other ideas. Everything below his waist tightened and stiffened, and the rush of arousal that coursed through him at the sight of Krista straddling him made the blood run hot and quick through his veins.

She cocked her head to the side as she took one of his hands and brought it up above his head, locking a cuff around his big wrist while fastening the other one to the big wrought-iron corner post of the bed.

"Oh, don't worry, you'll enjoy yourself ... I promise," she said, her smile triumphant and impossibly sexy. She finished her task, making sure that he was good and secure and wouldn't be using his hands anytime soon. Then, slowly, stealthily, seductively, she snaked her way down his body, planting warm, wet kisses over his ribs and pecs and abs.

Desire cut through him with a painful sharpness. Even vulner-able, bound and defenseless, he wanted her. He was coming to always want her.

"Lower," he said gruffly. "Suck my cock, baby."

Krista glanced up at him from beneath her lashes. "In good

time. Remember who is whose *bitch* today. I'll do with you as I please."

A carnal growl rumbled through him as he bucked his hips into her. "I'm nobody's *bitch*."

She smiled again. "We'll see about that. This is my game, and I'll play it how I please."

He tugged at the handcuffs that were fastened to the bed. They were police grade, possibly even hers, and unless he wanted to destroy his own bed, he'd have to sit tight until she released him. He glared at her, but his cock betrayed his fury and practically winked at her, begging her to come closer.

"So I met some interesting and very handsome men today," Krista said dryly, letting the backs of her fingers run down the length of his shaft. His balls tightened even more, and his breath hitched.

"In the grocery store of all places. Two were bald, and one had the most luxurious head of flaxen blond hair I've ever seen. He could do a campaign for Pantene."

Brock's whole body went stiff. Her nails tickled his inner thighs as she leaned her head over and slid her tongue up his cock from base to crown, sucking lightly on the tip. Her mouth hovered over the tip, and she bared her teeth.

Fear shot through him like a bolt of lightning. Gently, she nipped the tip. His hips shot up off the bed from the mix of extreme pain and hidden pleasure.

"Look ... I, uh ... "

But she didn't give him time to continue and instead rammed him to the back of her throat, not allowing him to finish his sentence, pumping him with her hand and devouring his length with her mouth.

Holy fuck. This was not at all how he saw this little scenario going. Brock thrust his pelvis up into her face, desperate for her to take him deeper. He was already close. The woman had the mouth of a goddess.

But then she stopped.

Why'd she stop?

Sitting back on her heels, her eyes glassy and her cheeks a pretty pink from her own arousal, she looked him dead in the eye. "It would seem all the blood has rushed from your brain, so I'm going to give you a moment or two while I jump in the shower to think about the choices you've made. Putting a tail on me without my consent, *tsk tsk,* Brock, I don't like that one bit." Then she got up and shut the bathroom door. A moment later, he heard the muffled sound of laughter.

———

IT WAS QUITE some time later that his captor emerged from the bathroom, looking refreshed and revitalized. She had a black towel wrapped around her lithe body and another around her unruly hair. Her cheeks were an even sexier pink than before, and the delicious scent that followed her out the door made Brock's pulse kick back into high gear.

But as turned on as he was by the sight of her, the smell of her and the memory of the blow job and orgasm that almost was, he was also full of rage. White-hot rage.

"What the fuck?" he growled, pulling at the handcuffs and shooting daggers at her from his eyes. "Take these off me!"

Ignoring his demands and appearing almost bored, she let the towel drop to the floor and crawled back onto the bed, inching her way up from his feet to his pelvis, once again grazing her tongue along his length. He couldn't hide it. Despite the fury, he was still turned on, still wanted her. Only this time, he wanted to be in control. *Needed* to be in control. A drop of pre-cum beaded on the crown of his cock, and using her finger, she swirled it around before licking it off and closing her eyes with a soft hum.

Brock swallowed. Fuck, she was something.

"Suck it," he said, his voice catching in his throat. The lack of control, the need to come—he was *not* in his comfort zone right now. And she knew that and was using it to her advantage.

She continued moving upward over his torso and chest until the scruff of his chin scratched the inside of her thighs. He glanced down toward the lips of her pussy, perfectly pink and glistening with arousal. He couldn't stop himself and licked his lips.

Her eyes flared as she watched him. "Apologize properly, and then maybe I'll consider releasing you." She lowered her cleft down onto his waiting mouth.

A groan rumbled through the woman on top of him as he carefully scratched her inner thighs with his chin and cheeks while flicking out his tongue to brush her clit.

She groaned again and shamelessly pressed into his face, taking what she wanted, what she needed. He loved how strong she was, how bossy and demanding. It would be a power struggle between the two of them for sure, because he was just as much a control freak, but he also liked a woman who knew what she wanted and wasn't afraid to fight for it. No, the mother of his child was no weak little kitten sitting in the corner. She was a lioness, just as ready to fight and defend as he was.

"Fuck my pussy," she demanded. "Fuck it with your mouth."

He did as he was told and sucked on her folds before letting his tongue dart in and out, plunging deep inside only to retract and then do the whole thing over again. She rode his face for a while, reveling in the power. He'd let her have the power—for now. Once the cuffs were off, she'd be beneath him and paying dearly for this little role-reversal trick of hers.

She continued to rock against him, soft moans and feminine sighs letting him know he was doing just what she liked. He drank her down, her sweet honey pouring across his tongue as her clit grew hard and swollen. She was close. Now if only she'd release his hands so he could feel her tight heat around him as well, fuck her with his fingers and truly take her the way she wanted to be taken.

Her hands drifted up, and she began pinching and pulling on her nipples. Brock loved a woman who wasn't afraid to heighten her own pleasure, to touch herself whether he was in the room or not. She cupped her breasts and rolled them in her palms as her lips parted and she let her head loll back.

"So good," she said with a sigh. "So. Fucking. Good."

Brock knew she was close, but for some reason she just wasn't getting there. "Release me so I can use my fingers," he said, sucking hard on her clit and making her body jerk against him.

Lifting her head again, she glanced down at him. "Not a chance." She nibbled on her bottom lip for a moment, gyrating her slippery cleft against his mouth. "But you are right, I do need more." Humming softly to herself, she let her body slide down his face until the apex of her thighs was positioned right at his chin, her buttocks on his chest.

Brock glanced down at her with curiosity.

"Deny it all you want," she said with a grin as she pushed her swollen lips and clit against his chin and began to move, "but you're loving this."

"No need to deny a thing," he said, his voice hoarse.

She pushed her labia against his chin again and began to move, swirling and thrusting.

"This feels good?" he asked.

She moaned an incoherent yes before trailing a hand down over the small swell of her abdomen to the V of her legs. She spread her lips wide and began to rub circles around her clit.

God, the sight was something to behold. Never in a million years did Brock think he'd ever get so damn lucky.

"It hurts ... kind of, but not in a bad way. Your chin is so prickly and my skin so sensitive." She moaned again. "So, so good."

He wiggled his chin back and forth and up and down, hitting the underside of her clit just right while her fingers did their job on top. She exploded in a matter of seconds, pushing her hips up harder onto his chin, letting the coarse hair rub against her slick flesh.

Seconds later, she rolled to the side of the bed, her arm casually draped over her eyes and her chest heaving with each ragged breath.

Brock's balls throbbed with a dull, painful ache between his legs. "You, uh ... you going to let me come or what?" he asked, taking great care to hide the desperation in his voice.

Slowly, almost drunkenly, she sat up on her knees and looked at him. "No. Not unless you explain to me why the hell you thought siccing Rex on me was a good idea."

He rolled his eyes. "I didn't *sic* Rex on you. I asked him to do me a favor. You need to be safe. You're carrying my child, and I think you're in danger. Even now that you've switched to light duty, Slade is still a problem. And as far as the other two dorks go ... " He actually was a bit remorseful for the other two morons ambushing her at the store. He'd have to knock some sense into them later. He glanced up at her. "Sorry."

She let out a huff through her nose. "Wasn't exactly how I wanted to meet your family. Dead on my feet after work."

A smirk tickled the corner of his mouth. Jeez, this woman made him smile a lot. It was weird. But not altogether unpleasant. "For the record," he started, fighting the urge to squirm from the throbbing need between his legs, "they texted me before you got home and said they like you and think you're cute."

"You knew I was coming home pissed?"

He nodded. "Though this kind of *punishment* is way better than the screaming match I'd been anticipating."

She gave him a half-hearted glare. "I ought to spank you."

He'd never been the *spankee* before, but his little lioness and the wicked gleam in her piercing blue eyes made him curious. "Okay."

Giddiness raced across her face and flared in her eyes. Before he could say, "but first release me," she was out the door and off to what sounded like the kitchen, returning seconds later with a wooden spatula.

She hopped back up onto the bed and straddled him again, quickly releasing his cuffs. Only instead of getting up onto all fours like a good little submissive, he grabbed her by the wrists, flipped her onto her back, and pinned her beneath him.

"Rule number one: Never believe the first thing that comes out of your captive's mouth," he said, his entire body relaxing with the much-needed power shift.

She gaped at him, too shocked to move or fight back.

"Rule number two"—he grabbed one of her wrists and began handcuffing her to the bed just like she had him—"don't leave your handcuffs where the captive can reach them and use them on you. That goes for your gun, your knife, your taser, or any other weapon or form of restraint." He did the same thing to the other wrist, and within seconds, she was lying naked, bound and spread-eagle on the bed.

He sat back on his knees. "Now that's more like it."

"You're an ass!"

"And you're going to be fucked properly." He covered her again, positioning himself between her legs, tempting and teasing her core. God, how he needed to come. "There's a power struggle going on here, isn't there?" He grunted, doing a diabolical little hip swirl.

"You better believe it." She moaned, pushing her pelvis up to meet his.

A low and raspy chuckle shook his body, and then he slammed

into her with all his might, his head dipping low until his teeth found a nipple.

"That's okay," he murmured, the feeling of her tight, wet heat surrounding him and making the entire world right itself on its axis once more. "I like a challenge."

CHAPTER TEN

KRISTA REALLY DIDN'T WANT to go to the Christmas party, like truly loathed the idea of stepping foot into the rented room above the swanky hotel and having to face the questions, congratulations and curious stares of all her colleagues. News had traveled like a wildfire in a windstorm about her pregnancy, and she was not looking forward to rehashing it with some and filling in the newly informed either. God, police stations could be such gossip pools. And if she thought being a field cop was bad, the gossip and rumors were ten times worse in the office. She'd even heard one rumor that she was having twins and they belonged to two different fathers.

So, no. The idea of yuletide cheer around a bunch of off-duty cops while sober wasn't what she had asked Santa for, not even close. But Allie, one of the few friends Krista had managed to make on the force in the past six months, was going and had all but begged Krista to go when they'd run into each other earlier in the week.

Krista just wasn't feeling up to it. And even though she now no longer worked nights and had bought a ticket to the party many months ago, thinking at the time it'd be fun and maybe she'd have a sexy new boyfriend she could show off, now things were different. Brock wasn't exactly her "boyfriend," and she'd bet dollars to doughnuts he had zero interest in coming even if she did work up the nerve to ask him.

"You're coming tonight, right?" Allie asked as they walked out to their cars. Krista hadn't hung out with Allie in quite some time, not since she'd moved in with Brock. She missed her friend dearly.

Krista made a reluctant face. "I don't think so."

"What? Why?"

Lifting one shoulder, she hit the fob for her car. "Morning sickness isn't always in the morning ... or so it seems."

Allie made a mock pout. "Oh, come on, you don't have to stay late. Just come for the dinner portion and then you can leave. Do you have a date?"

Krista thought about Brock again. He'd most definitely say no. She could tell he hated parties. The crotchety hermit vibe was strong with her roommate-slash-fuck-buddy-slash-future-co-parent. Jeez, they should really nail down a title for each other.

She shook her head. "No. No date."

"Well, come with Violet and I. We can all go together." Violet was Allie's wife. The two were beyond adorable together and had welcomed Krista as a friend since her first shift, when Allie took pity on Krista's newness and bought her a coffee and croissant, filling her head with all the detachment gossip.

"I don't know," Krista said with a moan, immediately irritated with herself. If she were Allie, she'd be pissed right off with Krista's pity-party behavior.

But Allie didn't seem fazed or irritated. She simply shook her head. "You're coming, end of story. You already bought your ticket, and the food at this thing is usually good. Just come, eat, dance a couple of dances, and then you can go home to your cat, okay?"

Krista let out weighted sigh. Allie could be pushy when she wanted something.

Resting her hand on Krista's shoulder, she gave her a friendly head tilt. "I'm worried about you. I know you're pregnant, and this wasn't at all in *your plan*, but it'll all work out. I promise. I also hate that Myles kept meddling in the schedule for so long. You know he deliberately had our schedules changed so that we never had a day off together?" Her eyes grew wary, and she leaned in closer to me. "I'm really glad you're no longer partnered with him. But still," she glanced at the door for a second, "you just be careful around him, okay?"

A noise at a nearby car had both their heads snapping up from where they'd been bent tight together. It was just another officer heading home.

Krista was about to ask Allie to elaborate on her warning, but her friend simply smiled, gave her a side hug and was off to her car. "I'll see you shortly," she called, winking as she slipped into her black Pathfinder. "Don't make me come get you."

————

"Nothing *fucking* fits!" Krista screamed, throwing another skirt at the wall and then crumpling to her knees. Her head fell into her hands as the tears came on like a freak monsoon. "I hate this!"

A warm, fuzzy tail brushed her leg, and she reached out and grabbed Penelope, bringing her into her lap to nuzzle her, though she didn't seem too taken with the idea of being used as a stuffed animal. But once Krista scratched behind her ears for a few seconds, her tears trickling onto the cat's soft fur, the beast began to purr and closed her big amber eyes.

A creak at the doorway made Krista's head pop up. Penelope was not nearly as interested and didn't even flinch.

"Everything okay?" Brock asked, looking about as lost as a man in a lingerie store.

"No!" Anger ratcheted back up through her, and she grabbed

the closest thing next to her, a sexy red stiletto she hadn't worn in years, and chucked it at his head.

Only instead of ducking, his ninja reflexes kicked in and he snatched it midair. A second later, and it would have conked him in the forehead. But the fact that she didn't hit him made her even more furious, and she searched for something else to throw.

"You had to go and knock me up, and now I've got to go to my staff Christmas party tonight and I have nothing to wear. Nothing fits."

She found a gray ankle boot and chucked it at him. He caught it and started to walk toward her, patience in his eyes and stride.

Only instead of crouching down to her level with his hand out, like people do when they're approaching skittish dogs, he moved past her and began perusing her closet.

"What are you doing?" she asked, her throat tight as she fought back more tears.

Ignoring her, he continued to flip through various hanging items. A few seconds passed, and he emerged with two dresses and a skirt and blouse slung over his arm. "What about these?"

She rolled her eyes. "Probably won't fit. Nothing fits."

She went to grab the other ankle boot, but he put his hand on her shoulder, squeezing gently. "Just try them, okay?"

Growling at him, she stood up, much to the irritation of Penelope, and undressed. "They're not going to fit, I'm telling you. Nothing fits. I'm getting fat, and it's your fault." Snatching the red dress from his arm, she glared at him and unzipped it. "I hate you ... I hate your penis. I hate what your penis did to me."

But he just remained quiet and waited for her to step into the dress. Turning around, she motioned for him to zip her up. She heard him grunt as he struggled to get it up to the top.

"It's too small, isn't it?" she asked snidely.

"Take it off and try the next one." He unzipped it so she could slink out. He passed her the black one, and she pulled it over her head. This one didn't have a zipper, so she didn't have to deal with the embarrassment of it not zipping up to the top.

She moved away from him and went to stand in front of the mirror. It was long-sleeved with a scoop neck and came just above her knees. Classic and simple and hell if it didn't look half bad. She shot him an irritated scowl. "Fine! You win this one, Hart."

As if appearing almost bored, he lifted a shoulder. "Not about winning or losing. It's about keeping you happy."

Well, fuck.

More tears.

Krista's butt hit the bed, and her face fell into her hands. What the hell was going on with her? Hormones sucked, that's what. One minute she was a crying mess, the next minute a homicidal maniac looking for footwear to decapitate the future father of her child. Sobs wracked her body. This wasn't her at all.

"Shit," Brock murmured, sinking down onto the bed beside her. His hand fell to her back. "I didn't mean ... *shit*."

She lifted her head, her eyes stinging from all the tears. "You didn't do anything wrong. It's me. I'm the hormonal nutjob." She sat up. "Did you know I bawled in the car on the drive home today from a song on the radio?"

His lip twitched, but he didn't say anything.

"A song on the fucking radio, Brock. I've never cried from a song. Not even the really super emotional ones that most people cry over, like 'Cat's in the Cradle' and stuff."

Brock's breath hitched for a moment.

Oh fuck, right. His dad died when he was a kid, and that song was about father and sons. Shit, she really wasn't herself. No, right now she was a terrible person.

She blinked back more hot tears. "I'm sorry, I didn't mean ... that shouldn't have been the song I used as an example. I know you lost your dad ... " Her voice caught in her throat, and new tears sprang from her eyes. "I'm really sorry."

With a warm and throaty chuckle, he scooped her up, and she suddenly found herself on his lap. "It's okay. I happen to like the song." Her lip trembled. He tilted her head up with a gentle knuckle under her chin. The pad of his thumb brushed along her bottom lip. "Who are you going to the party with?" he asked quietly.

"My friend Allie and her wife, Violet."

"Will that douchebag be there?"

She averted her gaze, searching the room for those damn ankle boots. The rumble in his voice turned into a gritty hoarseness. "Krista?"

She found her boots and slipped off his lap to go and step into them. Her brain was so easily muddled when he was touching her. "It'll be fine. There'll be a bunch of people there. Cops, don't forget. I'll just avoid him and stay close to Allie. Plus, everyone knows I'm pregnant now. It's the talk of the station."

Ignoring her again, he pushed past her with a low and beastly growl, leaving the room. And she thought she was moody. One minute he was the nicest, sweetest, most incredible guy, and then the next, he was a grumbling, growling bear with more animal sounds than words. He could be such an ass.

She went about fixing her hair, getting frustrated once again and nearly taking the scissors to it, it could be so uncooperative. But in the end, she managed to wrestle it into a ponytail behind her and gel down the top. Though she knew by the time she got home later that night, there'd be a halo of red fuzzies around her head.

Applying minimal makeup, because she'd never really been the makeup kind of girl to begin with, Krista grabbed her black wool coat and red scarf and then headed for the front door.

"I'll drive."

She spun around in the hallway and nearly fell into the wall. The man looked delicious. No, delicious was the wrong word. Hmm, sexy as ever-loving fuck? Yeah, that seemed about right.

Dressed up in a pair of ass-hugging black dress pants and a forest green sweater, the collar of a charcoal dress shirt peeking out at the top, and sporting just a hint of a beard, the man was drop-dead fucking stunning. And still, even all ready to go out for the evening, he practically oozed danger, control and power.

He took up the whole damn hallway, and that smell, oh dear lord, that smell: Old leather and citrus musk wafted up her nose, making her horny pregnant lady hormones leap into overdrive. He tossed on his black leather jacket, but she just continued to gawk at him. She couldn't stop herself. Panties instantly wet, and her nipples went diamond hard.

"We going? Or would you prefer to just stand there and eye-fuck me all night long?" he asked, a hint of humor in his tone.

She shook her head. "Excuse me?" Still not able to get over how damn good he looked.

"I'm going with you. As your date. You look beautiful, by the way." He made his way past her, down the steps to the foyer, grabbed his keys from the bowl, slipped into his black loafers and opened the door.

"I didn't invite you, you know," she finally said, wondering if he knew where the party was and not completely sure she was ready to volunteer the information. He'd been so sweet earlier, comforting her and wiping away her tears, and yet now the bossy, broody hard Hart was back, and she couldn't get a read on him. He'd just invited himself to her work party, insinuated himself into her evening.

He grunted. "I know."

She still wasn't ready to go down without at least a little bit of a fight. "So maybe you're not allowed to come."

He shot her an impatient side-eye. "I found your tickets to the party on your nightstand. You bought two tickets several months ago. People are allowed to bring their significant others."

She put her hands on her hips and glared at him. "Well, you're not my significant other."

"That's right, I'm not. I'm the father of your child, your room-mate, and your fuck buddy. I think we're more than just *significant* to each other at this point, wouldn't you say? And I want to see this douchebag who's been harassing you for myself. Size him up. Maybe if he knows you're with me, he'll back off. Might be as simple as standing next to you looking all big and scary."

She snorted. "Big and scary ... "

A smirk jiggled on his lips. "You don't think I'm big and scary?"

Sitting up tall, she shook her head. "No, as a matter of fact I don't. I think you *want* people to think you're big and scary, but in reality, you're just a big mushy teddy bear. It's easier to be scary and keep people at arm's length than let your guard down and let them get to know you."

Where the hell did she just pull that from? His jaw clenched, and a tension muscle began to tick just below his ear. But he didn't say anything. He didn't even look at her. Instead he opened the front door for her and waited until she walked out into the cool December night.

"Do you know where you're going?" she asked with a huff, the seat warmers doing an impeccable job of melting her butt until it was wonderfully tingly.

"Eagle's Lodge Resort, no?"

Damn it. "Do you even like parties?"

"No."

"Well, then, why are you coming if you don't like parties?"

The resort was in sight, and the idea of having Brock and Myles in the same room made the butterflies in her belly flutter around in an unmitigated frenzy of panic, like a storm was coming and there wasn't enough shelter for them all to hide in.

Brock found a parking spot, pulled in and turned off the truck, shifting around in his seat to face her. "I'm here because you're here. I'm here for you. Now, let's go."

———

BROCK FUCKING HATED PARTIES. And a party where he didn't know a soul and wanted to kick the living shit out of a cop in attendance was certainly not high up on his list either. His hand fell to the small of Krista's back, and he instantly felt calmer. Feeling her beneath his palm, no matter how slight, grounded him.

It also scared him.

Since the moment that little *thump thump* heartbeat had echoed around the small ultrasound room, Brock felt differently around Krista. His protective instinct was all-consuming, for both her and the baby, but he was also feeling other things. He loved the fact that she liked his cooking. He'd never cooked for anybody but himself before, and although he liked what he made, he was nervous if other people would too. But Krista devoured everything he made, humming contentedly to herself and closing her eyes with a sultry little tilt to her lips as she ate his creations. Some days he'd pull her laundry out of the dryer and catch himself smiling at the brightly colored socks with animal prints that fell out. She definitely had a thing for cats.

More than anything, though, it was the way she'd clung to him. Thrown herself into his arms when he'd barely made it to the top of stairs and cried on his chest. She'd needed him. Needed his comfort. Nobody had ever come to Brock for comfort. They came to him for a solution, to fix things or take care of a problem, but never just for comfort.

He reached for her hand.

She glanced up at him, her lips parting just so and her beautiful blue eyes twinkling.

They made their way up the stairs to the ballroom, where red, white and gold assaulted his eyeballs and the shrill chime of poorly selected Christmas music blasted over the stereo system.

A fat fake Christmas tree sat poised in one corner with enormous red and gold bows tied all over it, while frosted snow pictures had been craftily sketched onto all the surrounding windows, and garland and icicles hung from every imaginable ledge or surface. It looked like an elf had gotten food poisoning and projectile-vomited over the entire room.

"You came!" an attractive brunette cheered, tottering up to Krista on her flashy gold stilettos, her red dress accentuating killer curves like nobody's business. The two women hugged, the brunette towering over Krista, who had smartly decided to go with her flat gray ankle boots. The same ones she'd tossed at Brock's skull not an hour earlier.

"Yeah ... " Krista sighed. "I came. Not sure how long I'll stay, though. Still not feeling great." The other woman's eyes suddenly flew up to Brock's face and then back to Krista and then Brock again.

A thousand questions asked in half a second with just one look and a lone raised eyebrow.

Krista coughed and moved back into Brock's hand. He gently wrapped it around her slender waist and cupped her hip. How in the world this woman thought she was gaining weight already was beyond him. She still felt fucking perfect.

"I, uh ... Allie, this is Brock, my ... *friend,*" Krista finally said.

Brock snorted. She elbowed him.

Glancing up at him with a glare and mouthing "be cool" she continued to introduce them. "Brock, this is my friend and co-worker, Allie."

He held out his hand, and the two made the customary pleasantries, though Brock could see and practically hear the cogs of curiosity spinning like a squeaky hamster wheel inside Allie's head.

She wanted to know every bit of juicy gossip surrounding Krista and her mystery date.

Krista left his embrace and stepped forward to join Allie. The two looped arms, and like a reluctant puppy, Brock followed behind, his eyes surveying the scene to see if he could spot that Myles fucker.

They were seated with Allie and Violet, and a few other of Krista's colleagues, most of them civilian workers. Brock hadn't said more than two sentences in the last hour, but he was completely fine with that. Chit-chat was overrated, and he wasn't there to make friends. He was there to protect Krista and get some intel on Slade.

Sure, Chase's hacking and Rex's patrol had proven fruitful, but there was nothing like seeing the monster in the flesh, watching him in action and getting a real feel for the creep. Brock was just glad Slade was no longer Krista's mentor. But that didn't mean the scumbag was off the hook.

They were just finishing up dinner when Krista suddenly inhaled mid-sip of her water and began to cough. Wanting to help his date, he started to pound on her back, but his eyes also followed hers.

Krista's coughing began to ebb, but not before the man she'd been watching swung his head in their direction and his eyes zeroed in on Krista. Then they landed in on Brock and nearly doubled in size.

Was this Slade?

It had to be.

Brock was only half listening to Krista's friend while the other half of him continued to watch Myles. He was up to something, Brock was sure of it.

Krista's eyes followed Slade, too, though not nearly as intensely as Brock's. She still answered Allie and laughed on cue. Brock couldn't give two shits if Allie had just told the funniest joke of the century; his focus was Slade.

Whether he was ignoring Brock or had legitimately lost interest, Myles turned his back and began chatting up a pretty, very young woman at the bar. The woman looked no more than twenty-one, if she was that. Blonde with big doe eyes and an innocent smile. Too young to be a cop for sure. Maybe a civilian worker? Someone's date?

Her dark red dress left very little to the imagination, and the way she was laughing and giggling at everything Myles said told Brock she was Slade's target for the evening. He couldn't have Krista, so he was moving on to other prospects. Brock only hoped this prospect was willing and not forced or coerced.

Krista's hand linked with Brock's beneath the table, and she gave it a gentle squeeze. He squeezed it back, and she gasped beside him.

"Too hard," she whispered.

Damn it. He was tightly wound.

He glanced down into her eyes. "Sorry."

His eyes swiveled back to Slade and the young woman. He watched as she ordered a drink from the bartender, then excused herself to the ladies' room, leaving her beverage under the watchful eyes of Senior Constable Myles Slade.

And then it happened.

As inconspicuous as could be, but not nearly as stealthy as he probably hoped, Myles dropped something into her drink, quickly grabbed a stir-stick from the back and began swirling it around with the ice cubes until the tablet dissolved.

"Did he just ... " Krista started.

He did.

Brock was up and halfway across the room, stalking toward Slade like a bull after a red cape. Steam rushed from his ears as tunnel vision set in. Slade was in for a world of hurt.

Krista was by his side seconds later just as he came up nearly nose-to-nose with Slade.

"What did I just see you put in that girl's drink?" Brock asked, the threads of his self-control snapping as he took in the smarmy look on Myles's face and was forced to inhale that disgusting cologne he'd apparently bathed in before he came.

Myles rolled his eyes. The man appeared bored, but the tightening of his jaw told Brock otherwise. "I don't know what you're talking about, dude. I didn't do anything. Mind your own business."

Brock snorted. He could hear his pulse thundering in his ears. A soft, gentle hand rested on his arm, and instinctively, his muscles bunched and tightened.

Myles's eyes followed the hand before his gaze flew back up to Krista. "Are you with this muscle-bound moron, Matthews?"

Krista went to open her mouth, no doubt to try to diffuse the situation, but Brock cut her off. "She is. And I've seen the marks on her arms from your ... *interests*. Leave her alone or you'll answer to me."

Myles puffed up his chest and took a step forward. "Are you threatening me? Are you threatening an *officer of the law* in front of other officers of the law? At our *Christmas* party?"

Brock's eyes shifted just slightly.

Fuck.

He'd forgotten for the briefest of moments where he was and who he was surrounded by. Myles noticed the change and sneered. "You're just a big dummy. Really, Matthews? I thought you'd go for someone with more brains than this ox."

Brock's fists bunched at his sides, and red clouded his vision. Cop or no cop, this fucker was going to pay. One day.

The young woman with the now drugged drink returned, equal parts fear and curiosity on her heart-shaped face. Krista grabbed her drink and then dumped it into Myles's half-full glass.

Damn, his woman had balls.

Did he just call her *his* woman?

"You might want to watch your beverages around this guy,

Ingrid. He's having a hard time getting laid without a little *help* these days." She shot Myles a smug look before stepping in front of Brock. Could she feel his need to punch, kick and maim? Probably. He wasn't exactly practicing his poker face. "You going to drink your scotch *now*, Myles?" she asked.

Brock wanted to move Krista behind him to protect her and the baby, but the stubborn woman wouldn't budge.

Myles's cheeks were on fire. They had him.

Brock felt Krista shiver in front of him. He immediately placed his hands on her shoulders to ground her—to ground himself. Myles just continued to glare at her, his eyes growing fiercer and darker. They knew, and he knew they knew, that this was not his first date-rape attempt.

But Myles Slade wasn't going to go down without a fight. Call it pride, arrogance, smugness or the true disgusting belief that he didn't think he was doing anything wrong, the man was going to deny it.

His Adam's apple bobbed twice in his throat before he threw his shoulders back and adopted a cocky smirk. "I don't know what you saw, Matthews, but I didn't put anything in Ingrid's drink." Then with a feigned look of boredom and confidence, he picked up his glass and took the smallest of sips. Ingrid, the little civilian worker, had remained quiet and confused during it all and didn't seem to relax in the slightest when she saw Myles drink. She smelled it, too. The guy was garbage.

"Go find Helen and Cindy," Krista said quietly, resting her hand on Ingrid's arm. "They're sitting over at our table with Allie and her wife." With fear in her big brown eyes, the young woman nodded and scurried away.

Krista turned around and rested her hands on Brock's chest. Her scent filled his nostrils, and his body immediately calmed. She motioned for him to take a step back, but he didn't move a muscle, not when his woman, his child were still within arm's reach of Slade.

"Brock," she said through clenched teeth, "let's not make a scene. We should probably just go home."

"You stay the *fuck* away from Krista, you got that?" Brock said through his own clenched teeth, his voice a breath above a whisper.

Myles's mouth drew up into a sinister grin. "Let's not forget who has the law on their side. You come within ten feet of me, and I'll shoot your fucking face off and get away with it ... you got *that?*"

Brock stomped and motioned to lunge at Myles, his arms coming up as though he was ready to start swinging.

Krista pushed against Brock's chest, determined to get him to move. "Just stop!"

Myles chuckled. "Fucking Neanderthal ... "

Brock's entire body was in flames.

But before he could do anything, Krista was spinning back around, her finger right up in Slade's face. Brock could barely hear her over the thrumming of his own pulse, but he did.

"We're on to you, Myles. And we're coming for you. I'm sure Ingrid wasn't your first, and she definitely won't be your last, you sad, desperate prick. Watch your back, because you're mine."

Slade's pupils dilated, and his pallor slowly changed to a greyish green as her threat sank in.

"You are a disgusting piece of shit, and if I find out you've drugged other girls, I will take you down."

Her shoulders were high, and her ribcage expanded rapidly. She was just as tightly wound as Brock. They needed to get out of there before one or both of them took a swing at Myles. Then shit would really hit the fan.

Blinking once, twice, three times and shaking loose the homicidal feeling inside of him, Brock grabbed Krista's elbow. The woman vibrated.

No longer with concrete in his feet, he ushered them both to the door. Her elbow was on fire in his touch, and the way her nostrils flared told Brock that this woman was seconds away from blowing. He had to get her out of there.

The truck door slammed shut, and on instinct, Brock hit the lock button. He'd gone through loads of training on bringing his heart rate back to rest within seconds and switching his focus from one target to another. He was already calm, cool and collected again. The same could not be said for his date. The woman was like a jungle cat who'd just chased an antelope through the savannah for an hour. Her chest heaved, a sexy vein along her delicate neck pulsed, and the way she bunched her fists made her knuckles glow a bright white in the darkness of the truck. She was wound as tight as a top.

Brock did the only thing he could do. He hauled her petite frame across the center console and into his lap, holding her, absorbing her anger and letting each shake and tremble of her muscles flow into him and disappear. She didn't say anything, didn't even really acknowledge where she was or that she was in his lap, she simply stared out into darkness of the trees and shrubs and trembled in his arms.

He willed her to calm down, to settle. He ran his hand down her back and murmured shushes and other reassurances.

He could only imagine how she felt right now. Probably much like he did. It was never a thrill, never a good or empowering feeling standing up to a bully like Slade, threatening them and letting them know you were on to them.

And yet, he probably would have done the same thing. They couldn't just let Slade get away with it, let him drug that poor woman or any other woman for that matter. The man was scum and deserved to be treated as such.

"What can I do?" he asked softly, weaving his hands gently into the hair at the nape of her neck and lightly turning her head to face him.

She blinked a few times as if not really seeing him, her blue eyes dark and more pupil than iris.

Her lip wobbled. "I hate him."

"Me too."

"This doesn't feel *good*."

"I know it doesn't."

"Instead it feels as though I have opened up this giant can of flesh-eating worms and they're getting ready to wriggle and squirm their way into everyone's lives, destroying and demolishing souls and bodies as they go."

Well, that was graphic.

She shivered in his arms. He felt gooseflesh rise across her skin.

Shit, they'd left so abruptly, they'd forgotten to grab their coats. The truck was freezing. Her teeth quickly began to chatter. He had to get her warm. Get her home.

Delicately, he lifted her from his lap and placed her back on the bench seat, then started the truck and swung it around to the front of the resort. He rolled down his window and called the waiting valet over.

The young man was more than eager to oblige and was back in seconds with both their coats. Brock thanked the kid with a tip and handed Krista not only her own jacket but Brock's as well. Then he rolled up the window, cranked the heat and peeled out of the resort.

They were silent for the rest of the ride home, both of them exhausted from the altercation but also digging deep into their own souls. Myles had hit all kinds of nerves and stirred all kinds of feelings. And one of those feelings had certainly been fear.

It didn't matter that Slade was no longer Krista's coach; this monster worked with her. Worked with the mother of Brock's child. At any point in the day, she could be cornered by him, alone with him, assaulted by him—again. And although Brock knew she was a ballsy little thing and could hold her own, Slade had proven tonight that he had no respect for the law … or women. And Krista had poked the rapey bear, letting him know they were on to him. Slade was a problem.

He pulled into the driveway a short while later, but neither of them moved to get out. They just sat there, eyes focused on the front of the stark white garage door.

"I wanted to kill him," Brock said finally.

"I know," she whispered.

"You can't keep doing this, Krista. You can't keep doing this to *me*."

Slowly, dramatically, she swiveled her head until she was staring at him. "What do you mean, I can't keep doing this? I went on light duty just like you asked. But I'm not going to stop being a cop. This is my job."

"I know, but Slade is dangerous."

"You don't think I know that?"

An exasperated sigh escaped him, and he finally let the heavy weight he'd been carrying on his shoulders all night slip off. His body crumpled in his seat. "I don't think you realize how close I came to putting my fist in his face tonight. To making it so the guy would never walk again. And I would have … for you. I would have … for our baby. Consequences be damned." He shook his head. "The fact that you work with … so close with a guy like that, who has no qualms about abusing the law, hurting you, drugging women … " He trailed off. He pivoted to face her. "You're killing me here."

"What do you want me to do? Quit?" she asked, a mite of fear in her tone.

He blinked but slowly shook his head. No, she'd hate him if he made her do that. Resent him, possibly resent the baby. "Start thinking about more than just your job. Start thinking about you, about *our* baby … about me. You're being reckless. Irresponsible. You never should have threatened him like that. Now he knows we're on to him. Now he knows we're coming for him. What's to stop him from going on the offensive and coming after you first?" His chest expanded as he took in a deep and grounding breath. "I don't want anything to happen to you because you went all vigilante and tried to nail this guy to the wall. You have bigger things to consider now. Other people counting on you. I can't be the only responsible person raising this child. I can't be the only *person* raising this child because you took matters into your own hands."

Her bottom lip wobbled again. But instead of breaking down, she clenched her jaw and turned to face him, conviction in her eyes. "Will you help me?"

Slowly, he nodded. "I'll get my brothers on it."

"What do you want me to do?" She pulled her gloves on. Now that the truck had been shut off, the seat warmers were no longer working their magic, and even Brock was starting to feel the winter chill seeping into his bones. He'd toss the furnace on as soon as they got into the house.

He unbuckled his belt. "Stay away from him."

CHAPTER ELEVEN

THEY MADE their way up the steps to the front door. It was a frosty December night with plenty of stars and a biting wind. They'd most likely wake up to frost on the ground and their windshield frozen. Krista hugged both her and Brock's coats tightly around her body, thankful for the added layer of leather, which cut the wind nicely. Her boot hit the last step when suddenly she felt herself slipping.

There was a black ice patch on the top step, and her foot came out from under her. Immediately, all thoughts flew to the baby, and tossing off the coats, she windmilled her arms and did an awkward cha-cha dance to try to regain her footing. She couldn't fall, she just couldn't.

But then big, strong arms wrapped around her waist, and she found herself plastered against hard, warm brick. Brock's brick chest.

"Easy … " he hummed, his breath hot on her neck. "You wouldn't be nearly as beautiful with black and blue bruises everywhere."

She blinked up at him, having to flutter her lashes like a flirty little tween. And as if they were the stars of some Christmas romantic comedy made-for-television movie, flurries began to flutter down around them. Like cherry blossoms in May, gathering like clumps of dandruff in their hair and on their clothes. His eyes found hers. She wrapped her arms around his neck. Then, just to finish the scene before it faded to black, he lowered his head and took her mouth.

———

"Holy Jesus, it's freezing in here!" Krista shivered as she moved out of the way so that Brock could enter the foyer behind her. She was about to hang their coats up but suddenly thought better of it and instead put them back, toed off her boots and stuffed her feet into her slippers.

Without bothering to take his shoes or coat off, let alone muttering a word, Brock took the steps two at a time and headed to the control panel for the furnace down the hall.

"Shit!" he exclaimed. "Furnace is broken."

"Seriously?" Krista hugged her body and came up behind him. "Can you fix it? Or do I have to sleep in my clothes and coat?"

He shook his head. "I'll have a look at it in the morning. Might just need more oil. But for now, I think we might have to light a fire in the fireplace and maybe sleep out in the living room."

She nodded. "Okay. I'll go get some blankets."

He grunted, pushing past her again and heading downstairs or outside or somewhere, probably to go and find wood.

By the time she'd gathered all the bedding, Brock had returned and was crouched down next to the open hearth in the living room, blowing on flickering embers. Within seconds, larger flames began to dance, and soon it was beautiful orange and red wings of warmth pirouetting along the logs.

Krista let out a contented sigh. The cold that had seemed to embed itself in her very marrow once the adrenaline had worn off finally showed signs of receding.

"Go shower," he said with a grunt, not bothering to look at her. "Warm up, and the fire will be ready when you're out."

She pouted at his back but did as she was told, hoping that he'd join her and they could continue on with the romance from out in the driveway. But alas, no. She was forced to shower alone and scrub her own back.

Emerging a short while later in plaid flannel pants, a big oversize gray hoodie, her fuzzy green and pink cat socks and a French braid down her back, she found Brock in the kitchen with the sound of a kettle boiling. The fire was roaring, and the bedding had all been made.

Krista wandered over to the fire and sat down on the floor, bringing the covers up over her legs. She watched the flames dance, twirl and crackle, burning the once red-hued logs to a dark black.

"Tea?" he asked, making her jump out of her skin.

The man was like a ninja when he wanted to be, all stealth and silence. And then at other times, his big gladiator body stomped around the house and creaked on the stairs as he if were a giant toddler, adding to the paradox that was Brock Hart. A tough nut to crack, a hard man to get to know. Her hard Hart.

But she was determined to get to know him. Each and every time they were together, whether it be sitting on the couch watching a renovation show and eating a stir-fry or rolling around in his bed like sweaty teenagers, she thought she saw a new side of him. But the man was proving to be one of those dodecahedron things, multi-sided and endlessly complicated.

"Tea?" he grunted again, nudging her back with his shin this time.

"Oh, um, sure. Thanks," she said, shaking her head, letting the confusing thoughts rattle around and then slowly disappear.

He crouched down and handed her a steaming cup of what smelled like Sleepytime tea.

"You care to join me?" she asked, patting the empty space in the bedding beside her. "Plenty of room for two."

A slow and intriguing smile curved his lips, and in a moment, Brock's shirt and sweater were off and his pants soon followed, leaving him in nothing but those sexy black boxer briefs. He wasn't hard, but the line of his cock was hard to miss. Her man was hung.

Blowing the steam off her tea, Krista ran her tongue along the seam of her lips, eyeing Brock like he was a choice cut of meat she just couldn't wait to sink her teeth into.

"Tongue back in your mouth." His voice was low and gritty. A hunger echoed in those words, one of demand, one that met her own. He slipped in beside her.

Rather than punch him in the shoulder and tell him to shut up for his smart-ass response, she couldn't. She was on fire. Pushing the covers off her and quickly standing up, Krista began to undress. The fire, the tea, the flannel and hoodie, all combined with the insane heat radiating off the man beside her, and suddenly her whole body burned.

"You don't waste any time, do you?" he asked, a hint of humor to his tone.

She threw her hoodie onto the couch. "Shut up. I'm boiling." Next came the pants, then the socks, until she was in nothing but her underwear and a black tank top.

She stepped over his body before sinking back down into the covers. The whole time, their eyes remained locked. He watched her. She watched him. It was hard to tell who was the prey and who was the hunter at this point. Need and hunger seemed to percolate around both of them as pheromones bounced off the walls and the sexual tension grew thick and heady.

A low growl rumbled from the back of his throat, dark and dripping with promise. His green eyes glowed fierce and bright in the firelight, but as each moment passed, the pupils grew bigger and darker.

But she needed to find out more about Brock. That kiss outside had made those feelings she'd been having for him rachet up several notches, and her whole body had sparked alive in his arms. He was more than just a roommate. He was more than just the father of her child. He was more than just a lover. He was the man she was falling for, and she needed to learn more about him. She needed to learn everything.

The sex could wait.

Or could the talking wait?

Her nipples pebbled beneath her tank top, and her entire core clenched.

Her body certainly didn't want to wait.

But if they had sex now, he might just roll over and go to sleep after. Then when would they talk? She had him here by the fire. They'd just shared a romantic moment outside. Maybe he would be open to talking, open to sharing.

"Awful lot of thinking going on in that sexy brain of yours," he said, lifting one dark eyebrow.

Krista's lips twisted into a half smile as she grabbed her mug of tea and brought it beneath her nose.

"Care to tell me what you're thinking about? I'm assuming it's dirty."

She took a sip and let the tea sit on her tongue for a moment before answering. "Well, some thoughts were, yes. But I'm also curious about you. We've been living together for a while now, we have sex all the time, and we're having a baby together. Don't you think it's high time we got to know each other better?"

Something, she couldn't quite put her finger on what exactly, changed in him. He hardened. Wariness clouded his eyes, and he shifted uncomfortably in the bedding.

"You think so, do you?" he finally said.

She nodded. "I do. You can ask me questions too. It's not a one-way street."

All he did was grunt.

Nibbling on her bottom lip for a moment, she averted her gaze, pulling at a stray thread on one of the sheets. "How did your dad die?"

She lifted her head to gauge his reaction, but he wasn't looking at her either. His eyes were fixed on the flames, and in turn they reflected back in that gorgeous green. Like emerald fire.

"In a car accident."

"I'm sorry."

Brock sank down into the covers and put his head on the pillow, folding his arms up behind his neck and letting his eyes focus on the ceiling above. "I was in the car with him."

Krista gasped, her efforts in slinking down beside him halting in her surprise. "Oh my God."

Brock nodded solemnly. "He'd just picked me up from football practice, and we were on our way home."

Krista's heart physically ached at the idea of a young boy having to endure the pain that Brock did. No child, no person should ever have to witness such a thing.

"There was a guy speeding down a busy road. Even though my dad was technically off duty, he was still in a patrol car and heard the call. Figured he'd just park the car at the entrance to a shopping center and that the sight of his vehicle would make the driver slow down. Most of the time it does."

Krista nodded in understanding. It was true. Often, she and Myles would just go park their car in a school or park zone and have lunch or do paperwork, not even bothering to get out, because the presence of the law often seemed to be enough to enforce the rules.

He swallowed. "Only the guy didn't slow down. He didn't stop, and the nose of my dad's cruiser was sticking out just a bit too far."

Krista's hand flew to her mouth. "Oh no."

His throat undulated. "I was in the back. Otherwise I may not have made it. The speed of the other vehicle sent the patrol car into a pole, and both the driver and passenger sides in the front were crushed. My dad died instantly."

She shifted onto her side, propping her body up on her elbow and letting her hand fall to his rock-hard chest. "I'm so sorry."

He swallowed again.

"It wasn't your fault. You know that, right?"

He let out a slow breath though his nose. "I know that. Doesn't make it any easier."

Her fingers mindlessly played with the light scattering of hair between his pecs, but his hand came out from behind his head and stilled their efforts, bringing her fingers to his lips.

"I don't like that you're a cop. Even light duty. Because it's temporary. And that fucker Slade works there. I don't like that your job is dangerous, no matter how admirable a job it may be."

She let out an exasperated sigh. She didn't want to fight. But before she could say anything, he rolled her onto her back, covering her with his massive and powerful warrior body.

"But I also don't want to fight right now or talk about my family anymore. It's much more enjoyable being inside you."

Her legs spread of their own volition, and he nestled between them, his erection long, hard and eager, rubbing her clit just right.

Damn it. This was not what she wanted.

Well, yes, it was. But she also wanted to talk. They needed to talk.

"What's the dirtiest thing you've done, Constable Matthews?" He bent his head low and fished a dark, tight nipple out of her tank top with his teeth. Krista shut her eyes and fought back the groan that built in her throat.

"Um ... "

He ground his hips against hers. Even through her underwear, he felt incredible. "Hmm, that dirty, huh?"

Her cheeks grew warm. "I've been around the block. What about you?"

He lifted his head, a rare smile tugged at his mouth. "You didn't answer my question." He bit her bottom lip.

Krista swallowed past the lump in her throat. "Well, um, some spanking and bondage. Ass play. My ex was a kinky fucker."

The sound that rumbled at the back of his throat made her whole body stiffen.

Was he jealous?

"No ex talk," was all he said.

She rolled her eyes but quickly forgot why when his teeth found her neck and his big, warm hand cupped her breasts. Thumb and finger rolled her nipple until a dull, decadent throb pulsed in her chest.

"What kind of ass play?" he asked, his voice low and gruff next to her ear as he nibbled on that sweet spot right where her lobe met her neck.

"Ummm."

He lifted his head again. "Really?"

She nodded. "Yes, I have. Have you?"

He shook his head. "No, I haven't."

Liar! "Bullshit."

A sexy eyebrow slowly drifted up his forehead. "Why would I lie?"

"Because ... you had to have at least tried it once in your life. You're ... "

Levering himself onto one arm, he put his other hand to work lifting up her tank top and exposing her breasts. "I'm what?"

"Good in bed. Insanely sexy ... a fucking god. Pick one. You've probably screwed your way through a cheerleading squad."

"So?" His mouth found a nipple, and he bit down. She arched into him and shut her eyes.

"So at some point in your thirty-six years, you've had to have found your way up a woman's ass."

He snorted against her chest. "Well, that was rather graphic."

"Sorry, but when you're uh … doing … what you're doing makes my brain start to fart."

"Again, rather graphic."

Krista rolled her eyes. Her hand found him inside his boxers, and she began to stroke him. "So then why'd you ask me if I ever had?"

His head traveled down her body, warm kisses landing on her ribs and then the slight swell of her stomach. Krista's heart soared from how much love he already had for his child.

"Because I'm curious. Did you like it?" His fingers hooked into the waistband of her underwear, and he tugged them off.

"Maybe … "

"You want to do it again?"

"Why are you asking me this?"

His face was poised at the apex of her thighs. A surreptitious flick of his tongue had her melting into the floor. He lifted his head. "Because I thought if you *had* and were interested in doing it again, it might be a way for you to assume control. Teach me, boss me around. Tell me what to do, how to fuck your ass until you're a screaming mess."

Well, holy shit!

She gaped at him. "Really?"

His tongue flicked out again, and the caterpillars kissed as he closed his eyes. "Mhmm."

"I … I'd love to."

"Good," he murmured. "I don't know much about it, besides what I've seen from porn, but what I do know is that I'm supposed to get you good and turned on."

Krista nodded. "Yeah … "

"And then what?" A finger slipped into her folds and began stroking her inner walls. She clenched around him. "Let me know when you want another finger." He dipped his head back down and went to work with his tongue and mouth. Delightful circles and velvety licks had her thrusting into his face, panting and moaning and all but begging for another finger.

Their eyes locked for a brief second, and she nodded. She was ready, so very, very ready.

"Do we need lube?" he asked.

"I-if you've got it," she said through shallow breaths.

He grunted at the same time as the sound of a cap flicking open.

Krista chuckled. "You just so happened to have some?"

His big, wily smile made her heart soar. "A man's allowed to hope. I *was* a Boy Scout. Always be prepared."

She chuckled and then gasped as cool liquid silk dripped down between her cheeks.

"Do you want to be on top?" he asked. "In control and with all the power?"

Krista's grinned matched his. He really was trying to relinquish control. "Yes. That way you can play with my tits and stroke my clit."

The fire danced lambent in his eyes as he sat up. "You're the boss."

She snorted. "Damn right I am."

A low and carnal chuckle shook his body as they traded places and he reclined down into the nest of blankets. "At least for the moment."

She straddled him and, without waiting, sank down, taking him into her pussy in one hard and fast push. They both let out involuntary moans, and his hands came up to knead her breasts and tweak her hard, needy nipples.

She rode him slowly, long, languid, leisurely glides of his body disappearing into hers, stroking searing hot across her slick and sensitive channel. Her head tilted up and her eyes shut as she enjoyed feeling the big, gorgeous man inside her. Skin to skin, flesh in flesh. He cupped her breasts and relieved some of the strain of their weight. They'd grown again in the last few weeks, and when she went braless, they were a tad painful. He tugged on the nipples and twisted until a sharp cry broke past her lips.

Lost in the moment, in the feel of Brock, Krista's eyes flashed open when his fingers trailed down her body and wrapped around her hips, pushing her cheeks apart in search of her tight hole. He was watching her. Those green eyes glowed near gold in the flickering flames. His breath was ragged. His nostrils flared with each lift of his powerful hips, and with each lift, his pelvic bone grazed her clit. She was seconds from orgasm.

"Now?" he asked, the strain she felt in her own body equally evident in his tone.

She nodded, rising up on her knees and pulling him from her. He grabbed his shaft and held it firm. With her free hand, she grabbed the bottle of lube next to her leg and quickly squirted some on to his length, moving it around the soft, shiny crown with the tip of her finger.

A groan escaped him, and suddenly she ached to take him in her mouth. But they were on a different mission tonight. That desire would have to wait until tomorrow. Tossing the lube to the side, she lifted up again, making sure he was in position.

Gently, ever so slowly, Krista lowered her body. Her breathing relaxed as she pushed out again with her muscles. He entered her, and then there was that initial slight pinch of pain. It'd been a while since she'd indulged in such deplorable decadence, so the snap of pain was expected. She shut her eyes and pushed past the discomfort.

"You okay?" he asked, his voice thick with the effort of having to hold off his orgasm.

Despite the moment, a chuckle bubbled up in Krista's chest. Of the two of them, he was in far more discomfort than she was, she was sure of it. "I should be asking *you* that. You about ready to explode?"

He grunted. "Yes."

"Just a second." She sank down a little deeper, taking him all the way. And then she began to move, starting off slow at first, just bobbing up and down, her body tight around his, and then picking up the pace when her own climax began to brew and threatened to unleash.

"P-pinch my clit," she panted, angling over his body so that they were face to face.

He did as he was told, his other hand coming up to tweak and twist her nipples, but the combination of it all was just too much. His hands on her body, his cock in her ass, filling her, splitting her, taking her, and when she dared to look up and catch his eyes, the way he was looking at her, with so much ... possession, so much awe, she was a goner. Finding his shoulder, she bit down hard and gave over to the demand of her body. Unleashing the pleasure and letting it take over.

His shoulder muffled her pleas as she convulsed around him, every cell in her body on fire as the climax ripped through her in unyielding waves. White lights flashed behind her closed eyes, and the sounds of Brock's release filled her ears. She milked his cock and watched him as he gradually came down from his release, shuddering as the last of it drained him of all his energy.

When he finally opened his eyes, his beauty momentarily winded her. Especially since as soon as he saw her, he smiled. It was a boyish smile. A smile of thanks and gratitude. But also with the subtle lip tilt of a cocky bugger who'd just accomplished the unthinkable.

Tears burned behind Krista's eyes when the realization hit her like an anvil to the chest. Holy crap, she loved this man. She barely knew a thing about him, but what she did know, she loved.

They did the awkward post-coital dance and shuffle, and she tiptoed off to the bathroom, leaving him naked and possibly passed out in front of the fire.

When she returned, he had thoughtfully grabbed them each a glass of water and placed Krista's on the hearth. She took a greedy sip, not caring at all that a fair percentage of it dripped down her bare chest. Brock ducked off to the washroom and was back moments later. Then they went to the task of getting dressed and pulling up the covers. The fire had died down to a soft burnt orange glow, and the clock in the dining room said it was well past midnight.

As her head hit the pillow, she was suddenly overcome with exhaustion. This entire night had been a whirlwind.

"So ... can I ask how in your thirty-six sexy years you've never managed to have anal sex?" she finally asked after they'd lain there for a few minutes, quietly listening to the fire sizzle and pop and cast shadows on the far wall.

"Opportunity just never came up. I haven't been with *that* many women, you know."

Holy hell, were they going to have the numbers conversation? "How many have you been with?"

"Fourteen."

"Oh, that's not very many. You're right. Several long-term rela-tionships then?" Was he not going to ask her how many people she'd been with?

"No. Maybe one or two, but as you may have noticed, I'm not exactly ... "

She snorted. "Friendly?"

His body shook with quiet laughter. "I was going to say a

people person, but friendly fits. A few one-night stands, a few relationships, a few fuck buddies."

"Oh." They were quiet for a while again. Was he seriously not going to ask her her number? "You want to know my number?"

"Only if you want to share it."

She rolled her bottom lip between her teeth, suddenly grateful that they were both staring at the ceiling and he couldn't see her face and she couldn't see his. "I've been with eight."

Maybe it was her imagination, but she could have sworn she heard an exhale of relief. But to Krista, eight was high. She came from a town where most girls married their high school sweetheart, so their fuck number was one. So with a number like eight, Krista was a trollop in Tanner Ridge.

"Eight guys are not very many at all," he finally said. "The way you were breathing heavily just now had me thinking you were going to be in the triple digits."

She bit her lip again. "Uh ... eight *people*."

He turned over onto his side, propping his head in his hand. "You've been with women?"

She nodded, deliberately not turning to face him. The ceiling was much easier to look at. "Yes."

"How many?"

"Two."

"Was it ... ?"

"One was in a threesome. One was just the two of us." Finally, because she couldn't take it any longer, she shifted and faced him. "Does this change your opinion of me?"

Slowly his head bobbed in a nod.

Oh *shit*.

"I think it's hot."

"You do?"

He nodded more emphatically this time. "Yeah. Was it like an experimental thing? Or did you date this girl for a while?"

She mirrored him and propped her head in her hand. "It was when I went traveling. She's from Poland. We met in Guatemala and started traveling together, and one thing led to another and we had a couple of fun weeks together."

"So are you bisexual?"

Krista lifted one shoulder casually. "Maybe. I don't really know."

His hand came up, and he cupped her cheek. He tugged her in for a kiss on the lips that was more than peck. Seconds later he pulled away but didn't release her. "Bisexual, hetero whatever, I'm just glad you're in my bed now."

Reveling in the warmth and safety of his touch, she leaned her face into his palm. "Who are you, Brock Hart? I can't figure you out. I'm having a baby with you, share your bed and yet I know very little about you. And you know very little about me ... because you don't ask. Tonight is the first time we've ever really talked about ourselves and it's been so nice. I want to know more. And I'll tell you whatever you want to know about me. You just have to ask."

His brows knitted together for a second, and he studied her so intensely that she squirmed. Had the man even blinked? And then, all of a sudden, he changed again. The scowl returned, the walls or fence or whatever was back up, the mask was firmly on, and his eyes flitted to the clock on the mantel.

"It's getting late," he said gruffly. "We should go to sleep." Without waiting for her to respond, he pulled his hand away and rolled over.

Leaving her staring at the back of his head with a crushed heart and wondering what the hell had just happened.

CHAPTER TWELVE

THE TWO DAYS before Christmas had been spent in court. More prosecutions, more details, more horrible recounts of horrible events. So by Christmas Eve, which had been fairly uneventful, Krista was exhausted and with nary a flying fuck to give about flying men in red jumpsuits with presents, toys and reindeer. She'd been graciously given, by some holiday miracle, Christmas Day off but would be back working come Boxing Day.

After sipping peppermint mochas at Starbucks with Allie and the two of them exchanging equally corny gag gifts, she headed home. She was eager to shower, throw on her red and white striped candy cane flannel pajamas and settle down in front of a crackling fire with her ratty copy of *Little Women* as she sipped apple cider and nibbled on gingerbread.

She was crouched down and getting ready to build a fire in the hearth when the front door slammed and Brock stomped up the stairs.

Seemed they were on par with each another that evening. Both miserable. Both wanting to find a bearded man in a red jumpsuit to throat-punch. That made her quickly think of Mickey at the bar and how he was probably dressing up as Santa Claus for his grand-children. She didn't want to throat-punch him, but she did want one of his burgers. Her stomach grumbled at the thought.

"What are you doing?" he asked, his tone speaking volumes about just what kind of a mood he was in.

"Rhythmic gymnastics," she snapped, too tired for pleasantries. "What the hell does it look like?"

He shook his head. "Go pack a bag and let's go."

Krista stood up and gave him a dumbfounded look. It was threatening snow, and whatever harebrained overnight, wilderness Christmas campout he might have had planned, she was *not* going. She didn't even want to go out to her car and grab his Christmas present, which she'd stupidly left in the backseat. "Why?"

"We're going over to my mum's. It's a Christmas tradition. Come on, let's go." He headed down the hallway to his bedroom to start packing.

She chased after him. "What?"

As if elaborating was going to cause him some kind of physical discomfort, he rolled his eyes and scowled. "It's a Christmas tradition. We go over to my mum's house, play board games, eat pizza and drink rum and eggnog. Spend the night and then wake up and have Christmas morning. Been doing it for years. Now go pack. We're already late. Traffic was insane."

"I-I'm invited?"

He gave her another irritated look. "You think I'm going to let the mother of my child spend Christmas alone? Especially when her family is in another town? Besides, you've already met the Three Stooges, and my mum will love you. GO PACK!" And then, just to drive the point home even further, he came up behind her and shooed her out of his room, across the hall and into her room. "And don't bother changing out of your pajamas. That's pretty much the party attire anyway," he called back as he returned to his own room to finish packing.

It was a huge risk.

He knew that.

Bringing Krista to his mother's house. He'd rather have a bath with a toaster. But what else could he do? He'd be the king of assholes to leave her at home all alone on Christmas, and yet bringing her meant that the baby can of worms might get popped open before they were ready. Not to mention the woman he was confused as hell about would be given access to the only four people in the entire world who knew a damn thing about him, and what she uncovered, she might not necessarily like. He'd tried so hard to keep his distance, keep his walls up. But bringing her to his mother's could end all of that.

What other choice did he have, though?

"Have you told your family about the baby yet?" Krista whispered as they wandered up the cobblestone path to his mother's front door.

"No, not yet. Have you told yours?"

She glanced down at her feet. "No."

He didn't bother knocking and just opened the door. "We'll tell them tomorrow, and you can tell your parents tomorrow when you call them, okay?" He reached for her hand and pulled her inside. Better to just rip off the bandage and get it all over with. Almost eighteen weeks, the baby bump was still hideable beneath her baggy pajamas. Maybe they could wait until tomorrow ... or at least after dinner tonight to spill the baby beans.

The house was toasty warm and smelled the way you think Christmas should.

The big fake Christmas tree he'd helped his mother buy a few years ago took center stage in front of the giant bow window, while stockings and garland dressed the fireplace and a Christmas village among fake fluffy snow took up the coffee table.

The three other big black Chevy trucks in the driveway and on the side of the road told him that his brothers were already there. Dumb, Dumber and Dumbest, as he'd nicknamed them. Not that they were actually stupid; on the contrary, but they were younger than him and at times certainly acted like it.

But if it hadn't been for the Chevy dealership out front, the booming loud voices emanating from the kitchen easily gave them all away. Sudden laughter, followed by a "fuck off, you twat!" and then more laughter.

Brock took Krista's coat from her and instructed her to kick her ankle boots into the hall closet. She was doing just that as he hung up their coats when the voice of his mother and a red velour leisure suit came whizzing around the corner.

"You're late!" she chastised. Brock rolled his eyes. "Oh well, at least you made it. Was traffic a bitch?" She lifted up onto her tippy toes and wrapped her arms around his neck. She weighed next to nothing. But unlike Heath, the goofball, he didn't pick her up. Instead, he contorted himself and nearly bent double to hug her back, his body engulfing her small frame until she practically disappeared. She smelled like shortbread and baby powder, and he closed his eyes for half a second, squeezing her just a fraction harder.

Her breath hitched next to his ear.

She'd spotted Krista. Brock released his mother and spun around. Krista was practically cowering in the corner like a lost kitten. His chest tightened, and he fought the urge to wrap a protective arm around her. She was a strong, stubborn woman, though, and would probably bat his arm away.

"Wh-who?" Brock's mother stammered. Reluctantly, her eyes left Krista and zeroed in on Brock's.

Shit. Maybe he should have told his mother he was bringing a guest.

"Mum ... uh, this is Krista." He moved out of the way as best he could in the tiny foyer.

"Hi," Krista said softly, holding out her hand. "Nice to meet you, Mrs. Hart. You have a lovely home."

Brock's mother's midnight-blue eyes, the same shade as Heath and Rex's, went wide with surprise as they flitted back and forth between Brock and his Christmas Eve surprise. And then suddenly, as if being smacked by an invisible hand, she snapped out of it, took Krista's hand and gave her a big smile.

Brock sighed inwardly. Not that his mother wouldn't have ever been anything but kind, cordial and delightful to Krista, but he was still nervous.

"Well, isn't this a wonderful surprise. Brock didn't tell us he was bringing anyone. Or that he was *seeing* anyone. Lovely to meet you, my dear." Instead of releasing her hand, she pulled Krista close and brought her in for a hug.

The voices from the kitchen grew louder, and soon three enormous bodies took up the living room, all with rum and eggnog in one hand and cookies in the other.

Heath appeared to have a stack of cookies in his palm. "You came!" he cheered, a big, stupid, cookie-filled grin on his face.

Their mother spun around. "You've met her?"

"We all have," Rex added. "*Bumped* into Krista at the grocery store a couple of weeks ago and had the proper introductions. Right?"

Krista simply nodded, giving each of the brothers, including Brock, a steely glare before returning to their mother and tossing on a big smile. "That's right!" She eyed the boys again. "I was just coming off work, and who should be following me around the grocery store but three of the Harty Boys."

Heath snorted. "I like that ... the Harty Boys."

They made their way into the living room and sat down. Rex

brought Krista and Brock each a rum and eggnog, and Brock's mother, who had yet to stop grinning at Krista, decided to shove her son to the side and squeeze in between him and Krista on the love seat.

Oh, this was going to blow up so badly in his face. He just knew it.

"So, Krista, how long have you and Brock been seeing each other?" She laced her fingers through Krista's.

"I, um ... " Krista looked at Brock for help. Fuck, he didn't know. Were they seeing each other? She shrugged and turned back to his mother. "A few months, I guess. September, maybe?"

Brock had to keep himself from snorting.

"But it's serious?" his mother asked.

Krista shrugged again. "Maybe."

He had to hand it to Krista. She was playing it cool. They hadn't even discussed what they were yet. Which was stupid, but every time she tried to get him to talk, fear gripped his chest and he shut down. He never talked about himself, ever. It was just easier that way. Emotions muddled the fuck out of things. Facts were easier. When you had the facts, you could be responsible and get shit done.

Emotions were tools of the procrastinator.

His mother patted Krista's hand. "Well, he's never brought a girl home for Christmas before, so it must be."

Brock took a sip of his eggnog. The instant hit of rum to his brain immediately helped take off the edge. Heath always knew how to make a good rum and egg nog. Three parts rum to one part nog.

Krista did the same, but it must have occurred to the both of them at the same time, because just as Brock coughed and reached forward to take away the glass, Krista spat the contents back in. Four sets of eyes around the room looked on curiously.

"Dude," Rex said with a snort. "Control freak much?"

Brock glared at his brother.

"I, um ... " Krista trailed off, looking at him imploringly.

"Too hot?" his mother asked.

"Too much rum?" Heath joked.

Krista shook her head. "I, uh ... uh, no ... I ... "

Apparently, that was all his mother needed, because the light-bulb flicked on so bright over her head that it was practically blinding. She grabbed Krista by the hand and pulled her to her feet. "Come with me, dear. We'll fix you something better in the kitchen. If I've said it once, I've said it a thousand times, Heath adds too much rum."

"Go big or go home," Heath called after them with a laugh.

"What the hell is wrong with you?" Rex asked, giving Brock a what-the-fuck look.

But Brock didn't have time to deal with his brothers. He knew his mother knew. The woman had had four pregnancies of her own and certainly wasn't an idiot. He had to defuse the situation. He had to help Krista. Pushing himself up from the couch, he beelined it for the kitchen only to hear "How long?" whispered from his mother's mouth.

"How long what?" Krista stammered, her eyes darting up to Brock's.

"How far along are you?"

Krista made a sheepish look and let her eyes travel to her feet. "Mrs. Hart ... "

"Joy."

"P-pardon?"

"My name is Joy, dear. Call me Joy."

"Mum." Brock stepped up behind Krista.

"Let the woman speak," his mother snapped, her eyes hardening as they took in his frazzled state only to soften again when she glanced back at the equally frazzled Krista. "You were saying, dear?"

Krista swallowed with a nod. "Okay ... Joy. You have to know, I didn't trap your son. I didn't trap Brock. It ... it was a night of drunken stupidity."

Brock didn't know what to do with his hands, so he placed them on Krista's shoulders. The woman was tense.

Tears welled up in his mother's eyes, and she reached for Krista's hands. "It's Brock's?" Her eyes flitted back up to Brock. He nodded at the same time Krista did. "I'm going to be a Nana?" Krista nodded again. "Can I ... can I?" She lifted one of her hands from Krista's and made to touch her stomach, hesitating until Krista nodded again. A rogue tear dripped down her cheek, and she looked up at Krista with a smile. "Welcome to the family, dear."

Brock let out another sigh. Well, that had gone better than he expected. Much better.

"What's going on in ... here?" It was Heath, and had he been wearing shoes you would have heard them screech on the linoleum floor. Instead his socks slipped, and he nearly crashed into fridge. His eyes darted back and forth from Brock to their mother to Krista to their mother's hand on Krista's stomach.

Krista swallowed. "Hi, *Uncle* Heath."

———

"So ARE you guys getting married then?" Chase asked gruffly as they all sat around the dining room table a little while later, playing Risk and eating pizza. As was tradition, each brother had their own large pizza sitting in front of them. Obviously, Krista was free to have her own as well, but she chose to split one with Brock's mother. Seemed both women liked the idea of chicken, mushroom and spinach. Brock had shaken his head at their order. He went with meat and plenty of it. Always.

"I've asked," Brock grumbled, tipping back his drink and draining it. "She said no."

Krista rolled her eyes at him, and he snorted. "It's complicated."

Chase picked up the dice from the board and started shaking them in his meaty palm. "I don't see the complication. You're having a baby together. You have sex. Makes sense to be married."

Brock's mother joined Krista in another eye roll. "It's the twenty-first century, you big buffoon." She snorted. "Family styles are always changing. Would I *like* for my grandchild's parents to be married and in love? Of course. But let's let Brock and Krista figure out how they want to raise their family, okay?"

God, Brock loved his mother. A family therapist, she'd had nothing but patience for her sons as they grew up. When Brock's dad had died, Brock had been only twelve, and his mother was in the middle of getting her master's degree. She had planned on quitting to get a full-time job and just raise the boys, but Brock wouldn't allow it. Instead he took odd jobs on the weekends and after school to help make ends meet, and his mother alternated between part-time school and a night-shift job on a cleaning crew. It had taken her a little longer to complete school, but she'd never just quit. And eventually, she'd gone on to get her PhD as well and was now Dr. Joy Hart. There wasn't a woman in the world he was prouder of or admired more. And the way she had embraced Krista and her and Brock's unorthodox relationship just proved his mother was one hell of a woman.

"You asked her to marry you?" Heath asked, shaking his head in disbelief.

Brock lifted his shoulder. "It's the right thing to do."

His mother scoffed. "The right thing to do is be in that child's life. Whatever becomes of the two of you," she pointed her finger between Brock and Krista, "would just be a bonus."

Truth be told, though, he was beginning to have feelings for Krista. He was just total shit at showing it. Then she'd ask questions, and the fear would settle in and he'd clam right up. He'd never lived with a woman, never let a woman get this close, and for some reason, it scared the living shit out of him. But Krista, despite how much they butted heads and both seemed to be control freaks, made him want to open up. He just didn't know how.

"Are you going to find out what it is?" Rex asked, diving into another slice of pizza.

Krista shook her head. "Brock doesn't want to, and I kind of like the surprise aspect of it."

Heath laughed. "Well, for your sake, I hope it's a baby and a girl and has your size head. Brock's head was enormous! And all Hart boy babies weigh at least ten pounds or more at birth, right, Mum?" He continued to chuckle as he elbowed Brock in the ribs before devouring a piece of pizza in four bites.

Brock and his mother both winced at the same time. It was true. He and his brothers had been big babies.

"If they offer you the drugs, take the drugs," his mother started, "that's all I'm saying. Harts make big babies with big heads. I don't know about a girl, because I never had one, but if it's a boy, chances are he'll come out looking like a toddler."

Brock glanced over at Krista. Fuck, the woman had gone white as a sheet.

———

Krista yawned and then yawned again as she helped clear the table after dinner and board games. The clock on the mantle said it was closing in on eleven. She hoped the Harts weren't early risers on Christmas. She was exhausted.

After a rousing game of Risk that had Heath coming out victorious and Chase and Brock red in the face with steam coming out of their ears, they played Hearts (how fitting), dominoes and finished the night off with poker, which saw Chase and Brock getting redemption from their baby brother and fleecing him of nearly three hundred dollars. The boys were busy putting the board games away and stoking the fire, so Krista joined Joy in the kitchen to help put away dinner.

"I just wanted to say thank you for opening up your home to me," she said shyly, opening up the dishwasher and putting the dirty glasses inside. "And for being so cool with the fact that your son is having an illegitimate baby with a woman he hardly knows. Believe me, this was not how I saw my life going, either."

Joy stopped what she was doing and turned to face Krista. "No matter whether you two love each other or not, that baby will be so, *so* very loved. And Brock will be so, so very loved by that baby. He needs that. He's spent his entire life making sure that our family didn't fall apart after his father died. Making sure his brothers succeeded and didn't fall off the rails, making sure that I was always taken care of, that I could continue with school and finish my degree. He is the most responsible man I know. Almost to a fault. He made his family his life. So whether you're married or not, in love or not, I know that this baby is going to have the best daddy in the world. And that makes me incredibly happy."

Krista swallowed and then bit the inside of her cheek. "He's a good man."

"He's an amazing man. He spent nearly his entire life taking care of everyone else. He put his emotions aside to get the job done, and now his shell is extra hard. Extra tough to crack." Her eyes twinkled with mischief. "But I think you might be just the woman to crack it."

———

Krista pulled back the covers on the bed. Those big plush pillows looked so good. Her body was positively screaming to be horizontal.

"Hope you don't mind sharing a bed tonight," Brock muttered, pulling back the covers on his side of the queen-size bed in the spare room that used to be his old room. Unlike Krista's old room at her parents'—which was still a shrine to her younger self—Backstreet Boy posters and No Doubt concert tickets still tacked to the wall—Brock's room had been redone and was now just a soft muted brown with teal accents and a camel-colored bedspread.

She lifted one shoulder and climbed under the covers, sighing with pleasure at being off her feet. "We've done it before."

He snorted. "You mean that first night?"

"Mhmm."

"You snore, you know."

She punched him in the shoulder. "I do not!"

He nodded. "Do too. Almost had to go sleep in another room. It was like spooning with a grizzly."

"We didn't spoon," she said indignantly.

He lifted up onto one shoulder and rolled over to face her. "Yes, we did. You may have passed out right away, but later in the night, you snuggled up next to me and told me in your drunken lady mumble that you were cold and wanted to spoon."

"I DID NOT!"

He gave her a look of impatience. "Why is this something I would lie about?"

She crossed her arms over her chest. "I don't know."

"What do you know?" His voice took on a silky-smooth purr as his hand skimmed across the sheets and landed on her belly. She covered his hand with hers, but he pulled it away and made to push his fingers beneath the waistband of her pajama pants.

"In your *mother's* house?" she hissed. The idea of getting freaky in his childhood home, in his childhood bedroom, equal parts turned her on and terrified her.

But as always, her libido won out.

"I'm in charge tonight," she said confidently.

"Krista ... " he hummed, his voice stirring embers of arousal inside her into tall, licking flames.

"You shanghaied me into coming to Christmas dinner with your family, when your mother didn't even know about me. You owe me."

He was quiet for a moment, but then she was pretty sure she heard a barely discernible, "Fine."

Yes.

She swallowed. The power tasted divine on her tongue. "What was that?"

He cleared his throat. "I said *fine.*"

She had to keep herself from laughing. Some nights he willingly gave up the power, like that night by the fire, though he got anal sex out of it, so it wasn't *really* an exchange of power. But then other nights he was reluctant. It was nights like these that made Krista's inner dominatrix come out.

She knew that the power struggle between them was going to be ongoing, at least for as long as they decided to continue sleeping together. They both liked to be in charge in the bedroom and had a hard time (especially him) relinquishing that control. And even though they'd never really sat and discussed it, because they never sat and discussed anything, she appreciated that he was willing to give it a try, at least for a little while.

Then the thought occurred to her: Could she get him to open up while she was in control? Ask him questions, demand he answer her? Or would he shut down and call the whole damn thing off? Was it worth risking no orgasm for information?

Or she could pump Joy for information on Brock. Corner each of his brothers and make them dish the dirty deets.

She'd have to stew on it a bit.

"You know how hard this is for me, right?" he said quietly, his throat bobbing as he swallowed and ground his molars to control his nerves.

She nodded solemnly. "Yes, I know."

He licked his lips. "W-what would you like me to do?"

Grinning in triumph, Krista pushed him over onto his back and then sat up, looping one of her legs over his hips until she was sitting on top of him, straddling him.

"I want some answers," she said, running her hands up his hard stomach until her thumbs and fingers rested over each of his nipples. "I'm tired of being shut out. I'm going to ask you four questions, and you have to answer three. Deal?"

As if sticking a fork in an electrical socket, his whole body jolted, and the man went ramrod straight. Were four questions too many? Should she have started with two?

"Deal?" she asked again, tugging ever so slightly on his nipples.

All he could do was nod.

"Good. Question number one: What is your favorite color?"

He already appeared bored. She tugged up hard on his nipples until he clenched his teeth and sucked in air.

"Fuck," he gritted.

"They're my questions, and I'll make them as invasive or benign as I please. Got it?"

He swallowed.

"Got it?" she tugged up even harder on his nipples. He hissed but managed to grind out a barely discernible "yes."

"Good. Now answer the question."

His gaze landed on hers. "Blue ... like your eyes."

Her breath caught in her throat. Damn, the man could be seductive.

"Hmm," she hummed, averting her gaze, not wanting him to see how his words affected her. "Interesting answer. I'm guessing there's a certain part of your anatomy turning a shade of blue too."

He bucked up beneath her. "Probably."

She chuckled. "Then answer the questions more promptly so we can fix that. Question number two: What is your best memory?"

As if the man's body couldn't get any more rigid. His face

turned an almost unhealthy shade of white, and he shifted beneath her.

"Remember, you only need to answer three of the four," she said softly, worried that she might have pushed too hard too quickly.

"Christmas when I was ten," he whispered. "My dad had it off. We were all home. Heath was only two but the size of a four-year-old. It snowed like crazy that year. He tossed all of us into a huge sled, and we went tobogganing. Then we all, my parents included, slept in the living room that night in front of the fire in our new Ninja Turtles sleeping bags."

She couldn't quite tell, because he was looking anywhere but at her face and the room was dark, but the reflection off the clock on the nightstand glimmered in his eyes, and she could have sworn there were tears.

"Which Ninja Turtle were you?"

"Leonardo," he said, his voice hitching just a tad.

She struggled not to giggle. Krista didn't giggle. "Of course. The responsible, serious one. Makes sense."

"Also the smart one," he added wryly.

"Donatello was smart too. The techie nerd."

"That's Chase."

She hummed softly and ground her pelvis against his erection. "And let me guess, Heath was Michelangelo. And Rex was Raphael?"

He nodded. "Yes."

She licked her lips and swirled her hips again. "Leonardo was always my favorite. For a turtle, he was sexy."

His hands came up and he gripped her hips, forcefully pulling her down onto his lap so she could feel just how hard, how turned on he was. She felt the same way. Sitting atop Brock, riding him, even with fabric between them, was her favorite place to be these days. The way he looked at her as they both reached climax stole the oxygen clear from her lungs and made her whole body vibrate and burn.

She sobered and stopped her hip swirls, despite how strong his grip was on her hips and how much he was encouraging her to continue. "Okay, next question. What is the most reckless thing you've ever done? You're so responsible, so ... *grown up*, what's one thing you've done that is so out of character you didn't even recognize yourself when you were doing it?"

His lips curled up into a diabolical smile. "That's the fourth question. I don't have to answer it." Her mouth opened in protest, but her cut her off. "Favorite color, best memory, ninja turtle, this question."

Shit, he was right.

Making a mock pout with her lips, she glared down at him. "Fine."

Suddenly, she found herself up and off him and flipped over onto her back, her arms pinned above her in one of his hands.

"Damn, you really are a ninja."

That smile was back. The man didn't smile often, but when he did, holy hell. "Marry me, Krista."

She exhaled loudly and motioned to push him off her, even though her efforts proved to be futile. It was like trying to move stone.

Way to kill the mood, dude.

"Don't ask me that again until you're head-over-heels, can't-imagine-your-life-without-me, in love with me, okay? Because until that's how you feel, my answer will always be no."

His head dipped, and he took a nipple through her nightshirt into his mouth. She squeaked, followed by a groan from the blooming heat that spread through her chest and zoomed down between her legs.

"I do feel things," he said softly, lifting his head and gazing down at her. Krista's eyes went wide. "But if you're not willing to agree to marry me right now, can we at least make each other feel good ... as per our arrangement?" Levering himself onto one arm, he released her hands and went to work tearing off her pajama pants and relieving her of her shirt. She was already panty-free, so once the pants were off, she was bare.

She smiled. "We can definitely do that."

His grin widened, and his eyes morphed from green to black in two seconds flat. He cupped her face and brought his lips down to hers.

The kiss was slow and romantic. A kiss that she wasn't used to getting from this feral sex beast. Normally his mouth smashed down onto hers and his tongue challenged hers to a dance-off. But this kiss was gentle and so full of emotions that she had to suppress the lump that was forming in her throat. His hands traveled down her neck and body, cupping her butt and pulling her up to him, urging her to rock against him, accept him into her body. They both moaned as he finally entered her. The perfect fit.

His chest rumbled, and she was granted another rare smile before his teeth found her neck and his thrusts picked up vigor. Harder and harder he hammered into her, the sounds of their heavy breathing and bellies slapping the only noises in the room. And then, even though she was close to combustion, she couldn't help the fleeting thought that interrupted her brain—thank God the mattress wasn't squeaky, because they'd never hear the end of it in the morning.

"I ... I'm close," she panted, angling her head back into the pillows as his teeth raked down the vein. The vein that pumped her hot-for-him blood.

"Me ... too." He grunted.

"Look at me," she ordered. "I'm still in charge. Look at me."

Brock lifted his head and gazed down at her. What stared back at her in those endless pools of emerald was startling. A carnal need that mirrored her own along with a whole lot of other confusing feelings. And they did a bang-up job of confusing her, too. She knew she had feelings for him. Strong feelings. Yes, he was an overbearing control freak, but he was also kind and caring, and the way he'd stepped up to the plate with the baby spoke volumes of his decency. She just had to figure out a way to get deeper beneath his tough shell. Chisel through to the heart of her hard Hart and find out what he was really all about.

And then she broke. Completely and utterly. The look in his eyes, the way his body took hers in such a perfect and all-consuming way, she fucking shattered. Squeezing her eyes shut on impulse, Krista bowed her back and arched up into him, letting her nipples rub against his hard chest and his pubic bone slam mercilessly and divinely against her throbbing clit.

Her teeth sank into her bottom lip to stem her cries while Brock dipped his head again and smothered his grunts of release in her hair and the pillow as he poured himself inside her.

A few moments later, after Krista had hastily ducked out to the washroom to clean up, thankfully not seeing a soul—a big burly Hart, tiny matriarch Hart, or Santa Claus himself—she pulled her pajama shorts back on and climbed into bed.

"Should we talk about names?" she asked, running her tongue along the seam of her lips as she took in the sexy, sweaty beast of a man lounging on the bed. His eyes were shut, and his breathing had returned to normal, but a sexy dash of red still colored his cheeks, and his cock beneath the sheet hadn't completely returned to rest.

"Names?" he grunted, seeming to be almost asleep.

Damn it, were the walls back up?

"For the baby."

He didn't bother opening his eyes. "Oh. Uh ... yeah, we can."

"I like Hannah for a girl and Ansel for a boy. What about you?"

He shook his head and tucked his hands up and under it, the sheet shifting with his movements to reveal a dusting of pubic hair.

"All the men in my family have one-syllable names."

Well, now they were getting somewhere. He was going to talk about his family. She'd just spent the evening with them but all in all still knew very little. She turned over onto her side and propped herself up on her elbow, giving him her full and undivided attention. "And that's a tradition you want to stick with?"

He nodded. "Yeah. If you're okay with it, I wouldn't mind naming the baby after my dad, if it's a boy."

Krista nodded. She was a reasonable person. As long as his dad's name wasn't something atrocious or heinously feminine, she could probably go along with it. "What was your dad's name?"

"Zane."

"Zane?"

"Yeah."

"And is that your middle name?"

"No. My middle name is Lionel."

"As in Lionel Richie?"

A small grin lifted at the corner of his mouth. "Exactly. I was named after Lionel Richie because my parents were listening to him when I was conceived."

She couldn't control the unladylike snort that roared through her nose. "Really?"

He nodded again. "All our middle names are whoever our parents were listening to during conception. They had a warped sense of humor, those two. My mother still does." Krista noticed that from the start. Joy Hart was a little spitfire.

She shook her head and sat up higher, loving the glimpse she was getting into their baby's family. They were proving to be fun and loving people, people she enjoyed being around.

"What are your brothers' middle names?"

"Chase Marvin, for Marvin Gaye, obviously. Rex Barry, for Barry White, and Heath Leppard."

"Leppard?"

"Def Leppard," he said dryly, with an amused eye roll.

"Is *that* a tradition you want to continue with our kid, too?"

He reached over, and his hand grazed her hip. "No. Mainly because we didn't have any music playing when he or she was conceived, but also because we can start our own traditions, if you'd like."

She moved closer to him, allowing her breasts to touch his arm, the zing of arousal and need flying through her body once again, settling between her legs.

"Besides," he said, rolling her over onto her back and covering her with his menacingly powerful frame. She locked her ankles around his back and let her heels rest in the crevice of his butt cheeks. "A Pink Floyd song was playing at the bar before we left, and *Zane Floyd* just doesn't have a very nice ring to it." Then he shucked her shorts off and drove home, ending the conversation.

———

BROCK'S EYES flashed open at the sound of someone rattling around in the kitchen. Even though this was his childhood home and the sounds and smells were as familiar as the back of his own hand, it wasn't his *home* anymore, and he was wide awake at the simplest noise. Barely moving, so as to not disturb the naked, snoring woman next to him, he grabbed his phone and released it from the charger.

It said seven o'clock.

Jesus, couldn't his routine-obsessed mother sleep in even one day a year?

Of course not. She was probably up at five thirty like she was every day, ran on her treadmill downstairs for forty minutes, did thirty minutes of yoga and had a shower. Now she was getting the coffee going and preparing the Finnish coffee bread her mother used to make each Christmas. Joy Hart was a creature of habit and routine if he'd ever met one.

He pried himself out from beneath the sheets, grabbed what he needed from his duffle bag and slipped out the door. When he returned roughly thirty minutes later, he had to stifle a chuckle. Krista was taking full advantage of the empty bed now. She said she found sleeping on her belly painful, but that didn't stop her from getting comfortable. Arms and legs spread wide, head on his pillow, she was a sprawled-out, sexy naked starfish snoring louder than any man he'd ever met or any bear he'd ever come across while out grouse hunting.

She was something else, that's for sure. Fierce, hard-headed and frustrating as fuck. And as much as he told himself her stubbornness was annoying and just going to get her into trouble, he had to admit that it also made him admire the crap out of her. She was not a woman who just rolled over and exposed her belly at the first sign of a problem. She was a fighter. And fuck if he wasn't falling for her. Hard.

Careful not to wake her up, he stuffed his toiletries bag back into the duffle bag, then pulled out Krista's Christmas present. He'd driven around all fucking day yesterday looking for it. And of course, because he'd left it to the last minute, nearly every store had been sold out. But at the eleventh hour, for a price that made him damn near have a coronary, he'd found a suitable gift.

Would he have preferred something a tad more feminine?

Yes.

But at the eleventh hour, beggars and procrastinators can't be choosy. This would have to do. Next year he'd get her a better one if she wanted. A matching one with the baby if he could find one.

Fuck! Did he just think about *next year?*

Shaking his head, he laid the gift out on the bed for her, turned the receipt over, grabbed a pen from off the nightstand and scrawled, "Put this on before you come out" on it. Then with one last look at the naked mother of his child and a smile that made his face hurt, he headed to the kitchen to go and find some coffee.

"D<small>UDE</small>, *that's* the sweater you bought her?" Heath asked, causing Brock's head to snap up from where he'd been staring into his coffee, willing Krista to wake up. He glared at his brother and shook his head. Heath ignored him. "That sweater is more freaky than ugly."

It was true though.

He'd been desperate in his hunt for an ugly sweater—a Hart family tradition. They all had one. And Krista couldn't be any different. Though had he started looking sooner than December 24th , he probably would have found something better than a bright red sweater with a ghoulish-looking snowman on it who looked more like that character from *The Nightmare Before Christmas*. The figure was holding his head in one of his branch limbs, like some kind of headless horseman/snowman. And of course, he'd found it at some hipster novelty store downtown and it had been fifty bucks. He'd balked, blanched, choked and coughed as he took it up to the till and the goateed, man-bunned cashier in various patterns of plaid had rung him up, going on and on about how big of a seller this sweater had been this year.

To who? Brock had no idea.

But despite the moderately terrifying sweater print, Krista pulled it off. She'd tugged it over her nightshirt and had traded her shorts for those flannel candy cane PJ pants. Her untameable mane was pulled back into a messy bun on the top of her head, and fuzzy bunny slippers scuffed down the hallway. He'd never seen anything so adorably sexy in all his life.

Rex sat down on the opposite side of the couch as Heath and barked out a laugh. "Oh, poor little Krista. Brock really dropped the ball with your sweater." He clucked his tongue disapprovingly at Brock.

"It was all I could fucking find," Brock said with a growl. "I ran around for hours yesterday trying to find an ugly sweater, and they were all sold out everywhere." He made room for Krista next to him on the couch.

He watched Krista's eyes widen as she took in the sight. A comical one if there ever was. There was no getting around how big Brock and his brothers were. They were all well over six feet and two hundred pounds. So the fact that all four of them had crammed their muscles into various ugly Christmas sweaters was hilarious, even for them.

But they did it for their mother.

There wasn't much they wouldn't do for her.

"You guys look like bears in brightly colored leotards," Krista said with a snort as she leaned forward and grabbed a shortbread cookie off a tray. Rex and Heath both chuckled.

"Insulting, but accurate," Heath said with a head bob.

"I especially like yours," she said, nibbling on the cookie.

Heath beamed proudly at his outrageous sweater. He'd picked it out himself, the sick bugger. It had two reindeer, one of them being Rudolph, of course, engaging in some X-rated behavior. Rudolph appeared to be enjoying himself at least.

Brock's wasn't nearly as pornographic. Though he'd have to talk to Heath about his sweater next year when there was a kid crawling around. He might have to force his brother to get a more G-rated alternative.

Krista bumped Brock's shoulder. "Your floppy-eared puppy with holly on his collar is quite a bit tamer than your brother's. Who picked out yours?"

"Decaf coffee? Tea? Hot apple cider?" his mother asked, poking her head out of the kitchen.

Brock nodded in his mother's direction. "She did."

Krista chuckled before turning back to his mother. "Apple cider would be lovely, thank you." She made to get up and head to the kitchen, only Brock's mother and Chase were already emerging, a tray of cider and mugs in hand. Chase had a plate with more cookies and coffee cake, along with some fresh fruit and yogurt and granola. They always went light for Christmas breakfast in the Hart house, because for dinner they went *hard*.

Brock's mother set the tray of ciders down, and Brock heard Krista cough beside him, cookie crumbs flying all over the sweater.

"That's, uh ... that's *quite* the sweater you have on, Joy. Which one of the boys picked that out?"

Heath's grin was wide and jolly as he sipped his coffee. "I did."

Brock simply rolled his eyes. Heath had thought it appropriate to get their mother a sweater as X-rated as his. Only hers had two gingerbread people on it in the sixty-nine position, and both of their crotches had distinct bite marks on them, while the female gingerbread person appeared to have a face covered in icing.

"Next year you're both going to need some tamer sweaters," he grumbled, taking a sip of his Bailey's-laced coffee. "Can't have that shit around the innocent eyes of my kid."

His mother chuckled softly as she handed Krista a steaming, Christmas-themed mug. Krista brought her nose down to the rim and inhaled.

"Oh, dear," his mother started, "I didn't think I raised such a prude. Sex, oral, vaginal, anal and otherwise is all very natural and healthy. I was never shy about discussing such things with you boys growing up, and you all turned out just fine."

"Well, I'm a nymphomaniac," Heath said with a laugh. "I'm not sure how *fine* I turned out."

Their mother rolled her eyes and made a rude noise in her throat. "You are not."

Brock glanced down at Krista, and the poor woman's cheeks were nearly as red as her hair. "We, and by *we* I mean my mother, Heath and Rex, have a bit of a warped sense of humor in this family. Sex has always been an overly open topic here."

Krista swallowed and nodded, wincing slightly when she sipped her cider.

"Well, I am a therapist after all," his mother added, her bright blue eyes twinkling.

Heath and Rex had inherited their mother's eyes and coloring, while Brock and Chase were clones of their father, right down to the green eyes, serious demeanor and dark hair—though Chase, like Rex, kept his head shaved bald for some reason. It was days like this, especially, that he really missed his dad, missed their family banter and all the jokes, because for a serious, no-nonsense cop, Zane Hart could toss out some wicked one-liners.

"Is that what you do?" Krista asked, some of the color leaving her cheeks. "You're a sex therapist?"

Joy took a seat right smack dab between Rex and Heath on the couch. "Well, family therapist, but I specialize in sex, sexuality and relationships. But I'll still see you if you're not having issues in the bedroom." She winked.

Brock cringed slightly at his mother's wicked little smile. The last thing he wanted to think about was his mother's sexual prowess or knowledge about how to "spice" things up in the bedroom. As far as he was concerned, his mother had not had sex since the night Heath was conceived.

Oh fuck. Now Def Leppard was in his head.

He shuddered.

His mother rolled her eyes again. "I certainly hope he's not this big of a stick-in-the-mud at home," she said, not blinking and looking dead serious at Krista.

Brock's coffee tasted foul on his tongue.

The mother of his child in a godawful Christmas sweater chuckled next to him. "Not at all. No need for intervention."

His mother seemed pleased with that, nodded and leaned forward to grab a strawberry. "Shall we open gifts?"

Brock let out a long, loud sigh of relief that made everyone, including Krista, laugh until cookie crumbs were flying.

———

KRISTA WANDERED into the kitchen an hour so later, after all the hubbub of the gift opening, to find Joy elbow-deep inside a turkey, packing it full of stuffing.

Despite the fact that Brock was still so tight-lipped about his family and life, she loved how open and honest Joy was. Maybe she could get his mother to spill the beans about Brock, save Krista the headache.

She saw a few dishes in the sink that needed to be scrubbed, so without even thinking twice, she donned the gloves, poured in some soap and went to task. "Can you tell me about Brock?" she asked, not bothering to look up from the sink. "What was he like as a kid? What were his hobbies? What are his hobbies now? Does he have any friends?"

The men had all gone outside to shovel the driveway and bring in some more wood for the fire. Though when she'd peeked out the window a moment ago, Brock was shoveling, Chase was stacking wood in the wheelbarrow, and Rex and Heath were having a snowball fight. Now was the perfect time to get the skinny on Brock while he was out of earshot.

Wiping the sweat from her brow with her non-turkey hand, Joy paused and waited for Krista to look at her. "Let's just get a couple of things straight, honey."

Oh, shit, what did she say wrong?

"I know my son can be a closed book. A hard nut. A fucking frustrating grump who acts more like a caveman some days than a human being. But he's *my* son, and his secrets, his information is his to give and his alone. I know it's like pulling teeth to get information out of him. I'm his mother. I know that shit firsthand. But I won't be the one to tell you about him. If he wants you to know, he'll tell you. You have to figure out your relationship," she waved her hand flippantly, "whatever it is, on your own. With no help from me or anyone else. I've seen him do things for you I've never seen him do for anyone else. His shell is cracking, just maybe not as fast as you would like." Her eyes softened. "But I won't be the one to spill the beans. Just like if you told me all your dirty little secrets, I wouldn't breathe a word of them to Brock. You're both adults. Act like it."

Krista swallowed hard, feeling like a child who'd just been slapped with a strap across the wrist. Her cheeks burned, and her gut churned.

She averted her gaze, not sure if she should still be looking at Joy and fearing what could possibly be written all over her face when the wise woman spoke again. "I think you're a lovely young woman, strong and bright and beautiful and exactly what my son needs. You are so very welcome into this family, you and this baby. Lord knows I could use some extra estrogen in this house from time to time, but just know I'm not one of those meddling mother in-laws. You need to fight your own battles. I'm here if you need to talk, but I won't go to Brock *for* you. And vice versa. And I definitely won't fill you in on him just to make your life easier. That information is earned through trust and time."

Krista nodded. "I understand."

Joy mimicked her nod before going back to her task of violating their dinner with her tiny little hand.

"So, uh, a sex therapist, eh?" She needed something to break the tension, and the fact that her child's grandmother was a sex therapist seemed like as good a topic as any.

Joy tittered. "Well, I'm a psychotherapist and will see families and individuals for various reasons. But I specialize in sex and sexuality." She glanced at Krista, who was looking around in search of a second apron. "Hanging off the fridge there. The one with the owls on it."

Nodding, Krista slipped it over her head and tied it behind her back, wondering how much longer before a real telltale bump began to show beneath her clothes. "That's really cool. What made you want to specialize in sex and sexuality?" Noticing a pile of washed carrots sitting on the counter next to a compost bucket, she located the peeler and began peeling. She needed to keep her hands busy.

Joy grunted and rose up onto her tippy toes in her red velvet slippers to really jam the stuffing into the turkey. "It's always interested me. Maybe because my own sex life, before the boys' dad, that is, was not a pleasant one. My ex, who was also my first, was a misogynist. When I got out of that relationship and into one with Zane, I realized how good things could be and I wanted to help other women, help other *people* realize their entitlement to pleasure as well."

"That's amazing. And so cool." She felt a little stupid, standing next to this incredibly liberal and educated woman. What else could she say? *Amazing* and *cool* didn't seem like responses worthy of this woman's knowledge and expertise.

But Joy didn't seem fazed in the least and just kept talking and cramming the turkey. "Was upfront with the boys from the get-go. None of this 'pee pee' and 'wee wee' bullshit. Call them by their real names, 'penis' and 'vagina' or 'vulva' to be more anatomically correct."

This woman was raw and didn't pull any punches, and Krista loved it. Loved her, even if she was a tad spooky when her mama bear came out.

"And when the boys' father died, it was just me, so I had to be Mom and Dad. If they had any 'manly' questions, I needed them to feel comfortable enough to come and talk to me about it."

"That makes sense." Krista took a sip of her third mug of cider, allowing the warmth to flow down her throat. It tasted like Christmas.

"Masturbation, sex, relationships, anything they wanted to know more about, they could come to me." She scooped some more stuffing out of the bowl and started really giving it to the turkey, trying to cram every last crumb in there. "The same open-door policy stands for you, too, you know. And the babe. I don't judge." She blew her salt and pepper bangs out of her eyes. "The amount of conversations I've had about masturbation and safe sex ... " She snorted at her own mirth. "Guess I failed Brock on that last one, eh?"

Krista's eyes went wide, and she could feel her face getting warm once again. She knew it wasn't just from the piping-hot cider. "Well ... uh, thanks. I mean ... judging on my current *predicament,* I'm all educated up on how babies are made, and I'll be open and honest with our kids, too. But it's nice to know that they have a nana to go to if they have any questions."

Joy's face broke into a giant smile, her eyes glittering like Venus on a clear night. "You said *kids.*"

———

KRISTA SHOVELED a forkful of turkey into her mouth and had to stop herself from groaning in delight, especially since the juicy breast and well-seasoned gravy made her tongue want to have a spontaneous orgasm. She was sure neither she nor Brock would hear the end of it if she made even a peep that sounded sexual. So instead, she put her head down, shut her eyes and let the flavors envelop her in silence.

"Are you guys at least dating?" Heath asked over a mouthful of mashed potatoes. His plate resembled the Himalayas if the sky snowed gravy. "Is she your giiiirlfriend, Brocky Boo?"

Brock shot his youngest brother a stern look of warning, but Heath shrugged it off and grinned with puffy potato cheeks.

Krista looked up at the man on her left. What exactly were they? Well, besides parents-to-be, roommates and fuck buddies? Was it a relationship? Were they dating?

She had to catch herself from snorting. Dating. Ha. Besides her staff Christmas party, which he had invited himself to and had ended horribly, they hadn't been on one date. So no. They were not *dating*. But what exactly were they doing? Was there a label for it? Should they label it?

Brock lifted one shoulder. "Yeah, I guess so. I mean I like her, she's hot, makes killer gingerbread men, and I'd rather stop breathing than stop screwing her. So ... I guess she is my girlfriend."

The table went dead quiet, and all eyes, all eight of them, stopped and stared at the patriarch sitting at the head of the table. Krista's mouth hung open, and when she glanced around the table, she wasn't the only person sitting there with a goofy paper Christmas Cracker hat on her head who looked like a widemouth bass.

Brock made a rude noise in his throat and took a sip of his beer. "Pass me the brussels sprouts, Rex ... please." Then everything went back to normal. It was weird and odd and all kinds of crazy. And as they sat there eating the incredible dinner that Joy had prepared, Krista couldn't help the giddy feeling that bubbled inside her.

She was his girlfriend.

———

Uncomfortably full of dinner, but also Christmas cheer, Krista and Brock waddled through the front door later that night, gift bags in hand. Brock's brothers must have had a sixth sense or something about Krista coming to celebrate Christmas with them, or maybe Brock had told them he was bringing her and not taking no for an answer, but either way, all three of them had a gift for her. And really wonderful gifts to boot.

Heath had bought her a gorgeous forest-green wool scarf with matching gloves, while Rex and Chase went in on a beautiful black leather jacket, one that matched Brock's.

Joy had glowered for a moment at Brock for making her feel like a putz as she didn't have a gift for Krista, but besides Brock, Krista didn't have a gift for anyone, so if anything, she was the putz and said as much to Joy.

"Nobody is a *putz*," Rex said with a laugh. "Well, nobody besides Brock. He really shouldn't have blindsided you guys."

"Agreed," Joy and Krista had said in unison.

Brock had just sat there with a scowl on his face as he passed Krista her gift. And what a gift. Even though the scarf, gloves and jacket were amazing, Brock's gift was out of this world. Literally. He'd gone and purchased a star, an actual up-in-outer-space ball of fiery gas millions of light-years away, with the intention of naming it after their baby once he or she was born.

And of course, as hormonal pregnant ladies are wont to do, Krista had welled up with big, fat, ugly tears and cried when she'd opened the envelope.

His amazing gift had certainly put hers to shame. She'd felt like the putz of putzes when, after opening up the envelope that contained the star, she was forced to hand over her gift. A lump of coal compared with his diamond.

She had no idea what to get the sexy teddy bear. Mostly because she didn't know him. And every time over the past few weeks she thought of a gift for him, her mind immediately went to the gutter.

Thanks again, pregnant lady hormones.

Whipped cream and strawberries and her with no clothes on,

edible underwear and kinky sex toys. A coupon book for nights of whatever he wanted. Dirty shit. Lots and lots of dirty shit.

So, in the end, she'd bought him a book. A freaking cookbook. A cookbook consisting primarily of stir-fry recipes, because that seemed to be his go-to meal. She'd yet to have a bad one, but he was getting repetitive.

Fortunately, and almost convincingly, he seemed genuinely interested in her gift and leafed through it for several minutes.

Next year she'd do better.

Brock's house was cold, especially compared with the warmth and charm they'd felt at Joy's just moments ago, and an involuntary shiver raced up Krista's spine as she climbed the stairs. She was exhausted, even though she'd done nothing all day but eat.

"I'll light the fire in a second." Brock yawned, coming up behind her as she made her way down the hallway toward her room. He flicked on the furnace, and she heard it hum to life beneath her feet. "But first I want to show you something. It's your *other* Christmas present."

She groaned. "Another one? Jeez, you trying to make my gift seem even crappier?"

He shook his head and reached for her hand, his other one on the knob of the spare room that they never went in. "It wasn't a crappy gift. I'll get a lot of use out of my stir-fry book," he said with real and genuine affection in his voice. He turned the doorknob. "Now, it's not quite done. I thought you might want to have a hand in the final touches ... " He opened the door and flicked on the light.

She gasped and stared in amazement as she slowly spun around the room and took in the nursery. "Oh my God ... "

This man ...

"You'd mentioned you wanted to do the baby's room in yellow and gray with an owl theme, right?"

She nodded and ran her hand over the smooth, painted wood of the white sleigh crib.

"I haven't put up much art or anything, just a few things I've found. But feel free to go crazy."

"I ... " She shook her head "I can't believe you did all of this. When?"

He shrugged. "You work a lot. I had time."

"Did you make the crib?"

He shook his head and came up beside her. "No. I know a guy who does woodworking as a hobby. I commissioned it."

"It's ... " She ran her hand over the silky wood again. "It's incredible."

He shrugged and toed at a piece of nothing on the carpet. "I hope you don't mind. I just wanted to help you. Take away the stress. My brothers thought I was nuts, given how big of a control freak you are."

She was flooded with the need to be with him. Near him.

She ate up the distance between him and rested her arms on his shoulders, her hands tickling the nape of his neck. She had to lift up onto tiptoe to kiss his chin. "Thank you," she murmured.

His arms drifted around her waist. He grunted.

She chuckled against his skin. "That all you have to say?"

He grunted again, his head tilting down and his eyes finding hers. "What do you want me to say?"

She blinked up at him and smiled. "I dunno. You just grunt an awful lot."

He grunted again, and she giggled.

"I like the sound of your laugh," he whispered, still gazing down at her. "It's not a girly giggle."

She lifted one eyebrow. "No? What is it? A *womanly* giggle?"

The corners of his eyes creased, and his mouth lifted into a lopsided smile. "Yeah."

"I'm glad I moved in," she said softly. "I'm happy I don't have to do this alone."

His hands tightened around her, and he pulled her closer. "You're not alone."

"Not now."

His lips brushed her forehead. "Not ever. You, this baby, I'll always be here. Protect you both. Take care of you."

Emotion caught in her throat from his words. She pushed back up to her tiptoes again and lifted her head. He angled his down to hers and took her mouth. But unlike all their other passionate embraces that were fueled by lust and a carnal need, this kiss was slow, sweet and filled with something much more than Krista could even begin to decipher. Her heart constricted inside her chest, and a lone tear slowly slipped down her cheek as he continued to kiss her, to hold her, to protect her.

Her hands slid down from his shoulders and roamed across his big chest and down to the hem of his shirt. He was so warm. The heat from him radiated through the fabric and into her skin, swirling through her.

Seconds later, she found herself scooped up in his arms and being carried fireman-style down the hallway to his bedroom. He gently placed her on the bed and began peeling away her clothes. The way his eyes devoured her made her entire body pulse. He looked at her like no other man ever had. As if she was all he would ever need or want. Gooseflesh raced across her skin as he removed her pants and underwear. But his searing stare quickly warmed her. He wasn't nearly as patient with his own clothes and removed them with deft precision and speed.

The man was perfect. And he was hers.

She reached for him. "Make love to me, Brock."

Desire sparkled in his green eyes as he put one knee into the bed and covered her.

"Move into my room," he said, hovering above her, his lips just inches from hers. It wasn't a request. But she was used to his bossy alpha-hole ways, and for the most part, they only turned her on more.

She gazed up at him. This was the man she was falling for. Her mouth quirked up into a grin. "So we're boyfriend and girlfriend?"

He grunted and let the tip of his cock brush her clit. Oh, he was playing dirty now. "Sleep here tonight," he said. "Move into my room." He did one of his signature hip swirls and she nearly combusted on the spot.

"Why?"

"Because." He pushed deeper inside her. "I don't like you being across the hall."

"You like me in your bed?" she teased, squeezing her muscles around him. "Easy access?"

He pushed forward until he was all the way inside. They both let out contented sighs. Languidly, almost torturously slow, he began to thrust.

"I like you here. You belong here."

"I belong here," she said, more to herself than anything.

Until the police force, Krista had never really felt as though she belonged anywhere. She wasn't like the other kids in high school or even her older brother. She'd always felt like a bit of a screwup or a black sheep compared with everyone else. But with the RCMP, she belonged. And now, with Brock, as his *girlfriend*, in his house, carrying his baby, she felt like she belonged. She was part of something. This was where she was meant to be. In his house. In his bed. Beneath him. *With* him.

"You belong here," he repeated, his eyes not leaving her face. "You belong with me."

CHAPTER THIRTEEN

BROCK HAD BEEN DISAPPOINTED when Krista was forced to rush off to work the following morning. He had the day off and hoped they could spend the majority of it in bed. Lord knows he'd grown to love nothing more than hammering her into the mattress until she passed out from exhaustion with a smile on her face.

She'd loved the nursery, loved the star for their baby and had agreed to move into his bedroom. Despite the fact that he knew she'd be seeing Slade today at work, he was in a pretty decent mood. His mother had also confided in him, as he and Krista were leaving the house the night before, that she was smitten with his new "roommate" and couldn't imagine a better suited woman to "exorcise the miserable" out of him.

Jeez, thanks, Mum.

Chase came by shortly after Krista left, and the two spent a couple of hours downstairs in Brock's home gym, neither of them saying much, which was how they both preferred it.

Afterward, he showered, shaved and then spent the rest of the day cleaning the house. He had a housekeeper, but Marlena was on vacation, and shit still needed to get done, so as much as he loathed it, he knew Krista would appreciate it. Then he moved the rest of her things into his room. If she was going to live in his room, she was going to do it properly, girlie shit and all. After all her clothes were put away, he chucked out some of his own shit, tossing it into storage under the stairs. He made a new stir-fry from his cookbook and then sat and waited for her to come home.

Brock drummed his fingers on the armrest of his La-Z-Boy as he tipped up a bottle of beer into his mouth with his other hand. He glanced at the clock above the mantle. Where was she? She only worked until five, and it was almost six. Was everything okay? Was she okay? Was the baby okay? There was still a fair bit of snow on the roads, and in their neck of the woods, the plow only bothered clearing one lane. What if she'd been in an accident?

Fear, anger, frustration and worry gnawed at the back of his neck like a rabid badger until he felt it all the way down his spine. Where the fuck was she?

It wasn't until he heard the lock in the door that he realized he'd been gripping the armrest so tightly, his hand was cramping and his heart beat wildly in his chest.

"Get a fucking grip," he murmured, not wanting her to see him sitting here *waiting* for her like some lapdog. He was no fucking lap dog.

"Hello?" she called, the sounds of her hanging up her coat and ditching her boots following her greeting up the stairs.

He grunted and pushed himself up from his seat, wandering over to the top of the stairs to look down at her. She looked exhausted.

"You're late," he said with another grunt.

Ascending the stairs, she rolled her eyes. "So? It's snowy out there, and I had to finish processing someone. Just because the clock strikes five doesn't necessarily mean my day is over. If I'm in the middle of something I finish it." She lifted her head and wrinkled her nose. "Mmm, something smells good."

Damn her fucking cuteness. He turned away from her and glanced at the news on the television. "Call next time."

Her exasperated sigh niggled more frustration at the back of his neck. Why did everything have to be a fight? Why couldn't she just do what she was told?

Would you like her half as much if she did?

"Yes, sir. Sorry, sir," she replied with a yawn, appearing bored with him and his tyranny. "I'm going to go have a quick shower." She glanced at him, mischief twinkling in those gorgeous blue eyes. "That is, if I'm *allowed*."

He simply grunted again, turned his back and walked into the kitchen.

"Missed you too, baby," she called back, her voice already down the hall. "So happy to be home."

Unable to throw anything or pound the wall, Brock gritted his teeth and turned on the wok, angry, but why?

Because you care about her. Worry about her, and she's turning you into a sap with feelings.

"I'm not a fucking sap," he grumbled around fifteen minutes later as he scooped rice out of the rice cooker onto two plates.

"Who said you were a sap?"

Her voice made him practically jump out of his skin, though thankfully he was able to hide his surprise and simply shrugged.

"Hmm?" she asked, coming up behind him and resting her hand on his back for a moment. "Who said you were a sap?"

His entire body responded on instinct to her presence, her scent, her touch. His balls tightened and his dick lurched as heat flooded his veins.

"Nobody."

She leaned over the wok and grabbed a piece of broccoli, popping it into her mouth with a pleased hum. "All right then, Mr. CrankyPants."

He thrust a plate into her hands. "Go eat."

She saluted him. "Yes, sir."

Moments later, they were sitting across from each other at the dinner table—for some reason, Brock had decided that they were going to eat dinner at the table, rather than in front of the television —and he felt his foul mood slowly disappear with each bite. And that's when it hit him: He'd been so busy all day, cleaning and moving Krista's shit into his room, that he hadn't eaten. Had he even had breakfast? He didn't think so. He was "hangry," as his mother called it.

Son of a bitch.

Now he just felt like an ass.

Wanting to make amends and not ruin his chances of getting laid, or having Krista reconsider having moved into his room, he decided he needed to make peace. He needed to give her something she wanted, and that was a bit of communication and genuine interest.

Taking a sip of his beer and clearing his throat, he asked, "So how'd your parents take the news about the baby?"

But she didn't respond. Instead, she quickly shoved more food into her face, her cheeks puffy like a chipmunk.

"Krista ... "

Slowly, she swallowed, and with the same speed lifted her eyes to his. "I, uh ... I didn't tell them."

What the hell?

"Why not? I heard you talking to them on the phone yesterday, but then it was dinnertime and I didn't get a chance to ask you."

Her lips twisted, and she dropped her gaze back down to the wood grain of the table. "Because I'm just not ready, okay?"

"You have to tell them."

Was she ashamed? Embarrassed? Embarrassed of him?

Her head snapped up, and she glared at him. "I don't *have* to do anything. They're *my* parents, and I'll tell them when I'm good and ready. You have no idea what our relationship is like. How they're going to take the news. So just back off."

Wow! Where'd the sudden bitch switch come from? Hormones? He certainly hoped so. She's been so happy, albeit tired when she got home, this was like night and day.

Maybe she was feeding off his lousy mood?

He needed to lighten the mood and handle this, handle her delicately. So even though his killer stir-fry was calling to him, he didn't flinch, didn't pick up his fork. He didn't even breathe.

"Then tell me," he finally said, his voice calm. He wasn't letting her off the hook that easily. He wanted to know why she hadn't told her parents.

"Tell you what?"

"About your parents. Your relationship with them. How are they going to take the news that you're having a baby?"

She reached for her glass of water and took a sip. "Not well."

"Why?"

"Because ... because I was the wild child. The rebel, the ... the screwup. I was the one that dicked around in university for years, took off traveling to go and 'find myself.' Something that people in Tanner Ridge, the Matthews family in particular, just don't do. We're workers. We live to work, not the other way around."

She rolled her big blue eyes, clearly already fed up with the conversation topic.

Too fucking bad.

She went on, though it seemed painful to do so. "Compared to my brother, Vince, I'm a family embarrassment. He finished school with scholarships, both athletic and scholastic. Got accepted to numerous universities and then graduated law school with countless offers. He moved home and started working at my dad's small practice. Picked right back up with his high school girlfriend, who's a pharmacist, and the two are planning their wedding for next summer."

She shot him a sarcastic look. "Let's just say that if I called them up right now and told them I was knocked up from a one-night stand, they'd be disappointed but not necessarily shocked. This *behavior* is almost expected from me now. Hell ... " She snorted. "They thought for sure I was going to get knocked up in high school."

He couldn't see it. No, she wasn't as responsible as he was, but few were. But she certainly didn't strike him as the town bicycle or a careless person. Was it all in her head or did he really not know a damn thing about the woman he was having a child with? "What did you do that was so horrible that made you the black sheep?"

She rolled her eyes for the umpteenth time. "For starters? I didn't marry my high school boyfriend. Curt and I were together for three years, since we were fifteen."

Oh, good. Not the town bicycle. He didn't think she was.

Brock didn't say anything but simply nodded, encouraging her to continue.

"Then I went away to university, and he stuck around Tanner Ridge. We tried to do long distance, but it didn't work. So eventually we broke up. I had some boyfriends and partners in university, hooked up a bit while I was traveling." She must have caught his eyebrow rise. "I wasn't a slut, if that's what you're thinking. I've had fewer partners than you, don't forget."

Shit. Fuck. Damn. He needed to work on his blank face.

Brock raised his hands in the air in surrender. "Sorry. I never said or even thought you were a *slut*. Please, continue."

She grunted, made a face, but then went on. "Anyway, after traveling I came back to Canada. Finished university but still felt lost. I moved home to Tanner Ridge for six months. That's when I went to an RCMP information session. It lit a fire under my ass, and I finally discovered what I wanted to do. I spent those six months preparing for the police academy. Curt and I picked up again, and it was like no time had passed. He thought I'd apply for a posting in town or at least near Tanner Ridge, but I wanted to move. We broke up again. My parents were devastated that I moved. Devastated that Curt and I broke up. Devastated that I wasn't going to be like every other girl in Tanner Ridge and marry my high school sweetheart, work for a few years before hopping on the baby train express."

He shook his head and picked up his fork, finally feeling like the conversation wasn't so intense that he couldn't eat and talk at the same time. "That doesn't sound like a *screwup*. That just sounds like you didn't follow *their* plans."

Her shoulders slumped, and she let out another big, tired sigh before cramming more food into her own mouth and tucking it into her cheek to speak. "You don't know them. In their eyes, that *is* me screwing up."

"Have you actually *heard* the words '*screw up*' from your parents or brother? Do they call you that?"

She looked down at her plate. "Well, no, but that doesn't mean they don't think it."

"Uh-uh," he tutted. "Sounds to me like you're putting words in their mouth. Maybe you're the one that thinks of you as a screwup; they just think of you as Krista, their wonderful daughter who graduated university and became a cop. And you're just projecting your feelings of insecurity onto them. Because it's easier to blame others. Because in my opinion, you're not a screwup. You're a free spirit who decided to do things her own way. But you're still a college graduate, a well-traveled person, and now you're an officer of the law. How on *earth* could anyone consider *you* a screwup?"

She gaped at him. "What the fuck, Dr. Phil?"

His lip twitched. He was happy that she seemed to have ditched a bit of the bitchy mood. Hormones were the devil. "My mother's a therapist, don't forget. That shit was bound to rub off on me at least a little bit."

"Little bit," she murmured.

"You need to tell them."

"You need to back off." Oh fuck, her hackles were back up. For some reason, the woman wanted to fight, needed to feel the heat and passion of an argument coursing through her veins. Even though Brock had been pissed off when she got home because she was late, he wasn't looking for a fight.

He looked her calmly, squarely in the eye. "How would you feel?"

She sneered at him. "About what?"

"If this was our baby having a baby, and he or she didn't tell you?"

Those damn rolling eyes. He was going to have to take her over his knee pretty soon. "You're really grasping at some hypothetical straws. And I *will* tell them. Just not right now."

"When?"

"When I'm good and fucking ready!" She pushed her plate away, growled at him, stood up from the table and left. Seconds later, a bedroom door slammed.

Brock really hoped it was *their* bedroom door.

———

She definitely needed time to cool off. Something, a bee, a hornet, a wasp, something was in her bonnet. It would do nobody any good for Brock to follow her down the hallway and demand she continue their conversation from earlier. He chalked the majority of it up to hormones and the rest up to her feeding off his bad mood. He really needed to work on that.

So instead, he finished his own dinner, wrapped hers up for later, did the dishes and then waited.

It was nine o'clock and he was watching the news in the living room when he finally heard the bedroom door creak open.

Good. She'd locked herself in *their* room. At least there was that.

Quiet as a mouse, she padded her fuzzy slippered feet down the hallway. He glanced up to find a pillow-creased, tear-stained face with wild red hair frizzed out as if she'd stuck a fork in an outlet. She looked sad and beautiful and so damn tired.

He turned off the television and popped the footrest back into his recliner, inviting her to move into his lap.

With no hesitation, she perched her strong, petite frame on his thighs. Fuck, she smelled good.

"You okay?" he asked.

She nodded.

"Care to tell me what that was about?"

She lifted her gaze from where she'd been studying her intertwined fingers. "Shit at work."

His back stiffened.

Slade.

She ignored him. "And then I come home and you're all grumpy. I plastered on a happy face even though I wasn't happy, and then you get all Mussolini on me about telling my parents." She wrinkled her nose and glared at him. "Not cool."

"What happened at a work? Was it Slade? What did he do?"

She rolled her eyes again. Now he really was going to have to take her over his knee. A sigh escaped her. "*Nothing* ... to me. But I ran into Wendy and Marlise, and we're all going to go for coffee tomorrow. I asked them about their one-night stands with Myles, thinking I could get some information for our case, and they got all weird, said they didn't want to talk about it at work. I know something's up. Something happened when they slept with him."

Damn it. He'd told her to leave the digging to him and his brothers. He unclenched his jaw and rubbed her back. Now was not the time to get all tyrannical on her.

"You think it was rape?"

She shook her head. "I don't know. I mean, we both saw him put that pill in Ingrid's drink at the Christmas party, which means he's obviously not *above* drugging a woman to get laid."

The man shouldn't be *above* anything. He should be fucking six feet under.

"You're going to meet them in a well-lit, heavily occupied public place, right?"

There was that fucking eye roll again. "Yes."

"Good." He ran his hand up and down her back, squeezing the nape of her neck until he felt the tension begin to dissolve. "Now, about your parents ... "

Another sigh.

"Just hear me out."

Her petulant look was just screaming to be dealt with. "I get how you feel. But this is their grandchild, and they have a right to know. If they're as *disappointed* with you as you say they will be, I will fly to Tanner Ridge myself and deal with them. But I think you'll be pleasantly surprised with their response." He continued to knead the back of her neck.

She glared at him. "You were in a dickish mood when I got home. What was so terrible about your day that made you grumpy? Did someone switch your beer for piss?"

His lip twitched, and he wrapped her soft, rebellious hair around his hand, pulling until her neck tilted and she looked into his eyes. Her gaze softened, and that glimmer of defiance that he was coming to love so much returned. "I'm sorry," he said quietly. "I was worried about you. About the baby. I don't like you driving in the snow. Or going to work when I know Slade is going to be there."

Those big blue eyes batted thick lashes at him. And a slow, knowing smile flitted across her lips when she felt his cock jerk in his jeans. "Get over it, man."

A low growl rumbled deep in his chest. "Do you have any idea how many times you've rolled your eyes at me today?"

Her lids sank to half-mast, and her nostrils flared. "At least three spanks' worth?"

"Try six." And his mouth crashed down on hers.

.

CHAPTER FOURTEEN

THE FOLLOWING DAY, Krista pulled into the parking lot of the swanky little café that overlooked the breakwater at Ogden Point. The lighthouse at the end of the long, manmade L-shaped jetty shone bright and white against a dreary gray sky while people and their dogs or companions braved the nasty wind and walked the path. Harsh gusts threatened to shove them into the frigid green water if they weren't careful. The Juan de Fuca Strait sat in front of her with raging whitecaps on dark waves, and snow-capped mountains stood tall and authoritative in the backdrop on the Olympic Peninsula.

Knowing that she had fifteen minutes to kill before the girls were set to arrive—reluctantly, but knowing that cocky, disgustingly responsible roommate of hers was right—Krista pulled her phone out of her pocket and dialed.

"Hello?" her mother answered after the third ring.

"Hi, Mum."

"Krista? Is everything okay, dear?" Apparently calling twice in the span of a week was cause for concern.

She swallowed. "Uh ... everything is just fine, Mum, how are you?"

"Getting ready to tear the tree down."

"I thought you didn't do that until New Year's Day?"

"Well, as neither you nor your brother live at home, and your dad and I are busy with work, I figured I might as well make the most of my day off."

Krista hummed a response and let her gaze focus on a seagull caught up in a wild gust of wind. "Um, Mum?"

"What is it, dear?" She could see it now: Her mother had dropped whatever it was she was doing and wandered over to her chair in the living room, with her basket of knitting on one side and her stack of Danielle Steele novels on the other, with half a cup of long-turned-cold coffee perched on the coaster Krista had made her in the third grade sitting on the end table. It was her television watching chair, reading chair, knitting chair. But most of all, it's where Elaine Matthews went to think. The woman was anything if not predictable and set in her ways.

"I, um ... I'm pregnant." Good job, hardly hesitated at all.

Silence.

"Mum? You there?"

"Y-yes ... I'm here."

"Did you hear me?"

"Yes."

"And?" Well, now her mother was just being downright frightening. Krista hoped to God her dad was home, or at the very least a neighbor was within screaming distance, in case her mother went into cardiac arrest and needed medical attention.

"D-do you know who the father is?"

Riiiight—because she didn't marry Curt, she was a giant hussy, spreading her legs for any man willing.

Krista clenched her teeth. "Yes, Mum, I do. We're living together."

HARD HART   203

Her exhale of relief traveled through the phone, only to send the hair up on the back of Krista's neck. "When are you due?"

"Early June."

"And you're happy about this?"

She couldn't get a read on her mother's tone. "It was a shock at first, for sure. Not exactly planned, seeing as I'm a rookie and all. But we're happy about it now. Brock comes from a big family, three brothers, and his mother is wonderful. This baby is already very loved. And that's what's important, right?"

More silence.

"Mum?"

"All I want is for you to be happy, Krista. And I don't think you would have been if you'd stayed here."

Well holy hell, where was this coming from?

"Um ... thanks?"

"Are you and this ... Brock getting married?"

Too good to be true. Here we go. Get ready to be called a screwup.

Krista let out a weighted sigh.

"Not at the moment. We've got some things to sort out first."

"But he makes you happy?"

Well, now, that was a loaded question if she'd ever heard one. She really had to stop and think about her answer.

Did he make her happy?

Sure, whenever she saw the man, butterflies went bat-shit crazy in her belly, and her body got all warm and tingly. The way he looked at her, the way he smelled drove her wild. His voice, deep and throaty like a diesel truck coming to life, was music to her ears. And the way he unequivocally loved their baby, having jumped in and embraced fatherhood with both feet, made her heart swell. Was that happiness?

But then the man could be so infuriating as well. She could blame her mood swings on hormones and exhaustion, what was his excuse? The man had borderline personality disorder or something, and she was getting mighty tired of not knowing which Brock Hart she was going to wake up to each morning.

But her mother didn't need to know any of that, so instead, she gave her the short answer. "Yes, Mum. He makes me happy." She was still trying to figure out the long answer.

"That's all that matters. As long as you and baby are happy and healthy."

Krista wiped away the sudden tear that had sprinted its way down the crease of her nose. "Thanks, Mum. That means a lot."

"How do you feel?"

Krista caught herself smiling in the side mirror of her car. "I'm feeling pretty good. The first trimester sucked. I was exhausted all the time, barfed most mornings as many women do. But now that I'm into my second trimester, things are good."

"The 'Golden Trimester,' " her mother said with a chuckle. "Enjoy it. The third trimester is usually rough."

Krista half snorted, half laughed. "I'll try to remember that, thanks."

She tittered quietly on the other end, but then her tone sobered quickly. "Would you like to tell your father, or should I?"

Oh, crap, she'd forgotten about her dad. Her lip wedged its way between her teeth in thought. The image of Wendy's car pulling into the parking lot filled her rearview mirror. "You can tell dad," she quickly said. "It was hard enough telling you. I was really worried about your reaction."

Was that a gasp on the other end? "Never be afraid to talk to me, sweetie. I know we've had our differences, but no matter what, I'll always love and support you. Your father and I are very proud of the amazing woman you've grown up to be. We couldn't be prouder. A college graduate, world traveler, and now a respected police officer. And I'm certain you're going to make an incredible mother. I just wish you were closer so I could help you out."

Another tear. This time Krista let it fall. "Wow, thanks, Mum. I love you too."

"I wish I could hug you and congratulate you properly." The emotion was thick in her voice. Elaine Matthews was a crier. Movies, commercials, documentaries, books, a touching moment, you name it, the woman leaked from her eyes.

And apparently now that she was pregnant, Krista, too, had become an emotional geyser. She blotted her eyes with her sleeve. "Me too, Mum. But I'll see you guys soon, okay?"

"Okay."

They said their goodbyes, followed by more I love yous and more tears. When Krista finally hung up the phone, she felt lighter than she had in months. A heavy weight slid off her shoulders and dissolved into nothing but mushy feelings of love.

Her mother hadn't called her a screwup or a disappointment. She'd simply asked Krista questions and offered congratulations, support and love. All the things a mother is supposed to do.

Had it all been in Krista's head all this time, for all these years? Did she even know her parents?

Despite her light heart and weightless shoulders, her head began to swim with new thoughts. All these years, she thought her parents looked at her as nothing more than a screwup, a black sheep, a wild child, and maybe they didn't look at her like that at all. She'd simply compared herself with her perfect brother and all his achievements and just assumed her parents were doing the same.

Well, we all know what assuming does …

For the first time in nearly four months, she finally felt proud of her pregnancy. There was no more embarrassment or shame that she'd gotten knocked up on a one-night stand or as a rookie. Sure, the timing wasn't great, but she wanted this baby and would take the rest as it came.

Marlise's car pulled in beside Wendy, and with a quick wipe of her sleeve to her eyes, Krista hopped out to greet them. She'd have to thank Brock. Though she wasn't looking forward to telling him he'd been right.

"Hey, you!" Wendy grinned, having pulled a black toque over her silky blonde hair, the cool winter wind off the water whipping her day-glow green scarf behind her like a jet stream.

Krista shivered and rubbed her hands together. "Hey!"

"How's baby?"

Krista smiled, wrapping her arms around her midriff. "Letting me keep my breakfast down finally."

Wendy smiled. "That's always a plus. They say it's the most important meal of the day."

Marlise joined them, having pulled a big, puffy coat out of the back of her car and tossed it on. Even though it was only a few hundred yards to the door of the café, that winter wind off the water was enough to cause a wicked wind burn.

They each ordered a warm drink and a pastry before finding a table far off in the corner next to a window, where the view of more sea birds gliding in the sky like zero-gravity surfers was unencumbered.

They talked about this, that and the other thing. How their Christmases went. Both Wendy and Marlise had to work, and their shifts had not been without a shit-ton of holiday drama. They were still both up to their necks in paperwork. Eventually all three of them grew quiet, their minds drifting along with their gazes out to the blustery day and what Krista could only imagine were equally blustery thoughts.

But she needed to get it out. Besides catching up with two good friends, this meet-up had a purpose, and that purpose was to bring down Senior Constable Myles "Dirtbag" Slade.

"Can I, uh … can I ask you guys something about when you slept with Myles?" Krista finally asked, causing both women to snap back to reality and turn to face her.

Both their faces grew tight, and Marlise fidgeted with her mug. "What do you want to know?" she asked.

"Do you remember all of it?"

Wendy was the first to shake her head. "I don't ... no. I remember him asking me out for a drink. I don't know if I had more than one. Next thing I know I'm waking up in his bedroom naked. He then proceeds to show me pictures, disgusting horrible pictures of me, of the two of us, and threatens to take these to the media, to the superintendent and anyone else high up in the force. He said he'd make my life a living hell if I told anyone."

Marlise's eyes had filled with tears as she quietly nodded next to her friend. "He did the same thing to me," she finally croaked.

Motherfucker.

Krista nodded, biting her lip. "But the whole force knows that he's slept with you guys ... so it got out. I don't understand."

Marlise blew her black fringe bangs out of her eyes and started fiddling with her mug again, avoiding eye contact. "He was the one who bragged about sleeping with us. And in order to save face, we just played along. Corroborating his story with as few details as possible." She lifted one shoulder. "It's not unheard of, cops sleeping with each other. Scratching itches and all, but it's a power thing with Myles. It's always been a power thing."

Wendy's head bobbed up and down as she continued to look out the window.

"Did either of you take this to Staff Sergeant Wicks?" Krista asked, not understanding why two tough-as-nails female cops were allowing a little shit like Myles Slade to bully them.

Wendy nodded again. "I did. He said it was all he-said, she-said and that without any evidence, there was no proof. That Myles is a respected senior officer with a squeaky-clean record, and from what he heard, I'd willingly accepted his offer to go grab a drink after shift."

Marlise reached into her purse and pulled out a tissue, blotting at her nose and eyes as she sniffled and nodded, agreeing with Wendy.

"I think Myles might have something on Wicks," Wendy said slowly, bringing her voice down a couple of octaves.

Krista leaned in over the table, bringing her own voice down. "What do you mean 'have something?' "

Wendy shrugged. "Why else would the Wicks defend him? I threatened to take it to HR, and Wicks got all weird and snippety, saying he'd take care of it. Though nothing happened. He's Myles's senior officer; he shouldn't be afraid of him, and yet he is. He's defending the guy's behavior. Why?"

Shit. She'd never thought of that before. Maybe Myles did have something on the staff sergeant. It would make sense. She'd have to get Brock and the Harty Boys on it. Investigating a fellow officer, even a senior ranking one, was one thing, but investigating your staff sergeant, that was the equivalent of jumping into a shark tank with a gaping wound.

Wendy swallowed hard, taking a sip of her probably now cold coffee. "I've tried to not let it affect my job, and for the most part it hasn't. He wasn't my mentor, and I rarely see him, but when I do, that smirk, that arrogant, self-righteous smirk makes me want to vomit but also throat-punch the shit out of him. He loves that he has something over me, that he thinks he holds my career on his flash drive."

Marlise, who'd been quiet for the most part, blotted her eyes again before speaking. "I know he raped me. And it wasn't gentle. I ended up having to go to the doctor because I was having issues afterward. Lots of bleeding and pain. I confronted Myles about it and asked him what he did to me. He said it wasn't his fault I can't hold my liquor and couldn't remember. That at the time I'd been all about the '*kinky* shit,' as he'd put it." She looked like she was about to puke but instead took a sip of her tea, her hand rattling as she brought the mug to her lips. "I haven't been into any *kinky shit* in

my life." She glanced back out toward the lighthouse and breakwater. "I never did find out what he violated me with."

Krista's insides roiled. "Are you okay now?"

Marlise nodded solemnly. "I think so. Tough to date, though."

Wendy nodded solemnly. "I haven't been on a date in months.
Keep canceling at the last minute."

Marlise's jaw trembled. "Me too."

It wasn't just the hormones talking anymore. It was the rage, it
was the fury, the sadness and the injustice for her fellow officers,
her fellow females—her friends—that caused fresh, hot tears to well
up in Krista's eyes.

Marlise's face turned serious when she noticed Krista blotting
at her eyes with a napkin. "Did he do something to you too? God,
please tell me the baby isn't his."

Wendy looked up from her lap, her eyes pleading Krista to
say no.

Krista's lip trembled. "I didn't let it get that far. He's been
trying for months to get me into bed, but I've refused. He cornered
me in the staff room a few weeks ago. Tore open my shirt. Assaulted
me."

"No," Wendy whispered, shaking her head.

Krista nodded.

"Did you report him?" Wendy asked.

"Yes, but Wicks pretty much dismissed it. Said now that I'm on
light duty I don't have to worry about Slade anymore."

"Fucking useless prick," Wendy gritted out.

"I think we need to take matters into our own hands now,"
Krista said, fury tasting metallic in her mouth.

"It's dangerous to try to go after him," Marlise whispered.
"Myles is smart. And I don't want to lose my job."

"Plus," Wendy added, "it's embarrassing. We're cops." She
brought her voice down. "We should have known better. Should
have been stronger. Smarter."

Krista's heart ached for her friends. "You won't lose your jobs. But he can't keep getting away with this. He nearly did the same thing to Ingrid at the Christmas party and probably would have gotten away with it if Brock hadn't stepped in. If we band together, find other women in the department who Myles has or has tried to take advantage of and ask them to join us, we'll be a more powerful force. Wicks and HR can't dismiss us if we all come forward."

Wendy's jaw tightened, and her high cheekbones burned a bright pink. "We can't let him get away with it. I'm in."

Marlise wiped her eyes again with her tissue, but despite the red eyes and blotchy skin, she tossed her shoulders back and held her head high. "Me too."

Krista grinned and reached for each of her friends' hands. "We'll get him. I promise."

———

DESPITE THE MOOD at the café, Krista felt lighter, happier than she had in a long while when she parked her car in Brock's driveway later that day. She'd finally told her parents about her pregnancy, and they were supportive and accepting. Now she was building a case, a strong case, with witnesses and testimonies, against Myles. He wasn't going to get away with it. He wasn't going to hurt anyone else. Not if she had anything to do with it.

Brock's truck was in the driveway, too, which meant he was home. He'd been home a lot lately. Seemed to almost always be home when she was. Coincidence? Was he working at all anymore? Did it matter?

She wasn't going to let him gloat too much, but he did deserve to know that he was right. That her parents didn't view her as a screwup and in fact were proud of her. She was a big enough person to admit when she was wrong; she only hoped he played the

"I told you so game" with a wicked gleam in his eye and perhaps a heavy hand rather than get all cocky and smug about it.

As she opened the front door, the sounds of grunts and rhythmic pounding filled her ears, and they seemed to be coming from downstairs. She knew there was a home gym down here but hadn't actually checked it out yet. There were a few rooms with closed doors, and not wanting to be too snoopy, she hadn't bothered to open them.

The father of her child would tell her if he had a weapons or torture room, right?

Kicking off her shoes and slipping into her slippers, she hung up her coat, then took off in the direction of the noise.

The dimly lit hallway strained her eyes compared with the bright and spacious upstairs, and before long, she found herself feeling claustrophobic. All the doors were closed. She needed to open one soon. Reaching the door where the pounding and grunts were coming from, she hesitantly turned the knob, only to come face-to-face with one of the sexiest things she'd ever seen: Wearing headphones and no shirt, sporting boxing gloves and a glistening sweat that defined each and every muscle to chiseled perfection, Brock was kicking the shit out of a punching bag.

His back was to her, and there were no mirrors, so she took the opportunity to just watch for a moment. Revel in the way his arms and torso bunched and contracted each time his monstrous fist made contact with the bag. Even his back was magnificent.

She licked her lips and followed the line of his body past his shorts to his strong, powerful calves as he hopped back and forth on each foot like an agile fighter. Then without any warning, his body lurched up and leaned over as his foot made wicked contact with the bag, sending it flying backward. Krista gasped in surprise and shifted where she stood, her lady parts tingling the longer she watched.

Brock circled around the bag and lifted his head, and that's when he noticed her. His green eyes glowed under the harsh fluorescent lights, and those sexy lips that knew all too well how to make her burn tilted up into a cocky little smirk. "How long you been standing there?"

She strode forward, confidence in her gait. His hands were in the gloves, so he couldn't remove the earbuds, so she did it for him, even loving the way he smelled after a workout. All man. All Brock.

"Hmm?" he hummed. "You like what you see?"

They were less than a foot apart, and her entire body was on fire. Oh yeah, she liked what she saw. She liked it a lot. She wanted to lick him like a goddamn soft-serve cone dipped in Belgian chocolate.

"I owe you an apology," she said softly, resting her hands on his shoulders.

"Yeah?"

She nodded, resisting the urge to run her hands up into his hair. "Turns out you were right."

Interest piqued in those gorgeous green orbs of his. "Not very often that I'm not, but go on."

She snorted a laugh and swatted him gently on the ear. "About my parents. I called and told my mum today. She was very supportive and said she's proud of the person I've become." Emotion clawed at the back of Krista's throat at the memory of her phone conversation with her mother. It had been a really good talk. She hoped to have more just like them. A lot more.

Amusement and happiness filled Brock's eyes. "See? I told you."

"You did."

"So you've come here to ... "

"Eat crow."

His gloved hands fell to her waist, and he pulled her against his hard, sweaty body. "Hmm, crow, eh?" She melted into him. It didn't matter that he was damp from his workout. They could have a shower together and get clean. His lips hovered just over hers. "I think I'd prefer to take you upstairs in the shower than force you to eat some disgusting bird."

She hummed softly and flicked her tongue out against his salty lips. "That sounds good. I'd definitely prefer something else in my mouth."

He growled above her. "Oh, baby, that can be arranged." And instead of kissing her, with gloves on and all, he scooped her up and carried her upstairs.

CHAPTER FIFTEEN

AFTER A SEXY SHOWER where Krista let Brock gloat just a little, they shared a much more pleasant dinner than the previous night of leftover stir-fry and then watched television in companionable silence until Krista's eyelids were droopy.

She was just drawing back the covers on the bed when Brock stalked in, pulled his shirt off and went to work on his jeans. Like a well-trained soldier, he tossed everything into the laundry hamper and put his watch down in the same place as always, followed by his phone and wallet. The man was nothing if not disciplined and a creature of habit. Everything had a place; everything had a purpose.

She'd been taken aback when she first moved in by just how clean he was, how spotless his house seemed. Curt had been a slob, so the military level of tidiness in Brock's home was alarming. Though he'd quickly confided that it wasn't all him. He had a housekeeper, Marlena, who came once a week to tidy and do the floors and bathrooms.

It didn't mean Brock still wasn't a bit of a neat freak who gave her the stink-eye when she set her water glass down on his oak coffee table without a coaster.

"I'm the boss tonight," he said gruffly, dragging his side of the duvet down and sliding between the sheets. He hadn't bothered with boxers, and she could already see his erection springing to virile life.

Her eyebrows flew up. "Is that so? Seems to me you were *the boss* earlier today. I think it's my turn. If that's what we're doing here, switching?"

He shook his head. "Today was different. You were apologizing."

"And last night? What were those six spanks?"

"You being insubordinate."

She pushed herself up to full seated position and glared at him. "Insubordinate?"

He grunted again with a nod. "Rolling them baby blues at me like some cheeky Catholic school girl. Next time I'll get out the yardstick."

"What are you going to have me do, then?" she asked, being sure to add just enough sass to her tone to make his nostrils flare.

"You're going to tell me all about your time with your Polish friend while I go down on you." Then forgoing all customary acts of foreplay, not even a kiss, he slunk down the bed until he was positioned between her legs. An irritated and impatient scowl crossed his face as he pulled off her underwear, as if it was the most inconvenient and inconsiderate thing in the world for her to be wearing panties to bed.

"Now, what was her name?" He wasted no time in getting down to business and, using the entire surface area of his tongue, swept it up between her folds. She let out a contented sigh and closed her eyes.

"Her name was Maja."

"And how did you two come to be together?" he asked, managing to speak through his task.

She swallowed. "We, uh ... we met in Panama, at a bus station. We decided to get a hostel together to save money."

"And is that where you ... ?"

"N-no ... oh God, that feels good." Knowing that she loved it when he rubbed her with his stubble, he started using his prickly chin against her clit, exploring her cleft with his fingers. Alternating the torture with nibbles and nips on her inner thighs. "Oh ... God, yes."

"When did the two of you finally hook up?"

"Not until a bit later ... " She shamelessly bucked up into his face. Her hands traveled along her own body and cupped her breasts, pulling and twisting the nipples just hard enough that the pain was exquisite but not overwhelming. "We decided to go to the San Blas Islands, and that's where we first hooked up."

"How did it happen?"

"We were at a beach party. Dancing and drinking in our bikinis. There were a couple of guys who had just shown up that day. We'd been there for a few days at this point ... Oh God ... these guys were Spanish, I think, and pretty aggressive compared to the rest of the friends we'd been meeting along the way. And they wouldn't leave Maja alone. We stuck close together and as the night progressed started behaving more like a couple, just to get the guys to back off. We were dancing on the beach, and I'm not quite sure who kissed who first, but before I knew it, we were making out, our breasts knocking as our drinks sloshed into the sand."

"And then what?"

She exhaled. "And then we found ourselves back in our bungalow. A tangle of limbs and lips and curious hands. We were only in our bathing suits to start, so it was easy enough to get naked. At first, we just kissed. She was a good kisser, a really good kisser. She had a tongue ring and it ... " Krista squeezed her eyes shut tight, envisioning Maja and her perky breasts and hourglass hips swaying toward her, licking her lips. She was stunning. Soft curves, light brown hair, bright blue eyes, absolutely gorgeous. "I think at first I was surprised that she found me attractive." She went on. "I mean, she was supermodel beautiful, and I'm, well ... "

His head popped up. "You're what?"

"I'm ... me ... "

"What's that supposed to mean?" Brock's brows furrowed into a deep frown. Were they really going to do this now?

"I mean I know I'm not hideous or anything, but I'm no Maja. My hair is insane and uncooperative; my skin is near translucent; and I have more freckles than the beach has sand. Maja was perfect."

He fixed her with a fierce and menacing glare. "I think *you're* fucking perfect, and I don't want to EVER hear you say anything self-deprecating again, you got that?" He grabbed her leg, pulled it up so her hip left the bed, and a firm hard smack came right down on her exposed butt cheek.

Krista yelped.

His eyes were like hot daggers, boring into her soul. "I wouldn't have fucked your brains out four months ago and accidentally knocked you up if I didn't think you were hot as hell. And I wouldn't be continuing to fuck your brains out now if I still didn't find you beautiful, so shut the fuck up." And then he slid back down onto his stomach. "Continue with your story."

Krista's mouth just hung open. No one had ever spoken to her like that before, with such raw and heated passion. And to hear such things from Brock, a man who kept his feelings so closely guarded that one might suspect him a robot—if she hadn't been already lying down, she would have been knocked flat on her ass.

His eyes flashed open, and a growl rumbled up from deep in his chest and buzzed on his lips. "Continue with the story, Krista."

Licking her lips, she continued. "Uh ... so we kissed for a while on the bed, and then the booze must have hit my system, because I got brazen and bold and let my hand trail down her body, exploring her plump folds, pumping and scissoring until she was panting and begging me for more. I'm not going to lie, it was a pretty big high knowing I could turn her on and get her off like that. I wanted to see if I could do more. I slowly sank down onto my stomach and licked her. I'd never been with a woman before, never stared a pussy in the face before, and it was equal parts exciting and terrifying. But I just did the things that I liked."

"And what do you like?"

She glanced down her body at him and laughed. "Oh, you know what I like."

His own chuckle made her heart sing. "Tell me anyway."

"Long sweeping glides of the tongue up my folds, ending with a flick on my clit." He did just that, and she dissolved further into the mattress. "Rhythmic and predictable circles until my clit begins to swell." He followed suit, and she began to thrust into him again. "My fingers got curious, and I wanted to see what she felt like on the inside, so I slipped one in first and then another, stroking her walls, pumping and coaxing. It didn't take long for her to come again."

He opened one eye, and the brow rose with it. "Keep talking."

"Well, after she came, we switched positions and she ate me out. And, well ... it was great. She'd never been with a girl before, either, but she knew what she liked, and it did the trick. Little flutters of her tongue, long hard sucks, exploring and curious fingers pumping. It was weird at first to see a woman's head bobbing up and down between my legs, but after a minute or two I closed my eyes and it really didn't feel any different. If anything, she was a little gentler, and I liked that." His assault eased up a bit, an attempt at gentle. A smile coasted across her face.

"And then we sixty-nined and got each other off again, finally falling asleep cuddled up naked on the bed to the sound of the crashing waves and wind in the palm trees."

He didn't say anything, so she figured she'd just keep talking.

"We enjoyed one another's company and didn't really feel like hooking up with too many dudes on the trip, so we just started sleeping together. We saw more of Panama, Costa Rica, Honduras, Nicaragua and Guatemala together. Then she headed home, and I went to Belize. That's where I had the threesome."

"And how was that?" He added another finger and started to really thrust. His tongue went to work lapping and circling her clit.

She was getting close. She could barely whisper out her story, he was making her so frantic.

"It was good. They'd never had one before, and I'd never had one before, so we were all nervous little noobs. They were married and on a second honeymoon, a bit older than me. Had left the kids with the grandparents for a week."

"What did the three of you do?" His words sent a sweet buzzing vibration straight up through her core. She clenched her muscles around him, bucking up into his face. She was going to lose it soon. The man was a master at the craft of seduction.

"We, uh ... B-Brock, I'm really close."

"What did you do?"

Gnashing her molars together and silently cursing his name, she pushed all thoughts of an orgasm out of her head and focused on answering him. "Fine. I, uh ... I ate her out while he fucked her. Then he ate me out while she sucked him off. Then he fucked me, then her, then me again, and then finally we ended in triangle where everyone was eating and being eaten. It was filthy and wrong and so much fucking fun."

He twisted his fingers inside her pussy, drew his chin up along her clit, and she lost her ever-loving mind. An orgasm unlike any other, a force all its own, ripped through her body.

Krista bowed her back and opened her mouth, but no words

came out, nothing but a squeak and a silent plea to the heavens. She willingly leapt off the cliff and let the orgasm take hold, eviscerating her body, her mind and moving on to her very soul.

He sat up, his weight shifting the bed as he slid off. "Good girl."

Slinging one arm over her eyes, Krista melted like a popsicle in the sun, deeper into the mattress, her chest rising and falling in erratic breaths.

Did he just say, "Good girl"?

Removing her arm, she let one eye lazily peel open.

His smirk was smug and satisfied. "A little tired, are we?"

"Screw you," she muttered, choosing to close her eye again rather than engage in a sassy argument over the fact that he'd just said "good girl," like she was some labradoodle he was teaching to sit and roll over.

He growled. "You're about to." His knee dipped back into the mattress, and the feeling of his big body hovering over hers finally made her open her eyes again.

She pushed at his chest, but of course he didn't budge. "No, no more. I can't keep my eyes open. That was intense."

He did a little pelvic swirl and positioned himself at her entrance. And of course, her damn body betrayed her, always willing and eager for more of Brock's attention, and she spread her legs, lifting her hips to welcome him. "I'll be quick. Your little confession was such a turn-on, I'll be done in thirty seconds."

She laughed as her arms drifted up to rest on his shoulders, her eyes closing sluggishly. His lips found hers and she wedged her tongue into his mouth, tasting her release and getting turned on by the thought of what he'd just done.

"Oh, all right," she moaned, tugging on his bottom lip. "But make it snappy. I'm tired ... unless of course you're willing to let me be the boss? Then I think I could find the energy to paddle your sweet ass for a bit."

"Not a chance there, beautiful." He chuckled.

"You're a bossy fucker, you know that?" she said, bowing her back to welcome him.

"You love it ... God, I love fucking you." He grunted, lifted his hips and drove home.

CHAPTER SIXTEEN

New Year's Eve had been brutal for Brock. As hard as he'd tried to pawn off a security gig in Vancouver onto one of his brothers, he couldn't. Chase was on an assignment, and Stewart needed two guys, one of them needing to be Brock. So he dragged Rex along and left Heath to keep an eye on Krista and another eye on Slade.

But it was an assignment he wasn't looking forward to. Some local celebrity's twenty-something daughter was the target. Threats had been made on her life. Everything was supposed to go down on New Year's Eve at her parents' annual party at their yacht club, so they'd hired detail and upped the security.

The party had been boring as fuck, in Brock's party-hating opinion, and he was beginning to think nothing was going to happen until around one forty-five all hell broke loose. A smoke bomb went off, making the entire place a foggy mess of screaming bodies. Shots were fired, and Rex had been knocked to the ground and nearly trampled by the half-drunk mob of Richie Riches clambering over him to get out.

Thankfully, no one was severely injured. The daughter had

been a decoy target, and the assailants were actually after her father, who unfortunately sustained a gunshot to the arm, though it wasn't fatal. They made a weak attempt to kidnap his daughter but were unsuccessful. The whole thing, upon later reflection, seemed incredibly disorganized, so between the security team and Brock, and eventually Rex who was a bit bruised—both his ego and his limbs—they brought down the three kidnappers and had them in custody by two o'clock.

But Brock was exhausted. The paperwork, the cleanup, the reiteration of his account to the police seemed endless. By the time he and Rex checked into their hotel at six in the morning, he had a splitting headache and was dead on his feet. Neither of them moved or made a sound until noon, and even then it was just a series of grunts and grumbles coming from his wounded little brother as his injuries caught up with him.

He and Rex were forced to head straight to Stewart's for a debriefing once they got off the ferry. Then Stewart's wife insisted on feeding them dinner, so by the time Brock got home, the lights were out and Krista was in bed. He welcomed the idea of crawling under the covers next to her lithe, warm body and smelling that incredible scent as he drifted off. It'd become so much easier to fall asleep and sleep well since she moved into his bed. Her scent, her warmth, her presence, they all made him feel ... complete.

Was that the word? He didn't know.

But what he did know was that he liked having her in the house, liked having her in his bed and would do everything he could to keep her there.

Desperate not to let the creaky bedroom door wake her up, he took forever and a day to open the damn thing, his eyes zeroing in on her petite frame beneath the covers. She'd started grumbling the other day how it was no longer comfortable to sleep on her front, that it put too much pressure on her belly and she would wake up achy and uncomfortable. It seemed she'd found a solution, and that was his pillow, which she was hugging like a life preserver or some giant teddy bear.

Brock quickly showered off the day, didn't bother with boxers and slipped into the cool sheets, taking a deep inhale as his head hit his one pillow. He'd been right. It was honeysuckle. She had the body wash, shampoo and lotion in all the same scent, and it drove him wild every time he smelled it.

He was just drifting off to sleep when a fist landed square in the center of his back.

Groaning, he rolled over, coming face-to-face with an angry angel. "What the fuck was that for?"

"You're taking up over half the fucking bed." She growled.

He inched over just a bit. "Better?"

She glared at him in the dark, her little button nose wrinkling. "No. You're enormous. Easily taking up seventy percent of the bed and probably eighty percent of the covers."

Brock rolled his eyes. He was too tired for this shit. But he also didn't want her to go. "What do you want from me?"

"To give me space. You're a furnace, too."

"Do you want me to go to the other room?"

He didn't want to, but he would. For her. For sleep.

She grew awfully quiet. "No."

Grunting, he sat up, scooted over to the edge. Half his ass cheek was hanging off, but hopefully that would appease the mother bear in his bed. "Better?"

She nodded. "You just need to be more considerate while you're sleeping."

"Oh, for Christ's sake, woman, how can I be more considerate while I'm *sleeping?* I'm *sleeping.* I have no idea what I'm doing!" Grumbling and swearing under his breath, he pulled a bunch of covers off his side and draped them over her. "There! Better?"

She grinned. "Yes."

That sassy little smile. Fuck. It got him every time. Even when she was being an irrational, hormonal back-punching nut job, he wanted her. He always wanted her. Never one to care about having anyone to kiss at midnight, he'd hated the idea of Krista sitting home alone the other night, ringing in the new year alone.

"How'd it go?" she asked, rolling over onto her side and propping her hand under her head.

He grunted. "How'd what go?"

"Your job?"

He lifted one shoulder. "Everyone's safe."

Her lips twisted, and she drew circles on the bottom sheet of the bed with her finger. Her eyes followed her finger. "Maybe next time you could call me when you go out on a job." She lifted her head just a touch, her eyes pinning on him. "Let me know you're safe. I worry about you too, you know."

Brock's chest tightened, and his throat felt raw. Here he'd been giving her shit for not behaving responsibly enough, meanwhile he could be doing more, too. He nodded stiffly. "Okay."

Her smile was small but triumphant.

He gave her the side-eye. He needed a distraction, and the way her breasts squished together when she was on her side like that was doing a hell of a job. "Well, now that we're awake, you want to bang?"

Her eyes brightened, and her smile grew. She scooted across the bed, tossing his pillow to the floor, and looped her leg over his hip. "What did you have in mind?"

———

SEVERAL OF KRISTA'S orgasms later, and with a mildly numb tongue, Brock tossed the covers back again and crawled his way up the bed, his body hovering just over Krista's. Her eyes were shut and her breathing ragged as she came down from the last climax, a sexy flush rushed across her cheeks, and that wild mane of fire fanned out over her pillow in a curly, honeysuckle-scented arc.

Without even bothering to open her eyes, she spread her legs for him and wrapped her arms around his neck, pulling him down to her softness, a soft hum buzzing from the back of her throat, making his dick harder than granite. Fuck, she was a sexy little thing without even trying.

Brock was just about to slip his dick inside when he stopped and glanced down between them. The bump was visible, and it gave him pause.

Krista's eyes slowly blinked open. "What's wrong?" she asked sleepily.

He grunted. "Your, uh ... your belly is kind of in the way."

Her eyes widened, and she followed his gaze. Then she rolled those baby blues. An act he'd love to take her over his knee for. "Barely," she said with lack of interest. "I'm fine. Now are we going to fuck? Or can I close my eyes and legs and go back to sleep?"

Brock grunted again. "I don't want to hurt the baby."

Another eye roll. Oh, she was on thin ice now. "You won't." A little hip shimmy beneath him caused her center to swipe wet heat against the head of his cock. A groan built at the back of his throat.

But he wasn't having any of it. Doctor's assurance or not, he wasn't crushing his kid. Brock rolled to the side. "You were on top earlier. You want to go on top again?"

She shook her head. "No, I'm too exhausted to do the work."

He snorted, followed by a chuckle.

"Let's spoon," he said with a grunt of approval before he tucked himself behind her and helped her roll onto her side.

He was inside her in seconds, his hand snaking over her torso to caress her breasts, pulling and tweaking the nipples until she arched her back, squeezing her internal muscles around him as he pumped. It wouldn't take him long. And from what he could tell, despite her numerous orgasms moments ago, it wouldn't take her long, either.

"Come for me," she panted, pushing her backside into him and squeezing tighter. "Feel that?" Oh yeah, he felt it. She had him in a vice grip. Even if he wanted to pull out, he wasn't sure he could. "I want you to feel as good as you make me feel," she said, her voice a ragged whisper. "Feel as full and complete. Take what you need from me. Take everything."

If he wasn't seconds away from coming, Brock would have halted and pondered her words a bit more. But he couldn't. At the moment, her words just spurred him on, drew him closer to the edge. That sweet, luscious heat surrounded him, the wild and sweet scent of her hair, her rocking body. He was a goner. He inhaled deeply, burying his face in her hair, found her earlobe, nipped it and let loose. Not a second later, Krista cried out in front of him, her body going rigid and her pussy pulsing around him as she leapt off the cliff. Brock grabbed her hand and intertwined their fingers at the peak of his release. She gripped him tight, her knuckles going white as she rode out her climax.

When they both returned from the bathroom, she snuggled up under the covers, having made sure the distribution of the duvet was closer to fifty-fifty, and then pressed her butt into the crook of his body and reached for his hand.

"What are you doing?" he asked. Sexy time was over. It was sleepy time now. What was her angle?

She yawned. "Cuddling."

"Oh."

"Have you never cuddled before?" Her fingers laced with his, just like he'd initiated earlier. Only before they were in the throes of passion, mid-orgasm and mush-brained. The only thing he'd been thinking of was how could he get more of himself inside and on the woman whose scent and touch had gotten so deep down under his skin he found it difficult to breathe when she wasn't around.

Yeah, no, he wasn't a goner at all ...

She placed his palm against her chest, and her entire body relaxed into him.

"Hmm?" she hummed. "Never cuddled before there, Hart?"

Brock grunted as he shifted behind her, trying to figure out where to put his bottom arm. "Yeah ... I guess. We spooned that first night and then when the furnace broke."

"Exactly." She snuggled deeper into his warmth. "Tell me about your other relationships. What were they?"

He shifted again, but instead of rolling away, he pulled her tighter. "A girlfriend in high school. A girlfriend while I was in the navy. That didn't last long. She thought I was cheating when I would go away."

"Were you?"

"No."

"So what? You just pick up half-drunk girls in a bar who smell of cheap tequila and french fries? Buy them dinner and then fuck them silly?"

Brock grew quiet. How could he get out of this one unscathed? Yes, that was his MO. Though just because Krista was picked up and fucked just like any other woman he'd been with in the past eight or so years didn't mean she wasn't special. He hadn't realized it, but his grip on her hand had tightened. He loosened it but didn't let go.

"I don't care, you know," she said, breaking through the deafening silence that had fallen upon the room. His fault, of course. She'd asked him a question, and he'd yet to respond. She continued on, "I could have said no. And for the record, you're not the first guy I've picked up in a bar either."

"You were ... *are* more than that. I told you I haven't been with a lot of women, and although some *have* been picked up in a bar, you're the only one I bought dinner or asked to move in with me."

Her chuckle was raspy and dead fucking sexy.

He hoped that was the end of the third degree. He was tired and getting uncomfortable with her curiosity. Brock hated talking about himself, about his feelings and about his life in general.

"Tell me about your time in the navy," she said with another yawn.

Oh fuck.

He let out a pained breath against her neck, allowing the scent of her hair to calm him.

It worked.

Kind of.

"I didn't want to make a career of it, but I wanted to be a part of something. My dad had done a stint in the navy before deciding he wanted to be a cop instead, so I followed in his footsteps."

"But you didn't want to be a cop?"

"No. A retired naval officer buddy of mine recruited me to join his security and surveillance company instead. It's more my thing, less politics."

A snort rumbled her body. "That's for sure. Politics up the wazoo. Mickey said you did some black ops stuff, too ... "

Brock grunted. Fucking Mickey. A pretty lady bats her lashes at him, and suddenly it's as if he's been vaccinated with a gramophone needle. Normally the guy was almost as tight-lipped as Brock. "He did, did he? That man has always been a sucker for a pretty face. Did he tell you his bank PIN, too?"

Krista giggled. "Mickey certainly is a talker."

"Not normally," Brock said blandly.

She hummed in response. "So, black ops?"

Damn it. He'd hoped she wouldn't continue to pursue this vein of curiosity. Brock hated talking about his time with the Phoenix

Fire Special Ops. Sure, he'd done a lot of good, took out a shit-ton of monsters, but those memories were not ones he wanted to relive —ever.

She squeezed his fingers, urging him on.

Fuck. He had to give her something. The woman was like a dog with a bone. "Yeah, all four of us have done special ops, or black ops."

"What exactly do you do now with your security firm?"

Jesus, she was worse than Stewart's granddaughter, Lily, with the constant questions. At least Lily had the attention span of a gnat and eventually got bored with him and moved on to someone more interesting. But no, not this woman. This woman was relentless.

He let out an exasperated sigh. "Anything and everything." He'd almost been asleep, and happily so, then deep inside her, which had been great, but he was ready for that sleep thing again.

"Which is ... ?"

"Surveillance, security. I've been a bodyguard or an escort for people who feel they are being threatened or in danger. I've installed and monitored security systems. We do a bit of PI work now and again as well, though that's more Stewart's gig, not mine."

"And your brothers are in on this too?"

He grunted, hoping she'd get the hint he was done talking.

"So getting them to run intel on me was just another day at the office then, eh?"

"Mhmm."

Come on, woman, take a hint.

She nodded, her hair tickling his nose and causing him to fight back a sneeze. "And what did you do ... you know, besides surveillance and security. Did you go to school for anything?"

He rubbed his hand over his whiskers. "I also have a biology degree. Thought about medicine, but ... well, I don't have the people skills." Her giggle stirred heat in his belly. "I like what I do, and I'm good at it."

"Have you ever thought of starting your own company? *The Harty Boys*, and getting your brothers to come and work with you?"

He snorted, his eyelids incredibly heavy and fighting to stay open. "Maybe one day. Stewart's a great boss. Wants to retire. So maybe."

She spun around in his arms to face him. She cupped his cheek, brushing his lips with hers. "Thank you for sharing with me. I know that talking about yourself ... well, *talking* in general doesn't come easy for you. I really appreciate it. I like this side of you."

More heat, and this time just a tad too much, ignited inside him. His face was warm, his body even more so, and an itch at the back of his neck told him to get the fuck out of there.

He was a lone wolf, a bachelor, and he liked it that way. Now here he'd gone and invited this woman into his home, who also just happened to be pregnant with his child, and she was sharing his bed. That was all fine. But now she was asking him to *share*. Share parts of himself, his history, his feelings and emotions that nobody knew about.

It was too much sharing.

Way too much sharing.

Even his family was kept on a need-to-know basis. It was just easier that way. He was the fixer. He was the one everyone went to for help, not the other way around. And if no one knew his business, then they never knew when he needed help or fixing—which was never.

Fear, and some other unsettling feeling he couldn't quite pin down, clawed at the back of his head like a hangover headache that just wouldn't go away. He wasn't ready for this. Not fatherhood, not a roommate and definitely not telling a complete stranger all his secrets.

Swallowing past a hard lump in his throat that felt more like a piece of jagged glass and half a dozen razor blades, he ground his molars together and rolled away from her, staring up at the ceiling. "It's late. Thanks for the fuck. Goodnight." Then he rolled away from her completely and stared at the wall for what felt like hours.

————

BROCK WAS DOWN in the home gym when Krista woke up that morning. She could hear the subtle pounding of the punching bag and manly grunts coming up through the vents. It was probably for the better she didn't see him. She needed time to pack.

After he'd shut down and turned away from her last night, she spent the better portion of what should have been sleep time mulling over their conversation. She mulled over their entire whirl-wind, unconventional, accidental relationship.

But even after all that mulling, she came up with bupkis. What had caused him to do such a complete one-eighty all of sudden? What had she said? What had she done? One minute they were having a nice post-fuck cuddle, complete with pillow talk, and the next minute he was giving her the coldest shoulder in the history of cold shoulders, thanking her for the fuck and wishing her a good-night, as if she were some hooker and not his roommate, bedmate and carrying his child.

All she could do was wonder what the heck she had gotten herself into. Who was the man she was about to have a baby with? Who was the man in her (his) bed?

He was sweet and kind and sensitive one minute, catering to her every need, including needs she didn't even know she had. He'd painted and built a nursery, for crying out loud, and yet when she tried to find out who he was or thanked him for opening up, he put up mile-high fences around himself, shut down completely, and they were back to being strangers—sometimes for days.

She was tired of it. Tired of not knowing who she was living with or who she was going to "get" when she asked a simple question. Was she going to get sweet Brock, the Brock who called her his girlfriend and painted a nursery for their happy little accident, or the Brock who clammed up for no good reason and made her feel like she should pack up her clothes and head back to her pimp?

Hell, she didn't even know when his birthday was. Was he a Gemini? Was she dealing with a split personality? She was done trying to figure it out. If he wasn't going to open up, she was going to send him a big fat message to either open up or move on. She could do the single parent thing if she had to. She didn't want to, especially not after discovering how nice it was living with someone again, but she could do it. Because if she was going to live with someone, she wanted to know that person. If she was going to raise a child with someone, she wanted to know his goddamn birthday and a few other things, too.

She'd had enough. She'd asked him time and time again to open up. To let her in and help her get to know the father of her child, and when he'd give an inch, seconds later he'd pull away and back up an entire mile. She hauled her big suitcase from the closet up onto her bed and opened her drawers.

This thing between them obviously wasn't going to work. They were just too different.

Sure, they were both stubborn, strong-willed control freaks, but it wasn't enough. She was bending for him. Relinquishing control. For him. For them. But Brock wasn't bending at all. At least not enough.

Her bed was scattered with clothes, personal paraphernalia and a snoozing Penelope on a pile of summer skirts when his voice behind her made her jump.

"What are you doing?"

She ignored him. She could put up walls too.

"What are you doing?" he asked again.

She didn't bother to turn around, but she felt him take a couple of steps forward. Heat from his big body radiated off him in waves, causing her to practically sway where she stood. He smelled faintly of sweat, but it wasn't off-putting. She knew he was going to look goddamn irresistible all jacked up with ripped muscles and glistening sweat, so she resisted the urge to look at him.

He was beside her now, and his big hand fell to hers, halting her efforts of packing up a pair of jeans. "What. Are. You. Doing?"

She pulled her hand from his and resumed her task. "I'm packing."

"Why?"

"Because I'm going home."

He grabbed her hands again and tugged, forcing her to pull her gaze from her suitcase and finally take in his face. Confusion streaked across it. "This is your home."

She shook her head. "I can't live with someone I don't know."

"You know me."

She shook her head again. Her throat burned and ached from how hard she was trying not to cry. Fucking hormones. "I don't know you. I ask you about yourself all the time, but you only give me the bare minimum. I'm living with a closed book with glued pages. I can't do it anymore."

She pulled her hands from him and turned back to her suitcase. She folded up a shirt and placed it inside. He pulled it out and put it on the bed. She put in a sweater. He pulled it out, along with a pair of jeans, a tunic and three pairs of socks.

She let out an exasperated huff and turned to face him. "This isn't funny."

His face was stern. "I agree."

"Then let me pack in peace, please."

"You're not leaving."

Anger raced through her. She'd also had enough of the bossy

fucker telling her what do to. She could bloody well leave if she wanted to. Her mouth pinched into a scowl, and she glowered at him. "Don't you dare tell me what to do."

He grabbed the suitcase and dumped everything onto the bed. "You're not *fucking* leaving."

Resisting the urge to haul off and deck him, she planted her hands on her hips. "I can't figure you out! One minute you're chatty and funny and sweet, and then the next minute, you're throwing up walls and putting on a mask. I can't do it. I can't live and raise a baby with Dr. Jekyll and Mr. Hides-his-Emotions."

He swallowed.

"You need to talk to me."

His eyes fell to his feet. "I'm trying."

She shook her head. "Not hard enough, Hart. Because when I see that you're trying and thank you for opening up, it's like one step forward and ten steps back. The moment I acknowledge your efforts, you shut down and pull away. What the fuck?"

The muscle along his jaw jiggled as he ground his molars together. "You were right, you know."

She let out a huff of impatience. "Not very often that I'm not, but go on."

His lips twitched, but he didn't smile. "What you said to me in the truck, on the way to your Christmas party. About me wanting people to think I'm big and scary. You were right."

"Of course I was right. But you don't scare me, you just irritate the crap out of me."

A snort rumbled through his nose, and a smile threatened again but ultimately failed. "I'm a different person when I'm with you," he started. "I don't recognize myself." He scratched the back of his neck, and his eyes finally met hers. "I'm happy when I'm around you."

"And is that a bad thing?"

"It ... it's a strange thing. A foreign thing."

She nodded slowly.

"But I'm also really confused."

She shook her head, her own confusion beginning to build. "About what?"

His lips pursed in thought for a moment before he continued. "When you thank me for opening up or ask me who I am, it makes *me* question who I am. Because I don't know which one is the real me. The man who can't stop thinking about you or smiling at the thought of you, or the man who keeps the world at arm's length because it's just easier that way. You scare the hell out of me. I don't know who I am anymore."

Her heart lurched inside her chest. Well, if that wasn't opening up, she didn't know what was. Gently, she took a step forward, wanting desperately to touch him. "Which man do *you* like?"

"I like who I am when I'm with you."

Holy crap.

"I like who I am when I'm with you, too."

He took a hesitant step toward her. "But I don't recognize myself or these emotions. I'm happy when I'm with you, but I'm also terrified. Terrified of something happening to you or the baby. Afraid of being a dad and that the kid is going to be as angry as I am. Afraid that something might happen to me and he or she will grow up without a dad like I had to. I'm used to living alone. Nobody knows or solves my problems but me. It's worked for me all these years. I don't know how to function any other way."

She ate up the rest of the distance until nothing but the baby they'd made, on a cold and windy night, sat between them.

"Then be the you *you* like when you're with me. And be the other guy with everyone else. Be who you want to be."

His throat undulated. "I'm just worried that one day you'll realize I'm just the angry guy and want nothing to do with me. Or one day, that's who I'll become all the time."

She shook her head and rested her hand on his chest. "Tell me."

He gripped her hand like a lifeline. "Tell you what?"

"Tell me why you're so angry."

Brock's pupils dilated, but then he let out a heavy sigh and sat down on the bed, bringing her with him. "It started after my dad died. I was angry at the world. Angry that he was taken from me. From us. The drunk driver who hit us did a bit of time in prison, but not nearly enough. One night, when I was in my late teens, this was shortly after he'd been released from prison, I went to his house. I stood out front with a baseball bat in my hand and watched through his picture window as he played with his kids in his living room. I hated him. Still do. He took my father, and yet he still got to have a family, got to watch his kids grow up." He looked up at her. "How is that fair?"

She squeezed his hand and inched closer to him on the bed. "It's not."

His mouth dipped down into a tight frown. "I wanted to kill him. Smash his head in with the bat. Take his life, just like he'd taken my dad's."

Krista's breath hitched. "But you didn't."

He shook his head. "No, I didn't. I couldn't. Just like my brothers and me, his kids were innocent and didn't deserve to grow up without their dad."

Krista let out a ragged breath. She didn't think he'd killed the guy, but the way Brock was holding on to her hand, turning her fingers blue, made her suspect he'd at least taken a swing at the guy.

"It wasn't fair what happened to your dad," she started. "Wasn't fair at all. Not fair to your dad, to you, your mother or your brothers."

"But life isn't fair," he said softly.

"It's not." She shook her head. Her heart hurt for him. He'd witnessed something so utterly horrific and been forced to grow up way too quickly because of it.

"I joined the Navy Reserves just like my dad, hoping to do some good in the world. And I did. But I also saw a lot of evil. Kids dying. Mothers and babies being ripped apart.

"It all just made me so mad. Mad that I couldn't do more. Couldn't prevent more people from getting hurt. More people from dying. I felt even more helpless than I did that night my dad died."

She put her other hand on his thigh. "You were doing so much good. You can't save everyone."

He glanced up at her. "I know. But I saw too much. Didn't save *enough* people. Too many people I'd grown close to, friends and civilians, died. So I retired and went to work for Stewart. Now I'm protecting people but on a smaller scale. I know sometimes those people are spoiled little rich girls, but when they're with me, they're safe. I can protect them. I can save them."

"You're doing a pretty great job of protecting me and this baby, too," she said. "You can't stack so much responsibility on your shoulders. You have me now. Stack some of that on my shoulders. I can take it."

"Don't move out ... please." That last word was barely a whisper.

"Then let me get to know you. I think I deserve that, considering you've uncovered all my secrets, either by asking me outright or snooping via your hacking brother."

The smile finally beat up the eternal frown, and his face softened. "I don't know *everything* about you."

She lifted one lone eyebrow in protest. "No?"

He shook his head. "But I'd like to."

Her fingers bunched in the fabric of his shirt. "I'd like to know everything about you, too. The good, the bad, the beautiful and the ugly. You don't scare me, Hart, so stop pushing me away. Take down the walls, unglue the pages and let me in."

His head bobbed. "I'll try ... harder."

"Okay." She brought his fingers to her lips. "Thank you for sharing with me. About your dad and your time in the navy. I know it wasn't easy. Please, don't keep me at arm's length like everyone else. I want to be wrapped up in your arms instead, right next to your heart."

His fingers untwined from hers, and he tucked a knuckle beneath her chin. "I'll do whatever I can to keep you here."

Her lips twisted playfully, and her heart beat wildly inside her chest. "Even unglue the pages?"

He tilted his head down and brushed his lips over hers. "Even unglue the pages."

———

"THE SOONER WE get *all* your stuff back to my—*our*—house, the sooner we can bang," Brock said with a laugh as he plunked one final box of God only knows what into the trunk of Krista's car.

Krista grinned at him. "Thank you for coming with me."

"You going to go give your landlords notice?"

She shook her head. "Not yet. You *say* you're going to try and open up, but I need to see it first."

He glared at her over the hood of her car. She'd insisted they take her car, much to his chagrin. A power thing of course. But his truck was also getting the clutch replaced, so he was without a vehicle until the morning.

"Stare me down all you want, Hart. I'm not giving my notice until I know this is the real deal. And I don't know that yet. I need to know who I'm having a baby with. Who I'm living with."

He growled and muttered "stubborn woman" under his breath before opening the car door. He was driving. There was no argument there. "Get in, woman," he barked before slamming his door.

She opened the door and swung herself into the seat. "Besides, Mr. and Mrs. Geller are like surrogate grandparents to me. I'd like to take some time next month to come by and properly clean the suite, maybe help them paint it, spruce it up a bit and then help them find a new, suitable tenant. The guy before me was a knob. Played loud music, smoked pot, had an ugly little dog that wasn't properly house-trained and ate up part of the carpet. They were so happy when I applied, gave it to me on the spot. I can't leave them high and dry with no money coming in without at least helping them find someone new."

"Bloody bleeding heart," he grumbled.

She grinned at him. "You like that about me."

"I don't know about that." He pressed down on the brake and turned on the ignition. "Hmm ... "

"Hmm?"

"Brakes are a little mushy."

She lifted an eyebrow at him, her face half confused and half scared. "*Mushy?*"

He threw the vehicle into gear and then abruptly tossed on the brakes again. It lurched but still stopped. They still felt off, but not nonexistent.

"Everything okay?" she asked.

"Have to get this looked at once my truck is back. Need new tires."

She scoffed.

"You're carrying my baby. If I had my way, you'd be driving a goddamn tank."

They rode in silence for a while. Every so often Brock would glance over at her, sitting there quietly watching the snow fall out the window. It had grown dark as they were packing up inside her place, and by the time everything was loaded, night had fallen completely. Driving down the narrow back road that had been turned into one lane by the piled up snow from the plow made Brock glad Krista was going to be done with this place. There were no streetlights anywhere, no curb, nothing. Nothing besides a rock bluff wall on one side and a big ravine into a dense wooded area on the other. To know his woman wasn't going to be driving this death trap anymore eased his mind. He'd push her to wait until the spring to come back and clean. Maybe by that time she might be too pregnant and grumpy to want to.

"Fuck, I hate this hill," Krista muttered, one hand falling to her belly and the other gripping the handle on the door.

Brock hated it too. It was steep as fuck and had a hairpin turn at the worst part of the slope. It'd frozen hard yesterday and was now a sheet of ice where the plow had missed.

He pressed his foot to the brake, but nothing happened.

They weren't slowing down.

They weren't stopping.

Holy fuck! They had no brakes.

The car began to rattle on the front right side.

Shit. The tire.

They hit a bump and suddenly the car dipped on Krista's side, only slowing down slightly.

"W-what's wrong?" Krista asked, her eyes going wide and her knuckles turning white on the door handle.

Brock slammed his foot down. "Brakes. We don't have any brakes."

"Don't kid!"

"I'm not fucking kidding, Krista. We have no fucking brakes, and the tire is fucking loose."

They were gaining speed now. The tread on her tires was shit, and they were slipping down the ice and at an alarming speed.

"What are we going to do?" Both hands fell to her stomach now.

Brock pulled the emergency brake, and the car hitched and made a disturbing *clunk* and grind sound but didn't slow down much.

He gripped the steering wheel to keep them on the road. "Fuck!"

Panic flooded Krista's face in the dark cab of the car. "What now?"

"Now? Now we crash."

Brock knew that if they didn't stop before the hairpin turn, the car might not make the turn at the speed they were going, and they'd go over the embankment. They needed to turn into the rock bluff and hope to God it slowed them down and stopped them without crushing them.

He geared down, steered into the wall and prayed.

The sound of metal on stone filled the silent winter night, only competing with the thunderous pounding of Brock's heart as the car ripped down the hill, grating against the bluff. But it was slowing down.

Sparks and green paint chips flew from the front of Krista's Tercel as it continued on down the hill, scraping against the bluff. There was a pile of snow bigger than her car coming up, and if they kept going, they were going to hit it. Brock only hoped the snow-bank would be strong enough to sustain the impact of her vehicle and would stop them rather than just breaking apart and letting them keep going down the hill.

It was coming up. Forty feet, then thirty, then twenty. Brock held his breath. Ten feet ...

Crunch.

Crash.

Smash.

Followed by what could only be described as a vehicle going *oof,* the airbags going *whoosh,* a hard punch to the chest. And then everything was still. Everything was quiet.

Brock felt the airbag slowly begin to deflate. "Krista?" He took inventory of his body. Nothing hurt too badly, his limbs all seemed to work and his neck didn't ache ... that much.

A groan next to him had him turning his head and unbuckling his seatbelt. "Brock?"

His driver's side door had taken the majority of the impact—thankfully—but now he wasn't sure he'd be able to open it.

"Brock?" she said again.

Fuck! The baby. Was the baby okay?

"I'm here. I'm here."

Krista's airbag slowly started to deflate, and she shifted in her seat to face him. "You okay?"

He let out a relieved sigh. "I'm fine. You? The baby?"

Her whole body began to shake. "I don't know."

Fuck.

Brock reached into his coat pocket for his phone, pulled it out and dialed Rex.

———

"WELL, THAT WAS FUCKING SCARY," Rex said, tipping his beer back as he sat on the couch in Brock's living room later that night. Brock was right behind him and took up roost in his La-Z-Boy, followed by Chase who sat on the opposite end of Rex's couch. Heath was out on a mission. They didn't know where.

"Yeah," Brock said with a nod, leaning back in his chair. His body ached, and he failed at keeping his groan of discomfort silent.

"You think someone cut her brakes?" Chase asked, sitting down on the opposite end of the couch from Rex, his green eyes, the same as Brock's, looking far more serious than Brock would like.

Brock tipped his beer back and grunted. "I do," he replied, wiping his mouth with the back of his wrist. "It'd been running perfectly fine just days ago. I meant to get her some better winter tires; the tread on them wasn't great. But the thing had no brake fluid left, the lug nuts on the right front wheel were loosened and someone had punctured the tire."

"Slade?" Rex asked.

Brock grunted. Who else would want Krista silenced? Only they had no way to prove it.

"I'll see if I can pull up any traffic cam surveillance, see if he's been out this way," Chase offered.

Brock grunted again and nodded. He was just thankful that Krista was tucked safely in bed. They'd rushed her to the hospital, where both she and the baby had been thoroughly checked out. The impact of the airbag deploying had scared Brock shitless that something might have happened to the baby, but thankfully—sort of—poor Krista's face had taken the majority of the impact and was bruised and banged up pretty good. So was his. But her belly and the little monkey inside were A-Okay.

"I'll continue to keep an eye on Krista," Rex added. "At least when she's at work, we know she's somewhat safe. There are too many other cops around, and now that she's on light duty, she doesn't have to be alone with him. We just have to watch her when she goes to work and when she leaves. And she can drive Heath's truck until he gets back from his assignment." Rex didn't appear to be bothered that he was now the only one talking.

Chase nodded in acceptance and tipped up his beer.

Brock did the same but drained his. His mind wasn't in the living room. It was in the bedroom, under the covers with his child and his or her mother. He belonged with them right now. It's where he needed to be.

Pushing himself up to standing and not even bothering to look at either of his brothers, he walked into the kitchen, rinsed his beer bottle and placed it in the recycling. "I'm heading to bed." And with that, he left Rex and Chase in his living room and headed down the hallway to his bedroom.

She was asleep

Peacefully.

The hospital had given Krista Tylenol and Gravol to help with the pain and help her sleep. Her lashes fanned out across her purple mottled cheek, and her wild hair of fire looked as though someone had spread out copper threads on her pillowcase. She was stunning. Even battered and bruised, she was the most beautiful woman he'd ever laid eyes on. And he'd nearly lost her tonight.

Emotion clung hard and thick in the back of his throat, like a glob of stubborn peanut butter that just wouldn't go away.

He'd almost lost them.

Swallowing that lump, he quickly did what he needed to do in the bathroom before silently slipping into bed next to her. His side of the bed was cool, but he needed warmth. He needed Krista's warmth. Inching slowly, carefully behind her, he turned onto his side and tucked in behind her, protecting her and their child the way he should have done earlier that night. He let his top arm fall over her body, and his hand fell to the soft swell of her belly, where their child slept soundly.

"You're cuddling," she murmured, still half asleep.

"Hmmm," was all he managed. The words just weren't there. Only fear and anger resided inside, and they were too big, too fierce to say out loud.

"We're okay, you know." Her fingers intertwined with his over her stomach. He held on tight.

Still he couldn't say anything.

Krista craned her neck around to look at him. "We're okay. Me, you, the baby. We're fine."

Brock gnashed his molars together until a dull ache ran up the side of his jaw. He liked the pain. The pain was good.

She cupped his cheek. "Do you hear me? We're okay."

In the darkness of the bedroom, staring down into the eyes of the mother of his child, he realized he wanted it all with her. Forever. But first he had a few things to take care of. There was a threat out there, and that threat needed to be neutralized.

"Brock?" Her face grew serious. "We're okay."

He swallowed down the razor blades and went nose to nose with the woman in his arms. "Not yet, but we will be." Then he buried his face in her hair, pulled her more tightly into his body and willed them both to sleep. Tomorrow he'd figure out a way to take down the bad guy, but tonight he just wanted to hold his woman, yes, *his* woman, his child, and forget everything but how good it felt to have something, *someone* to hold on to.

CHAPTER SEVENTEEN

Krista took the next few days off work. She couldn't very well go into the station looking like the train wreck she saw in the mirror. She'd been fine that night, no residual pain besides that in her face, but the next morning and the morning after that, an achy stiffness took hold of her body and just refused to let go.

The doctors had her on Tylenol round the clock and bed rest for a few days, just to make sure that there was no internal hemorrhaging and no delayed complications with the baby.

Bed rest sucked.

And bed rest in a house with Brock Hart sucked even more.

He didn't let her do a damn thing.

Never one to sit idle and do nothing, Krista was ready to pull her hair out and knit it into a shawl just for something to do.

"I keep telling you, first-hand testimonials are going to be our best route," she said, grinding her teeth together and giving three big, muscly Hart men her best stare-down. They were in her bedroom, standing at the foot of her bed for a much-needed meeting of the minds. "I need to sit down with Wendy and Marlise, get their statements and maybe see if I can talk to some of the other female officers and civilian workers. I'm sure he's put the moves on more than just the three of us and Ingrid."

Brock shook his head.

Krista narrowed her eyes at him. "You're not the boss of me, you know."

Rex made a pained face, while Chase just averted his eyes.

"I'm not, but when it comes to your safety, I'm not taking any chances. I'm running this op, and I say you take early medical leave and get out of that place until we can dig up enough evidence on Slade to put him away for good." He crossed his arms in front of his big powerful chest for good measure and stared down at her sitting up in their bed. She didn't flinch.

"Monday," she whispered, her eyes not leaving his. "It's Thursday now. I'll be back to work on Monday."

The man growled.

The man growled a lot.

But he didn't scare her, so instead she just rolled her eyes. "I'm compromising here, Hart. I have a job to do, and I intend to do it until this baby pops out. I'll stay away from Slade and only talk to Wendy and Marlise, but you're not running squat. I'm the only police officer in this room. The rest of you are behaving like vigilantes who are above the law, hacking into the RCMP database and whatnot." She leveled her gaze at Chase and gave him her best glare. The man didn't so much as blink. "Knock it off."

Was that an eyebrow twitch?

Was he even breathing?

Brock let out an exasperated sigh. "We'll discuss Monday on Sunday night, but for now, you and the baby need rest."

Now it was her turn to growl.

Rex's face split into a grin so big, both dimples winked at her. "I really like her."

"Out!" Brock barked.

His brothers both spun on their heels like good naval officers, and with straight backs and heads facing forward, they practically marched out of the bedroom.

Brock met her gaze again. She met his just as intensely. But suddenly his softened.

"I only want what is best for you and our baby," he said, his tone nowhere near as harsh as a moment ago. Two long-legged strides and he was at her bedside, sitting on the edge. His big, sexy palm landed on her belly.

She linked her hands with his. "I know. But what is best for me is being productive and getting back to work. I'm going stir-crazy being cooped up here."

He nodded. "Okay, but I need you to quit your investigative work. Leave that to Rex and Chase."

"Wendy and Marlise aren't going to give them their statements. That shit is personal. Besides, Wendy's roommate, Stella, is a lawyer and has agreed to represent us. We're going to meet with her soon and find out what we have to do. Whether she wants us to go to HR as a united front, wait for her to build the case or what."

"It'll come out in court eventually if they testify against him," Brock said.

She shook her head. "Doesn't matter. I want to be the one to talk to them. They need a friend, a woman there, when they discuss what happened to them. Not a big mountain of muscle with a voice recorder and a scowl on his face."

"I wouldn't have Chase do it."

She snorted. Yeah, Chase, the man who she wasn't sure even knew *how* to smile. "Either way, it has to be me ... or at the very least Stella. But I want to be there for my friends."

His gorgeous green eyes sparkled. "You're a stubborn little thing, you know?"

She grinned back at him and squeezed his fingers atop her belly. "Would you like me any other way?"

This time his growl spoke of promise and sent a pleasant ache to settle right between her legs. "No, I really wouldn't."

———

It wasn't until the following Friday that Krista felt well enough to not hide her face in a vacant office or in her cubicle whenever possible. She turned down the option to do booking and processing and instead hid her purple and blue face in the evidence lockup or in front of a computer screen.

Obviously, people at work had been curious. How could they not be? A fellow officer walking into work looking like she'd seen the end of somebody's fist multiple times over definitely draws attention, and not the good kind. Mallory had even pulled her aside and asked if things at home were okay. Krista had almost burst out laughing and nearly said that the only marks Brock ever left were on her ass or her shoulder, and she'd never complain about those in a million years. Instead she'd just been honest and said she was in a car accident and the airbag had deployed.

Slade was conveniently absent for the entire week, which made confronting him about Brock's theory a moot point. Not that Brock would be pleased at all if she did such a thing. But it did make interviewing Wendy and Marlise easier. She sat down with each of them separately to get their testimonials, taking advantage of the vacant interrogation rooms and voice recorders on site. Neither woman had been in a good head space afterward and promptly headed home, so it wasn't until Friday that the three of them had an opportunity to get together and discuss things and plan their next move on Slade.

Wendy and Marlise had returned to the station to grab Krista and the three of them were going to wander down the road to the bakery for lunch when they ran into Allie. She was just exiting the woman's locker room, and her face was as white as a sheet.

"Hey," Marlise chimed. "You okay?"

Allie swallowed and stiffly shook her head, her chestnut hair swishing off her face and revealing red-rimmed eyes.

Worry gripped Krista. She looped her arm around Allie's shoulder, and she and the other two women led her outside the back of the building and into the parking lot.

It was threatening more snow, but so far nothing besides bulbous dark clouds hung in the sky, along with a chilly wind that threatened to freeze off their fingertips.

Nobody said anything. It was too cold, and they all knew that whatever had a strong woman like Allie looking like a complete mess had to be important. They grabbed a booth at the back of the bakery-café and peeled off their jackets.

"Soup and sandwich combos all around?" Wendy asked, locking eyes with Krista.

Both Krista and Marlise nodded. All Allie could do was shrug.

Wendy disappeared to place their order at the counter while Krista and Marlise watched Allie, hoping that what had her so upset had nothing to do with Myles. God, not another one. Please not another one.

Wendy returned a few minutes later with four mugs of coffee on a tray and a number for their table. She grabbed a seat next to Marlise, then all three of them sat there and stared at Allie.

"Go on," Krista finally said, wrapping her arm back around her friend's shoulder. "What happened?"

Allie swallowed, her throat bobbing hard as she fought to suppress her emotions. But her eyes gave away her pain as they welled up with tears, and her body began to shake.

Krista gripped her tighter. "It's okay. You're safe. You're among friends. You can tell us."

Allie nodded. "I'm, uh ... I'm pregnant."

Wendy, Marlise and Krista all locked eyes across the table. You could practically smell the fear, it was so dense at their little table.

"Okay," Krista said slowly. "Weren't you and Violet planning on having a baby? Isn't this good news?"

Allie and Violet had confided at the Christmas party that they were indeed trying to start a family. They had chosen to go the anonymous donor route, as neither of them knew any men they were interested in asking for some swimmers. Nobody knew when they were going to start the procedure, though. They'd remained vague on that.

Allie looked up from where she'd been staring at the table, tears dripping down her blotchy cheeks and on to her pale blue sweater. "We were," she said softly, her voice a strangled whisper. "And this would be cause for celebration if … " Her words got hung up in her throat as more tears fell and her body trembled even harder.

"If … ?" Krista probed, hoping to God that what she thought wasn't going to be Allie's answer.

"If … " Allie's lip wobbled. "If Myles hadn't raped me in the station gym three days after I'd been inseminated at the fertility clinic."

Gasps echoed around their small table as Allie's face fell into her hands and she sobbed.

Holy. Fuck.

Myles had raped Allie, too. Oh, God, and now she didn't know if the baby she was carrying was his or her donor's.

Both Wendy and Marlise looked how Krista felt— gutted. Totally and completely gutted. Muscles began to tick at the corner of Marlise's jaw, while Wendy's nostrils flared as she struggled to keep it together.

Rage was quickly replacing disbelief in all of them.

Because they could believe it.

This was Myles Slade they were talking about. The man had no soul. There was no line he would not cross to get what he wanted.

"You didn't take a morning-after pill," Wendy asked slowly. "Because that's what I did after ... " she trailed off.

"Me, too," Marlise whispered.

Allie shook her head, slowly lifting it. "I didn't want to risk terminating the donor baby. We've been trying for a family for so long."

How soon could they have the DNA test done? Krista wasn't a biology wiz, so she had no clue. Maybe Brock would know. Would they have to wait until the baby was born to do the test? And then what? If it was Myles's child, then what?

Krista felt like she was going to be sick.

"I think I'm going to be sick," Allie murmured, covering her mouth with her hand and motioning for Krista to get up out of the booth pronto.

Krista did just that, and they all watched as Allie fled through the door marked "Ladies" as if she were being chased.

"Poor Allie," Wendy whispered, her hazel eyes a mix of sympathy and anger.

"We should have done something sooner," Marlise whispered. "I'm sorry, Allie."

Krista's gut churned. "Me too."

Wendy nodded. "Me too."

"We'll get him," Krista replied. "We have to. We can't let him get away with it or do this to another officer."

"Another *woman*," Marlise corrected. "Who knows if he's done this to civilians, too? He was gearing up to get with Ingrid at the Christmas party." Venom dripped from Marlise's tone, and fury radiated off the tiny Asian woman in pulsing waves. She wasn't a big person, but Marlise was all muscle and as tough as they came. Krista had witnessed firsthand just how tough her friend was as she watched Marlise take down officers twice her size during combat drills. She was also just as good at target practice, often tying with Krista when they'd go to the shooting range.

"Guys," Wendy murmured, her hazel eyes fixed on something outside, "I think we're being watched. Does Myles drive something besides his blue Blazer?"

Krista's eyes followed where Wendy was looking, and she immediately rolled them. She recognized that big, black, beefy truck. Hell, she was driving one of those big, black, beefy trucks herself right now. It was one of the Hart boys. Their beacon. A vehicle in their fleet.

"It's Rex ... or Chase. Probably Rex though," she said dryly. "Brock is having his brothers follow me to make sure I stay safe."

"That's sweet ... in a violating-your-privacy kind of way," Wendy said with a chuckle. "I mean, you *are* a cop. You can take care of yourself."

"Yes," Krista agreed, "but I'm also in a *delicate* state, and the man takes zero risks when it comes to this baby."

Marlise's dark brown eyes softened. "I think it's nice. And hopefully you won't need a detail for long. We need to put our heads together and come up with a plan to take down Myles."

The door to the women's room opened, and out came a pale-faced Allie, looking much worse for wear than when she'd left. Krista pushed in closer to the window so Allie had an easy escape if she needed to flee again.

"How about Wendy and I work on figuring out what Myles has on the staff sergeant?" Marlise offered. "Krista, you and your man and his brothers work on Myles's background some more, keep digging. Now that you have our statements, we can get to other females in the precinct and see if they have anything to add. We need to go en masse to HR. The more women the better. And Wendy's roommate has agreed to represent us."

Wendy nodded. "Stella is a shark in the courtroom."

Krista fixed Allie with a look. "It's going to be difficult, but are you prepared to give a statement about the rape?"

Allie looked like she was going to be sick again. But she swallowed, put her fist to her mouth and nodded. "Anything to make him pay."

They all locked eyes around the table, fire and fury igniting inside them.

Senior Constable Slade was going to pay dearly.

CHAPTER EIGHTEEN

BACK AT WORK AFTER LUNCH, Krista's mind raced.

A fucking serial rapist was on the loose.

And he was a cop.

A serial rapist cop.

Something had to be done. Myles couldn't be allowed to hurt anyone else.

Tears welled up in Krista's eyes as she stared at the contact list of her phone. She needed to talk to Brock. Not only because she wanted to fill him in on what she and the other women had talked about, but also because she just needed to hear his voice.

She got up from her desk and wandered to Mallory's empty office. Mallory was away for the afternoon, and Krista wanted more privacy than her cubicle allowed.

"Hey," Brock answered. "I was just about to call you."

Krista hiccupped as more tears filled her eyes.

"What's wrong?" Brock asked, his tone laden with fear. "Is it the baby? Is it Slade? What's wrong?"

She shook her head and swallowed hard. "No. The baby's fine. I'm fine … I just needed to talk to you."

There was silence on the other end for a moment. "You want me to come to you?" he finally asked.

"No. I'm okay. I just had lunch with the girls, and Allie gave us some pretty terrible news." She proceeded to fill Brock in on what Allie had told them.

By the time she was finished, her eyes burned and her cheeks were wet.

"That motherfucker." Brock growled. "Doesn't deserve to live."

"We're going to get him," Krista said though sniffles. "We can't let him get away with this."

"We will, baby, we will," he said. "You're okay, though?"

Her heart ached just a little less at how concerned he was for her. He really was trying. He really did care.

He was quiet for a moment again, but she took the opportunity to dab at her eyes with a tissue and collect herself. She had to walk past half a dozen desks to her own, and red-rimmed eyes would certainly draw attention. "The timing kind of sucks," he finally said, "but I was actually just going to call you."

"Oh?"

"Yeah, what are your plans tonight?"

"No plans. Why?"

"I was wondering if you might want to go out on a date ... with me?"

"You, uh ... you want to go out on a *date?*"

She could practically see his shoulders shrug over the phone, black leather moving just a fraction of an inch as one lone eyebrow quirked up. "Yeah. I mean we told our families that we're dating, but we've never been on a date."

"Oh!" Where was this sudden bit of romance coming from? Had his mother intervened? It seemed like something Joy would berate him about.

"So, dinner and a movie?"

Krista caught herself smiling in the window reflection. "Yeah, that sounds great."

"I'll pick you up at seven."

Before she could make some corny joke about the fact that they lived together and would be getting ready to go out together, he said a quick goodbye and hung up.

Well, that was strangely wonderful.

———

FOR THE REST of the day, despite her heartbreaking lunch with the girls, Krista was happy. She was going on a date with Brock Hart. Brock Lionel Hart had asked to her go out with him. And then the gooey, mushy girl in her really kicked in, and she envisioned the two of them sitting in the movie theater, his arm casually draped around hers as she snuggled under his big leather jacket, because theaters are notoriously cold. She would have stupidly left her coat in his truck. And then they'd share a goodnight kiss on the front porch and talk about wanting to see each other again, only to then both go into the house, take off their coats and shoes, brush their teeth and hump like bunnies. Of course.

She thought for sure he'd be home when she got home just after six o'clock, but he wasn't. Figuring that dinner and a movie was a casual date, and that ninety percent of her dress clothes no longer fit, she went with dark wash skinny jeans, only she didn't do up the button and wore one of those belly band things instead and a black cashmere long-sleeve sweater.

She was just adding a touch of lip gloss in the hallway mirror when the doorbell chimed. And there he stood. With a beautiful bouquet of flowers, a box of chocolates and a nervous smile. Looking drop-dead freaking gorgeous in dark jeans, a gray sweater with a white collared shirt poking out the top, and of course, his customary leather jacket.

"Hey."

Krista mentally told the butterflies in her belly to calm down and then took a deep breath. "Hi."

He leaned in and pecked her on the cheek. "You look beautiful tonight."

She opened the door so he could come inside. "You look really great, too." And that smell, oh lord, she was ready to skip the date and just get to the naughty parts of the night.

"These are for you."

She accepted the gifts, then started to climb the stairs. Was she supposed to invite him up? It was his house. This was weird. But he followed her and took a seat in his chair.

"Can I ... can I offer you a beer?" After all, it was *his* beer.

He shook his head. "No, thanks, I'm driving. Reservations are for seven thirty. Are you about ready to go?"

He made reservations? She was busy bumbling around in the kitchen looking for a vase. Could she ask him where he kept the vases in this little role play of theirs? Or was that against the rules? Were they even role playing?

He found her in the kitchen looking mighty frazzled. "What are you looking for?"

"A vase," she murmured, opening cupboards and drawers, even though she knew damn well a vase couldn't fit in a drawer. The man and his romanticisms were throwing her completely off guard.

"Oh. I don't have any."

She shot him a look. Then where were the flowers going to go?

He must have read her mind and the slight bit of frustration radiating off her; abandoning his role as suitor, he knelt down on the floor next to her feet and opened the cupboard beneath the sink.

His head still buried in the deep recesses of the cabinet, an arm came snaking out. "Here, will this work?" He thrust a beautiful old glass pitcher into her hands. It was rather heavy and had floral etchings on the sides. Something that would go perfectly with an afternoon brunch, carrying cool, crisp pink lemonade. So why on earth did he have it?

"Why do you have such a lovely pitcher?" She began to fill it with water. He went to the job of extracting his monstrous frame from the cupboard, joints snapping as he stood up.

He shook his head dismissively. "I think my mother may have given it to me or something."

She hastily put the flowers in water, looked longingly at the chocolates, promising them she wouldn't be long, that'd they'd be together soon, grabbed her coat, slid into her ankle boots, and they were out the door.

"So, a date, eh?" She couldn't stop herself. It was like a giant elephant between them.

Why had he all of a sudden asked her out? He held her door open, and she leaped up into the cab.

He slammed his own door a few seconds later and turned on the truck. "It's about time, don't you think?"

She smiled, a sweet warmth settling into her belly and across her cheeks. They were on a date. "Yes." She nodded. "It's about time."

As far as first dates went, this one was one of the better if not one of the best she'd ever had. Dinner was delicious. Gourmet handmade pasta in a decadent saffron and cream sauce with seafood, peppers and fennel. And then dessert—if she wasn't already falling in love with the man, the dessert would have sealed the deal. A chocolate ganache tower with raspberry coulis and fresh raspberries, topped with Irish Cream whipped cream and gold leaf.

They chatted about life: baby-proofing, their upcoming prenatal classes and the next midwife appointment. Besides the first appointment, where he hadn't even known he was a father yet, Brock had been at every one without fail.

The entire night was weird and wonderful, and she felt herself falling deeper and harder for the man the longer they sat there.

He was trying.

He said he was going to try to open up, and he was. She could tell it wasn't easy for him to let his walls down, to answer her questions without deflecting them, but he tried, and the more he tried, the easier it became.

After dinner, they still had some time to kill before the movie, so they wandered into a grocery store to buy candy and popcorn to smuggle them in Krista's purse and under her coat. She was already pregnant, so with the giant bag of M&M's, she just looked like she was ready to pop.

They were snuggled up in the back of the theater, and Krista decided that what she wanted to do more than anything was rest her head on his shoulder. But she was nervous. And then she mentally chastised herself for being nervous.

You let the man do far dirtier things to you, but yet you're nervous about putting your head on his shoulder? Well, that's ass-backward.

She shifted closer to him, their arms sharing the armrest, and then slowly, almost timidly, she let her head fall to the side of his arm. He was warm, and the smell of him—leather and ... Brock—it was perfect.

He glanced down at her, and at first, she thought he was going to shrug her off because he pulled his hand from the armrest where their wrists were touching. She had to lift her head, and a sudden flood of disappointment raged through her, but he lifted his arm up and wrapped it around her shoulder, pulling her close.

Ah.

Krista snuggled in and closed her eyes, letting her other hand rest on his chest.

The movie sucked. It was boring and corny and in places where they were trying to be funny, it was just plain awkward and uncomfortable. About halfway through, Krista found herself restless and frisky. The night was going so well and she was falling so hard that all she wanted to do was get home and get the man next to her naked. But then the wild child in her started to whisper things in her ear.

"This might be your last night out for a while. Make the most of it. The theater is practically empty. You're all the way up at the back in the corner. You know what people do in the back corner. You'll regret not taking a chance."

She tried to tell the voice to shut up. That she was a cop, a respectable woman and a mother-to-be. But that bitch was loud. And the more she told her to be quiet, the louder she yelled. And before Krista knew it, her hand drifted down Brock's belly and made its way into the front of his pants.

His free hand landed on hers. "What's the plan?"

Sassily, she glanced up at him from beneath her lashes. "No plan, just bored."

A huff of a laugh escaped his nose. "This is dangerous." But then his hand lifted from hers, allowing her to continue her quest.

He was already starting to rise to the occasion.

"What's life without a little excitement?" she asked with a feline purr, beginning to stroke him, reveling in the soft skin and the way he grew harder and harder in her palm. She got a serious high knowing she could rev his engine so easily.

"So, uh ... should we just get out of here?" His tenor was a little shaky. Krista grinned. Men were so easy.

"Of course not. Let's finish the movie. Just watch."

His hand fell back on top of hers. "Krista ... "

But she was too into the moment, too into him, into the date, into the romance of the night, and instead of answering him, she lifted her chin and went in for a kiss. It started out sweet and inno-cent at first, the soft brushings of lips against lips, but soon it turned heated and frantic, driven by more than just the passion of the night. They were both geared up and ready for more. His mouth was firm and his tongue seeking. Brock Hart definitely knew how to kiss. She took him in, returning the kiss and wishing she could press her body against his, into his warmth and strength. Feel his power. When she was with Brock, everything feminine inside her rushed to the surface—soft and powerful all at once, sending a craving though her that almost hurt.

She rolled her neck to the side, and his teeth scraped up the tendon. He breathed her in, sucking on that sweet spot just behind her ear, the spot that drove her wild and brought out her inner beast.

She thought for sure he was going to scoop her up and whisk her away, tossing her into the back of his truck and ravishing her just to feed the craving until they got home. But instead, he wedged his hands into her pants and began to rub wet and rough circles around her clit.

She continued to pump him. He was rock hard now, and the way he thrust into her hand, she knew he wasn't far off. But where would it go? Could she drop to her knees? Her inner wild child wanted to straddle him in his chair and ride him like a pony.

His fingers picked up vigor, and before long, Krista was bucking into his hand, eager for the orgasm that hid just beyond the bend.

"You're going to destroy me," he whispered, his teeth catching on her ear, his breath ragged and strained.

She nipped his chin. "That's the plan."

His hand fell back down to hers to halt her efforts. "You can stop ... I can wait."

They locked eyes, his own digits tirelessly tormenting her inside her jeans. "B-but."

"Come for me, Krista. And then we'll go home and I'm going to fuck you properly."

She swallowed. What a promise.

"Come for me."

CHAPTER NINETEEN

ONCE THEY GOT BACK to the house, Brock grabbed a black fabric bag he'd deliberately left hanging on the coat hook and tossed it to Krista. "Put this on."

She snatched the small bag midair as they stood at the bottom of the stairs.

She opened up the bag to peer inside, and Brock had to work hard at keeping a straight face. Her head snapped up, her eyes wide.

He didn't so much as blink. "I'm in charge tonight, but that doesn't mean you can't look the part of little Miss Authority."

A smile tugged on her lips.

He nodded, spun on his heel and headed downstairs. "I'll meet you downstairs in the study."

Now he had to get things ready. Most of it already was, but he wanted to light a fire, dim the lights and double-check he had everything he needed. The night needed to be perfect.

It didn't take his woman long to get dressed. She was probably just as eager as he was.

He was already sporting a raging hard-on just thinking about her in the getup he'd found for her to wear. Now he was finally going to see it.

"Come in," he commanded after she'd knocked on the door.

Slowly, almost painfully so—no, definitely painfully so, his dick was practically throbbing in his jeans—the doorknob turned, and there she was. The sexiest sexy cop he'd ever laid eyes on.

Even though the date night had been all his mother's idea, Brock thought up and executed the "sexy police officer" costume all on his own. Thankfully, the adult novelty store next to his dry cleaner had exactly what he needed, and Krista wore it perfectly. She'd braided her hair into a single plait down her back before fixing the big costume officer's hat on her head. The way her breasts filled out that navy and brass-buttoned crop top made his balls ache and his cock jerk. And of course, what officer's uniform wasn't complete without a miniskirt, black thigh-highs and black stilettos? He hadn't included shoes in the bag, so she must have found a pair of her own. He loved that she was into this as much as he was.

Brock had never role-played before, but the way Krista was so open to things, and the fact that she constantly battled him for control, made him all the more eager to really get his sassy little officer on her knees. He'd ditched his leather jacket and sweater and now just sported his white dress shirt with the sleeves rolled up and the first two buttons at his neck undone.

"You've been bad, *Constable* Matthews," he said, causing her eyes to fly up to his.

She swallowed. "Have I? How so?"

"You're supposed to be an officer of the law, and yet you choose to act above it. Behaving the way you did in public, in a movie theater no less."

Her long, sexy throat undulated.

"Those are grounds for some serious punishment."

She swallowed again and then nodded, her sapphire eyes glittering as an amused smile tugged at her lips. Slowly, she made her way across to the room to stand in front of him.

"You're right. I'm sorry."

He nodded. "You still need to be punished, though."

The pulse along her neck picked up and she licked her lips. "Yes, sir. Of course."

Oh, she was good.

But he couldn't lose his cool. Gruffly, he murmured, "Safe words."

He waited until she nodded.

"*Stop* will make me stop. *Slow* will make me ease up. And *more,* well, that speaks for itself. Do you understand?"

She nodded again.

He narrowed his eyes at her. "What was that?"

She fought to stow another smile. "Yes, *sir.*"

"Good. Now suck my cock, you dirty little thing. You got me all riled up earlier with nowhere to finish. On your knees." He began to unzip his jeans.

She dropped to the floor in front of him, bringing him out of his boxers and licking her lips as he continued to grow in her palm. Her plump lips encircled the crown, and then she immediately took him to the back of her throat, letting him bottom out until sexy tears sprung out at the corner of her eyes. He pulled her hat off, chucked it across the room and fisted her braid. She took all of him. Only she could satisfy him.

He was close in seconds, but he didn't want to finish this way. He needed to be deeper inside her. Using her braid, he pulled Krista's mouth off him with a wet *pop* and helped her to her feet, angling her over the brown leather ottoman he'd placed in front of the fire. Without any further ado, he impaled her. Two quick, growl-fueled pumps and he was coming, biting her shoulder blade as he dug his fingers into her hips, claiming her, marking her.

His.

She was his.

When he was finished, he stood up and tucked himself back into his jeans. A firm hand on her back told her he wanted her to stay there. He reached to the mantle and grabbed his weapon of choice.

"Do you know what this is?" he asked, circling in front of her.

"A flogger, *sir*."

"And how do you feel about it?"

Her legs trembled as she looked up at him from her willing but also vulnerable position on the ottoman "More, *sir*. Please."

"Good. How many spanks do you think your little 'public display of affection' has earned you this evening?" he asked, bending down until his mouth was right down next to her ear. He reached below her and inside her shirt, fishing out a nipple. He tugged hard enough to earn that delicate little squeak.

Chuckling softly and removing his fingers from her breast, he stood up and circled around behind her, lightly dragging the flogger across her exposed flesh.

Her ribs expanded and released quickly. She was panting. "H-however many my *sir* thinks I deserve."

He grinned. "Good answer. Well, I think you've earned twelve."

"Yes, *sir*."

"If you want me to stop at any time, just say 'Stop.' "

"Yes, *sir*."

He decided to ease her into it. The first one came sweet and innocent and light against her back. Like a gentle tap with a sting at the end. Krista twitched slightly on the ottoman and her breathing quickened.

The next few flogs were a little harder and faster, landing closer to her butt. He couldn't wait to flip up that slutty little skirt and get her ass good and pink, watch her pussy drip down her inner thighs as he made her wetter and wetter with each flog.

"You okay?" he asked. She'd been surprisingly quiet. Barely an inhale of breath or a squeak.

"More," she breathed. "More."

A big, satisfied smile stretched across his face. Fuck, she was perfect.

He got down to business.

Hard smacks landed across each cheek and the backs of her thighs until her whole body trunk region was bright red and screaming at him for more.

"Your skin is so beautiful," he murmured, his fingers tracing the curve of where her leg met her buttocks. "Pink and soft ... and ... mine."

She was his.

His.

"How are you feeling?"

A sob caught in her throat. "M-more, *sir* ... please."

"Then *more* you shall have."

And more he gave her. Flog after flog came down, and with each one Brock felt his brain slipping into a euphoric state of bliss. The redder her ass got, the slicker her pussy lips became, the more entranced he grew. His cock was already rock-hard again in his jeans and aching to be let free, but a part of him was enjoying the torture. Krista was being punished, then so could he be ... just a little.

"Sir," came a faint whisper. "Sir?"

Brock shook his head, clearing his mind and halting his efforts. "Yes?"

"Fuck me ... please."

Well, she didn't have to ask him twice.

He'd lost count of how many flogs he'd done. All he knew was that his dick was raging, and he'd never seen anything more beautiful than Krista's bright pink ass and dripping pussy. Within seconds he was back inside her, taking her at his will.

Taking her.

Because she was his.

INCH BY LUSCIOUS INCH, he took her with a deliberation she felt in every nerve, every cell. A faint growl behind Krista had her craning her neck to look. Brock, a big beautiful force inside of her, was taking what he wanted, what he needed and giving her so much in return. The entire evening had been perfect, from his adorable pickup at the front door down to the sexy cop outfit and flogger. The man thought of everything.

Her ass and back burned with a slow, decadent sting as Brock's skin slapped against her with each primal thrust. She'd be feeling those flogs tomorrow. For sure.

His hand wrapped around beneath her, and he cupped her breast roughly, taking a nipple between his finger and thumb and tugging it until her breath hitched and her pussy clenched around his length.

She felt the orgasm. It was slow to ascend and sweet and beautiful in its release. A decadent crescendo that took her almost by surprise. His pounding was so raw and rough that for something so sweet and beautiful to come of it nearly brought a tear to her eye.

Just as that orgasm ended, a bigger, more intense one took its place, shocking her system and making her whole body explode into a million little pieces. Her eyes flew open, as if looking for those pieces so she could collect them later, but it was impossible. And Brock held the biggest piece of all—her heart.

She panted and whimpered as the waves of the climax crashed into her. Her body bowed and flexed as the sensations flew through her. Tremors—big and small—cascaded inside her, catching on his shaft. She pressed back into him, desperate for more of his length, for more of the burn from his thigh hair rubbing against her flogged skin. She wanted more of everything.

More of Brock.

A harsh grunt was followed by sudden stillness. He jerked behind her, sighing with his release. She squeezed her muscles around him, wanting every drop he had to give her. Because as much as she was his, he was also hers. And she wanted all of him.

It could have been seconds, or it could have been hours, but eventually Krista felt herself being pulled off the ottoman and Brock was wrapping her up in a buttery-soft blanket. All she could do was hum. Folding her against him in the big chair in front of the fire, he kissed her temple and asked her if she was okay.

She wasn't sure if she responded. Maybe a moan or a whine of some kind, but definitely not any words. Krista was deep in la-la land and fully content staying there for a while. That last orgasm had rocked her world and then some.

He chuckled against her ear. "That's enough for tonight. Here, drink some water." He pressed a cool glass to her lips. She chugged it greedily, her eyes closing as her head lolled against his chest.

"Wh-where'd you learn to do that?" she mumbled, still not bothering to open her eyes. "Are you a secret Dom?"

He chuckled again. "I've been doing some reading. You seem interested in this kind of thing, and I certainly don't dislike it, so I wanted to do something to surprise you. Besides, you know me, I'm most relaxed, most myself when I'm in control. We should go and get you some chocolate." She smiled against his warm chest. Yes, she *was* getting to know him. And what she knew so far, she loved.

She lifted her chin and pecked him on the cheek, not bothering to open her eyes. "Well, you definitely surprised me."

Her head was back against his chest, and she was slipping off into dreamland, and maybe it was just wishful thinking, who knows? But she could have sworn she heard him whisper, "I love you."

CHAPTER TWENTY

It'd been nearly six weeks since anything new about Slade had come to light, and Krista was losing her mind. Wendy's roommate was representing them, but according to Stella, attorney at law, there was a process to these kinds of things, and all the paperwork needed to be filed. They were still trying to get in touch with the women at Myles's former detachments too. Stella figured the more evidence and statements they gathered, the harsher the sentence.

But Krista was getting antsy. Brock had asked her to lay low and she'd complied, but it was getting more difficult to not take matters into her own hands as the days ticked by. Valentine's Day had come and gone, and the first day of spring was just days around the corner. Slade was still slinking around the station, popping up like a creepy weed that stinks, stings and chokes the life out of all the other plants around it. He made "kill" eyes at Krista whenever he could, but otherwise he'd been staying away. Allie had officially gone on light duty as well, so she and Krista spent every free minute they had digging into Myles Slade any way they could. From stalking his social media to carefully mentioning his predatory ways around the water cooler, they were on the hunt.

Hunting a predator.

Thankfully, things between Krista and Brock were going well. She was so over having chaos in every realm of her life that the fact that her "love life" finally seemed to be on the upswing was a serious plus. After their date night and evening with the ottoman, things seemed to fall into a comfortable and pleasant routine between the two of them. He was attentive and slowly opening up, and she was as horny as ever, ready and willing to jump his bones the moment she walked in the door. It was the perfect relationship.

"Can you explain to me why Heath's truck has dual tires on the back, while the rest of the Harty boy fleet only have single tires?" Krista asked one night as she and Brock were lying in bed. They were both a tad breathless, and Krista's ass stung like a bitch, so now it was time for pillow talk. Their new deal was, if she let him be in charge, he had to give her fifteen minutes of pillow talk afterward where she could ask him questions and had to open up.

She didn't normally like relinquishing the control, but it was definitely nice getting to know him. Plus, the man was really coming into his own with that flogger.

"Because my baby brother is immature, and his vehicle is proof of that," Brock said with a yawn.

Krista wrinkled her nose. "Meaning ... "

"Meaning, he has the biggest dick and therefore needs the biggest truck because he *is* the biggest dick."

"H—" She scrunched up her nose again and spun onto her side to face him. "How do you guys know he's the biggest?"

Brock rolled his eyes. "You're having *my* baby. Don't be fantasizing about my little brother's big dick. It's not *that* much bigger."

Krista scoffed. "That's not what I meant. I meant, like, did you get them all out and measure?"

He made a face as if he'd just sucked on a lime. "No. We've obviously measured before. Wrote the measurements down and put them in a hat."

Oh, okay. That made sense. It was still weird, particularly to Krista, who had just the one brother. If she'd had a sister, would they have compared breast sizes? She didn't know. Men were weird.

"I'm driving around in a big penis truck?"

"Yep." He yawned and rolled over to face her, pushing her over to her other side in the process. He scooted in behind her and cuddled up close. Spring was in the air, but it was still damp and cool outside. The cuddling was welcome.

"I'm not sure how I feel about that."

"It's not for much longer. Heath will be back soon. And then we'll get you a new car."

"I want a truck."

His chuckle ruffled the hair at the nape of her neck.

"A big beefy black one."

"We'll see," he said softly, pulling her tight.

"Or maybe a white one. Show less dirt. The yin to your yang."

"You are that," he replied sleepily. His hand cupped her breast gently before traveling down her abdomen to the swell of her belly. "Sleep now. More sex and questions tomorrow." His lips found her neck, and it was if he knew exactly where the button was, because she sighed instantly, her eyes closed, she melted into him and was asleep in seconds.

———

IT WAS JUST after lunch on a Friday, and Krista was itching to get home. Brock had brought out the flogger again the night before, and a delightful tingle on her backside was a pleasant reminder all day.

She sat down at her desk, a fresh cup of decaf Earl Grey tea in hand, when she noticed her phone flashing. She'd left it on her desk when she stepped out to go and grab a sandwich for lunch.

One missed message. One voicemail. It was from Marlise.

She punched in her code and listened.

"Krista, hey. You'll never guess the shit Wendy and I uncovered. We know why Wicks lets Slade get away with murder. The shit Myles has on the staff sergeant is huge. Call me back ASA—" Then the message cut out.

Krista replayed it three more times, hoping to hear a background noise or another voice or something to give a clue as to why Marlise's message cut out early, but she heard nothing. It made sense in some ways. Marlise wasn't dumb enough to be leaving a message like that out for anyone to overhear. She was probably home or in her car or the empty locker room or something. Maybe someone came in and she didn't want them to hear.

Wrinkling her nose in confusion and about to call Marlise back, a text message from Wendy pinged her phone just as Krista put it to her ear.

"Hey! We've got news on Slade and Wicks. Meet Marlise and me at your old place ASAP."

Krista texted her back right away. "Awesome. I just got the message from Marlise. Why my old place?"

It was roughly five minutes before she got a reply. Five *long* minutes.

Wendy: "Privacy. Come now."

What the hell? That wasn't like Wendy at all. If anything, they'd all go back to the Ogden Point coffee shop to discuss things. It was out of their jurisdiction and in a public place. Something was up.

She texted back. "Are you okay?"

Wendy: "Come NOW!"

It had to be a setup. Fuck. Had Wicks gone to Myles and let him know what was going on? Did Myles or Wicks find out they'd all been investigating them? Had Stella filed anything to alert Myles they were on to him? Did Myles have her friends? Did Wicks? Or was this a setup to get her alone?

Either way, she had to go. If her friends were in trouble, she couldn't just leave them.

She called Brock as she headed out to her car, but there was no answer. She sent a mass text to all the Harty Boys about the call and text, swung her belly behind the steering wheel and peeled out of the police station parking lot.

At her old place, Marlise's sporty little Honda Civic sat around back where Krista used to park her car. There were no other vehicles around. Her old landlords must be out. But where was Myles's car? Was it a setup after all?

She quietly shut the door of Heath's penis truck, drew her gun and made her way toward the house. Instead of going straight for the front door, she snuck around back to do a bit of recon. The blinds were all closed. Had she done that before she left last time? Had Mrs. Geller? She was going in blind.

Slowly, she crept around the house, careful not to let the gravel crunch under her shoes. She paused next to the living room window for the suite and held her breath, hoping to hear something —anything.

Should she text Marlise?

No.

If it was a setup that would give her away.

Making her way around the house to the Gellers' front door, she tried the knob. They rarely locked it. It was open and she let herself inside, once again careful not to let her footsteps make any noise. She padded softly over to the vent on the floor in their dining room that she knew was situated directly over her living room. Kneeling down, she put her ear to the floor.

Nothing.

Fuck.

If it was just Wendy and Marlise they'd definitely be talking.

But maybe Wendy hadn't arrived yet and Marlise was just sitting down there quietly playing on her phone.

"Hey there, darling!" came a whisper from the living room.

Krista jumped where she knelt and spun around only to see Collette, the Gellers' African grey parrot, bobbing her head in her cage.

"Hey there, darling. Hey there, darling. Lookin' good. Lookin' good."

Krista shook her head and let out a *phew*. Her heart beat a million miles a minute and her stomach was in knots. "Don't do that, Collette. Not cool," she whispered.

The bird squawked. "Not cool. Not cool."

"Shut the fuck up," Krista gritted out.

"Shut the fuck up. Shut the fuck up. Shut the fuck up," Collette mimicked.

Krista growled low in her throat, shot the bird a dirty look and then put her ear back next to the vent.

Collette skittered along her perch, knocked her bell and then skittered back. "I want Wonder Bread, Joyce. None of that multi-grain shit," she said. "Multigrain shit. Multigrain shit. Hey there, sexy."

For fuck's sake. Krista was about to get up and go throw the sheet over the stupid bird's cage when the heavy stomp of a boot behind her on the wood floor caused her to pause. The cool steel barrel of a gun pressed hard against her temple.

"So lovely of you to join us."

That voice. It would haunt her every day for the rest of her life.

Hands up, she turned around to face him.

His smile was disgusting. Full of triumph. He thought he'd won.

"You bitches just had to dig, didn't you?" He snagged her elbow and took the gun from her hand before dragging her back outside and down to her old suite. Marlise and Wendy were both hand-cuffed and gagged, sitting wide-eyed on the couch. "Now I have all my *girls*." With a jerk and a shove, he pushed her toward the couch, the gun still pointed directly at her. "Well, except for Mullins ... but I'll take care of that dyke later. No witnesses."

"You okay?" Krista whispered to both Wendy and Marlise.

Mirror-image eyes of panic stared back at her, but they both nodded.

The toilet in the bathroom flushed.

Who else was here?

"Ah, good," came a familiar voice as Staff Sergeant Wicks came into view, doing up his fly. "They're all here."

"Staff sergeant?" Krista whispered. "Why?"

Unlike Slade's, the staff sergeant's light-brown eyes showed he still had a conscience. He wasn't entirely on board with whatever Myles had planned. His gaze landed on Krista, and his eyes softened. "I really hate that it came down to this, Matthews. You're all good cops."

Wendy squeaked next to her, her eyes growing fierce as she glared at the staff sergeant.

"What did Wendy and Marlise find out about you?" Krista asked. Maybe if she kept them both talking, she could come up with a plan to disarm Slade or, at the very least, give Rex or Brock time to get here and rescue them.

Wicks looked a bit embarrassed. A flush colored his cheekbones, and his jaw tightened. Myles was definitely the one calling the shots here.

Myles rolled his eyes, the gun in his hand wobbling slightly. "Junior detectives Lee and Dougherty discovered that I've been blackmailing the staff sergeant here."

Rolling her eyes at the glee Myles was getting from it all, Krista turned her attention to the man who she still believed had a soul. "What does he have on you, sir? Surely it can't be that bad? Whatever it is, we can help you. You help us, and we'll help you. You don't want to do this. You don't *have* to do this." She was determined not to let her voice crack. She needed to remain calm, collected and confident. If either man knew she was terrified, they'd use that against her. She had to save her friends. Her hand fell to her belly, and a new thread of fear wormed its way through her. She just had to save them.

"I found out that the staff sergeant here has been accepting bribes from a well-known crime family here in town. He looks the other way when it comes to some of their more"—his grin made Krista's stomach do a somersault—"lucrative business practices, and they pay him handsomely."

Wicks' eyes burned with hatred as his gaze swung up to Myles.

"When I discovered that juicy bit, I began using it to my advantage," Myles went on, clearly enjoying the entire scene more than the rest of them.

"That's why all our sexual assault claims haven't gone anywhere," Krista stated. It wasn't a question. Wicks had the power to stop the complaints in their tracks. He could even erase them from the database and lean on HR to drop the case altogether. Krista glanced at Wendy and Marlise, and they both nodded to confirm it. Then she looked back up at Wicks. "Sir, is it really worth the safety of your officers? Myles is a predator. He needs to be stopped."

Myles snorted. "It might be, if ol' Wicksy here didn't have a massive gambling problem and wasn't in the hole up to his eyeballs. He needs that payout from Yanni. Big time."

Wendy made a noise next to her to confirm.

Krista went to stand up. Perhaps she could appeal to the human within Staff Sergeant Wicks. She just needed to figure out how. But Myles was quicker, and the cold barrel of the gun was suddenly pressing into her temple once again. "Sit your ass down. The three of you are going to pay for your nosiness. And then I'm going to go take care of your friend."

"Allie," Krista breathed.

"Neither she or her dyke wife were home when I went there

earlier." He snorted and tilted his head toward Wendy and Marlise. "But these two morons were, and it was so easy to immobilize them and get them here."

The gun was still pointed at her head, but Myles was busy nattering away. Like a true narcissist, he wanted to regale them with just how clever he was. How he'd managed to outwit them all. But this gave Krista time to think. She still had the spare holster on her ankle as Brock had suggested, so if by some chance she could reach down beneath her pants and bring out her gun, then she and Myles would be at a standoff, or he'd have her riddled with bullets before she even stood up. And her only allies were currently tied up and gagged. Myles's unwilling ally would probably rather shoot her than take the high road and have his countless indiscretions as a staff sergeant brought to light.

She'd seen Myles at target practice. He was good.

She was better.

Could she knock his arm and disarm him without the possibility of the gun going off and hitting Wendy or Marlise?

Was the staff sergeant armed? Now that his secret was out—and it was a doozy—he'd probably feel as though he *had* to silence them all.

Fuck.

They were stuck.

"Myles," she whispered, "you don't have to do this. We can all keep our mouths shut."

He snorted and knocked the barrel harshly against her head until she saw stars. "Fuckin' rookies. You all had to just go pokin' your noses where they don't belong. Couldn't leave well enough alone. I had a good thing going, you know? And you," he pushed her again with the gun, "fucking prude. Wouldn't give it up. Had to make me work for it. Then I tried to just get rid of you altogether, but your stupid moron of a boyfriend had to be there to save the day."

Oh God. Her brakes. Her tire.

Krista bit the inside of her cheek. She could not let him see how scared she was. Terrified for Wendy. For Marlise. For her baby.

"Please, Myles. Don't do this. You're a good cop. Don't do this." She glanced at the staff sergeant. "Sir, please."

"I'm afraid it's too late for that, Matthews," Wicks said with reluctance in his voice.

Myles appeared almost bored. "All right, I'm gonna fuck you, and then I'll get rid of you all."

Krista's hand fell to her abdomen, her eyes roaming Wendy and Marlise's faces. Tears welled up in Wendy's eyes, and Marlise shook with fear.

The staff sergeant nodded, his face betraying his disgust in Myles. "You want me to take care of these two, then?" He jerked his strong chin toward the other two women.

Myles frowned before bobbing his head. "May as well."

"No!" Krista screamed, trying to wrench her arm free from Myles. "NO!" But he was stronger than her. She was no match. His fingers dug painful trenches into her arm as he lugged her farther down the hall toward her bedroom. "Please, Myles. Don't do this. Don't hurt Wendy and Marlise. You're better than this. Please don't hurt my baby."

He tossed her onto the bed, and with the gun in one hand, he kneed her legs apart and climbed on top of her. His fingers wrapped around her throat. "I bet you like it rough, don't you? Like that big Neanderthal boyfriend of yours fuckin' you hard." He slapped her hard across the face with the gun-heavy hand. Stars burst behind her eyes and her stomach lurched. He was straddling her belly, and the pain, the pressure was too much.

"Myles ... please," she cried.

"That's right, bitch, beg for it."

He smacked her hard again across the face before lurching off her and standing at the foot of the bed. Refusing to let go of the gun, his hands fumbled with the high Spandex panel of her maternity jeans.

Her mind, as throbbing and fuzzy as it was, immediately went to the gun on her ankle. He was going to find it.

She lifted her head and noticed her foot was right between his legs. He was struggling to get her pants down her thighs. She needed to act fast before she was immobilized.

His head was down, and he was deep in concentration, so she levered herself up and kicked him hard in the balls. Then, pushing herself up, she head-butted him, sending a cursing and groaning Myles back against the wall.

"You fucking bitch!" he wailed, his hand over his crotch. Blood gushed out of his nose. She'd gotten him good. Krista quickly took inventory of his hands and realized he was gun-free.

Where was the gun?

Ignoring the pounding in her skull, and with lightning reflexes, she reached for the gun on her ankle holster. She cocked the small snub-nose .38 just as Myles lifted his head.

"You're under arrest," she whispered.

His chuckle made her skin crawl. And now with the red blood all over his face, he really did look like the creepy clown that wanted to peel off her face.

Then he charged her.

She pulled the trigger. Twice. Double-tapped center mass to stop the threat. Myles stopped, a stunned expression on his face just before he collapsed forward on top of her.

Shoot to kill.

Or be killed.

Thunderous footsteps coming down the hall had her cocking her gun again and aiming it at the door. Even with Myles's body on top of her, she could still defend herself, defend the baby. The door flung open, and the staff sergeant, gun in hand, stood there.

Without a second thought, Krista shot him in the shoulder, causing the gun to fly from his hand.

Then she leveled the barrel at his chest. "It doesn't have to end this way, sir," she said smoothly even though her entire body hurt from the weight of Myles on top of her. "Let us help you."

"I'm afraid it's too late for that," he said, regret in his voice. His free hand pressed into the gunshot to stop the bleeding. "If only the three of you didn't know so much." He stepped forward, no fear on his face. Only ... acceptance?

She had no idea if the staff sergeant had "taken care of" Wendy and Marlise yet. She only hoped that he hadn't and she could get out and save them. His eyes landed on Myles's gun on the floor by the door. He reached for it.

Only Krista was faster.

Shoot to kill.

Or be killed.

He didn't even have a chance to stand back up before his body crumpled to the ground.

Krista's ears were ringing from the gunshots, and her body raged in pain from Myles's dead weight. She wasn't sure if that was just her pulse pounding in her ears or boots thundering down the hall.

Suddenly, Myles's body was being pulled from hers, and there was Brock, his face a mix of terror and then, when she blinked at him, relief.

"Oh thank fuck," he breathed, hauling her up and pulling her into his chest. Rex and Heath appeared in the doorway as well, their eyes surveying the scene.

"Holy shit," Heath murmured. He knelt down and checked the staff sergeant's pulse. "He's still alive."

Rex checked Myles's pulse. "This one's not."

"Wendy? Marlise?" She was going into shock, but she had to know if her friends were okay.

Brock's arms around her loosened, and he held her by the shoulders. "They're okay."

Krista finally let out a full breath, the tears of relief tumbling down her cheeks as her body began to shake.

Brock pulled her back into his arms, shushing and stroking her head. "It's okay. It's over. It's all over."

Wendy and Marlise appeared in the doorway, Chase looming behind them like a grumpy mountain.

"Thank God," Wendy whispered, pushing her way into the room. Brock released Krista, and Wendy went to hug her when Krista doubled over from the sudden stab of pain to her belly, crying out as it spread around her entire midsection and into her back.

Brock's hands landed on her shoulders. "What's wrong?

Another shard of pain, this one harder and longer. She fell to her knees on the bedroom floor, and that's when she noticed the dampness between her legs and the blood staining her gray pants.

"I—I think there's something wrong with the baby."

CHAPTER TWENTY-ONE

GUTTED.

Shredded.

Broken.

That barely scratched the surface of how Brock felt sitting in the hospital room, staring at Krista as she slept. Her face, her beautiful porcelain face was all purple and bruised from that bastard Slade, and cuts above her eye were held together with butterfly bandages.

He didn't want to close his eyes, but he couldn't fight it any longer and let them drift shut.

"Where is she?"

His eyes popped open to meet confused blue orbs of perfection.

"Where is she?" she asked again.

A lump bounced thick and heavy in his throat. "She's in the NICU."

"Is she ... " She batted away a tear. "Is she going to live?"

Krista licked her lips, and Brock leapt to his feet, bringing a straw to her mouth so she could drink. Staring up at him with conviction, she chugged her water. She had more to say, but her thirst was winning the war at the moment. Goddamn, his woman was fierce.

She finished and pushed the cup away. "Brock?"

He closed his eyes for a moment and felt a hand on his. She squeezed him tightly, and he opened his eyes. She moved over in the bed and invited him to join her. The springs and gears squealed and groaned from the strain of taking on his big, tired body.

She turned on her side with a groan of her own and rested her hand on his chest. "Tell me."

"They say she's strong and a fighter. She's twenty-eight weeks; twenty-four weeks is viable, remember? She's got four extra weeks of viability. She's a fighter, just like her mama."

God, his heart hurt. The baby was so tiny. And Krista, fuck, they'd nearly lost her. She'd tried for a natural birth, labored for hours, but just couldn't, and they ended up rushing her into the OR for an emergency C-section. Then right after the baby was born, she started to hemorrhage and was losing too much blood. She was bleeding internally, and they needed to operate. The baby hadn't even been born for five minutes before Krista was being put under and Brock and the baby were being rushed down the hallway to the NICU. All the while, Brock didn't know if either of his girls were going to make it. His heart hurt from how close it'd come to shattering.

"I want to see her," Krista whispered.

He fought back a yawn before kissing the top of her head. "You need to rest."

"I *want* to see her. She's my baby. I need to see her. I need her to know that her mother is here and loves her." She looked up into his eyes pleadingly. "I need to see her. If she doesn't make it, I ... " She choked on her words. "I at least need to know what she looks like."

He nodded before prying himself up off the bed to go and retrieve the wheelchair.

"She's so small," Krista croaked moments later after they'd bullied and cajoled their way into the NICU. It was after hours, but like hell was his woman going to let them dictate when she could and couldn't see her child.

Emotion choked him. "She's a fighter," he said once again. She had to be a fighter. Her mother was the strongest, most stubborn woman Brock had ever met, and if that little girl had even half the strength and ferocity of Krista, she was going to pull through and then give them all a run for their money. Challenging them at every turn.

He couldn't wait.

Her hands were the size of a thimble, while her teeny tiny feet looked like no more than doll feet, pink and wrinkly and absolutely perfect. She had a chest tube and was intubated, as they said she was struggling to breathe on her own when she was born. A series of monitors were on her chest and head to check her heart rate and brain activity. But even preemie, she had a full head of red hair beneath the tiny pink and green toque, and her mother's tight fists of determination.

"She's perfect." Krista put her hand on the glass. They both wanted so desperately to touch her, to feel her pulse beneath their fingertips.

He crouched down beside her and laced his fingers through Krista's. They couldn't touch their child, but they could still be connected to each other.

"So, Hannah?" she asked quietly.

Brock studied the baby. She didn't look like a Hannah. Hannah was a pretty name, but it wasn't the name of a warrior, and this little girl was a warrior. She had to be. He shook his head. "No, she doesn't look like a Hannah."

She nodded and pursed her lips together.

"What about Zoe?" he suggested.

Taking her eyes off their amazing little human for just a second, she looked at him. "Zoe?"

"Yeah. I found it in that baby name book you had lying on the coffee table. What do you think?"

"What does it mean?"

"It means *Life*. Which I think is quite fitting, don't you? She's *our* life."

She blinked back tears and cupped his cheek. "Look at you being all sentimental."

He smiled and leaned into her hand. "I have my moments."

She nodded and looked back at the baby. "It's perfect. Zoe ... Zoe Elaine Joy Hart. I love it. It's perfect, just like her."

Brock took the opportunity of her distraction and dropped to one knee. "Marry me."

Her head flew back, and she gaped at him. She shook her head with utter disbelief on her tired, beautiful face. "I told you not to ask me until you were—"

He cut her off. "I know. Marry me."

"Brock, I—" But instead of waiting for her to answer, he took her hand and slid the ring onto her finger. It fit perfectly. There was always going to be a power struggle between the two of them, he just knew it.

"I love you. I think I've always loved you. From the moment you asked me if my place was stumbling distance and then proceeded to pound back tequila like a frat boy, I've loved you. And yesterday you could have died, our baby could have died, and the thought of not having you or Zoe in my life makes me want to die, too. Marry me, Krista."

She swallowed and traced the beautiful diamond solitaire with her finger. "Can we do it now? Like tomorrow?"

"Tomorrow?" There was no hiding the surprise in his voice.

She nodded. "I don't want to wait. We can do a big ceremony later on if we want, but I want to be your wife now. I want to have the same last name as Zoe, as you. We can do the legal bit with the license later when I'm out of the hospital. But in the eyes of our family, in our hearts, I want to be your wife now."

His head bobbed up and down with frantic conviction. "I'll call Chase and have him come by first thing in the morning."

Tears trickled down her cheeks. If it wasn't for the big smile he'd be worried. "Why Chase?"

Brock quirked one eyebrow as he dug out his phone. "Because among other things, he's also a marriage commissioner."

Her laughter was music to his ears. "Well, that's convenient."

CHAPTER TWENTY-TWO

THE NEXT DAY Chase showed up, along with Rex, Heath and Joy. Although Krista would have liked to have had her parents and brother there as well, she didn't want to wait any longer. They knew what had happened to her and were on their way. They would be arriving in the next couple of days. But a couple of days was too long; she wanted to be Mrs. Brock Hart immediately.

Looking at herself in the mirror after a painful shower, she burst into tears. Her cheeks were cut up from Myles's beating. She was sore from Zoe's birth, the emergency C-section and surgery. This was not how brides were supposed to look on their wedding day. Along with lacerations and scratches, she was black and blue across half her face. She hardly recognized herself, and what she did recognize she didn't like.

"Everything okay in there?" Brock asked through the closed bathroom door. She knew his whole family was waiting for her in her room, waiting to start the ceremony, but she couldn't face them. She couldn't let them see her looking like one of those women from the domestic violence cases she used to go out on.

"Just fine," she called back, wiping the tears from her cheeks, their saltiness causing her scratches to sting. "Be out in a second."

There was another knock at the door, but this time the person didn't wait for her to answer, and the knob turned. It was Joy. "Sorry, dear, you can kick me out if you like, but it ain't nothing I haven't seen before. Do you need some help getting dressed?"

Krista thought for sure Joy was going to gasp and cry or turn away when she saw her face, but she didn't. Instead she held out a big, plush, white bathrobe—where on earth did she get it? It was a hospital, not a hotel. Krista slipped her arms through it. It hugged her body like a fuzzy polar bear.

"Brock's daddy saved me from an abusive relationship," she started, tucking a strand of hair behind Krista's ear as she tightened the belt on the robe. "I remember bruises and scratches like these ones, and not fondly." Krista's eyes went wide. Joy nodded and continued. "Zane was my neighbor in an apartment building. He heard my boyfriend at the time roughing me up and came over. Kicked the crap out of him and whisked me away. We were together after that. And nine months later, Brock joined the party."

"B-Brock was a ... "

"One-night stand?" She shook her head. "No. But I'd only been with Zane for about a month before I found out I was pregnant. We got married right away, of course. Because that's what you did back then."

Krista hadn't even been paying attention as Joy was talking, but she'd pulled some concealer and blush out from somewhere and was mindlessly touching up Krista's face.

"He was the love of my life. And I'm sure that if he were still alive today, we'd be married and happy. Celebrating the birth of our first grandchild."

"H-how did you know?"

"Know what, dear?" She motioned for Krista to close her eyes and then brushed shadow across the lids.

"That he was love of your life?"

"I felt it in my very marrow. Sure, I've had lovers over the years ... "

Krista opened her eyes. Joy's wink was playful with just a hint of sass in her smile.

"Don't tell the boys. We may be open about sex in the house, but some things need to be kept private." Krista nodded and closed her eyelids again. "But Zane, he was my other half. We balanced each other out. Where I am mellow and methodical, he was hot-headed and spontaneous. We fought like crazy over the years, but we always made up."

"I'm in love with Brock." Krista swallowed, feeling that for some reason she needed to let Joy know how she felt about her son.

"I know you are. I saw it instantly when you walked through my door on Christmas Eve, and every look you gave him after that. A love like that can be hard to hide and even harder to find."

"We're both control freaks, though."

She smiled knowingly and held out a tissue for Krista to blot her lipstick. "Makes the sex interesting, doesn't it?" Krista's eyes went wide. Joy lifted one shoulder. "So your relationship is unorthodox. Most good ones are. But don't let that hold you back from love because you think it's going to be a constant power struggle. Zane and I had the same problem. He was an alpha just like his boys, and I like *things* a certain way as well."

There was another knock at the door. "Everything okay?"

"We'll be right out," Joy called, giving Krista a motherly smile. "If you're not ready, it's okay. We don't have to do this today. Just because he's my son doesn't mean I won't support you in whatever decision you make." She reached for Krista's hand and gave it a squeeze.

Krista caught a glimpse of herself in the mirror. Joy had done an incredible job. She almost looked presentable.

Krista flashed her a giant grin. "I'm ready."

She was just coming out of the bathroom, ready to marry the man of her dreams and the father of her child, when her hospital room burst open.

"We didn't miss it, did we?" Krista's mother asked frantically, her hair all askew. Dark gray bags glommed on to the normally tight skin beneath her eyes, making her look at least ten if not fifteen years older.

"Just in time." Joy smiled, walking over to Krista's parents and brother, introducing herself.

Krista gave Brock a curious look. He lifted one shoulder cavalierly. "I know you said it didn't matter, but I know it does. I know a guy who knows a guy who owns a private jet."

Before Krista could hug her fiancé, her mother lunged at her. Krista winced from the pain, and her mother immediately withdrew, a look of terror on her face. She cupped Krista's cheek gently as tears welled up in her sapphire eyes. "My baby."

Krista swallowed and leaned into her mother's touch. "I'm okay. Zoe's going to be okay."

"Shall we begin?" Chase asked, not one for small talk or delay. Of all the Harty Boys, he was the one Krista was having the hardest time figuring out. The man held secrets and demons, and he kept them hidden well, only it was clear it pained him to do so.

Krista nodded. "Dad, will you give me away?"

———

"So," Krista started, leveling her gaze on Rex, "what took you so long to come save the day?" She was officially Mrs. Brock Hart, and they were all sitting around her hospital room eating cake.

Rex snorted. "I didn't save anything. It was all you, you little badass cop."

Krista's cheeks grew warm. "Seriously, though?"

His smile was electric. In fact, all the Harty boys had incredible smiles; just Brock and Chase gave them sparingly. "I was still on your detail but had gone to grab lunch. I'm really sorry I didn't get there sooner. I didn't expect you to leave." Remorse flooded his handsome face. "I'm really sorry."

"It's okay, Rex," she said softly. "Please don't blame yourself."

He swallowed and nodded, but he didn't appear to be convinced. She'd have to have a chat with him later.

"Wicks?" she asked.

"He was taken to hospital for his injuries and will be trans- ported to prison from there," Brock said with very little emotion.

She nodded. "And there will be a trial, of course."

"Most likely," Heath agreed, cutting himself another giant piece of cake and diving in. "They're launching a full investigation into the detachment, the crime family Wicks was accepting bribes from and Slade's previous detachments."

"We'll throw the book at Wicks, honey," Krista's dad said, venom in his tone.

Krista laughed. "Thanks, Dad. I would expect nothing less from Matthews and Matthews."

"And Slade is rotting in hell," Krista's brother piped up. "So no need to drag his victims to trial."

Krista breathed a sigh of relief. Yes, there was that. Her friends wouldn't have to relive their horrible ordeals in front of a courtroom or see Myles ever again. Her mind immediately went to Allie, though. Her poor friend. Pregnant and not knowing if the father was the donor she chose or a monster.

"And you can tell your friend Allie that the baby isn't Slade's," Heath added.

Krista's head whipped around to her new brother- in-law. "What?"

"Chase hacked Slade's medical records. You know, 'cause he can. Turns out Slade is shooting blanks. He had the mumps as a teenager, and it rendered him sterile."

Krista stared at Heath for a moment and then her eyes, welling up with tears, focused on Chase. She was about to open her mouth and thank him for doing some seriously illegal shit when something new and alarming passed across his face. They locked eyes for just a moment, but then he blinked, looked away from her, and the moment was gone.

Yeah, Chase had some serious demons. Some serious secrets. She only hoped one day he'd find the right woman to help him conquer those demons. One who would sit and listen and accept all his secrets.

"Thank you, Chase," she said softly.

This time she got a nod out of him.

Taking a deep breath, she smiled at everyone around the room —her family. "All right, then, who wants to meet Zoe?"

————

"You should go home to sleep." Krista yawned, resting her head on her laced hands as she sat in the chair next to Zoe's incubator box.

"I'm not going anywhere," Brock murmured.

She glanced up at him, her beautiful face scrunched in mild impatience.

He loved her spirit.

He loved her.

"At least go lay down in my bed for a few hours. I'm going to stay and watch her for a bit."

"I'm not going anywhere," he said again. Damn woman didn't listen. "My world is here. I'm not leaving. Deal with it."

Her twinkling eyes made his heart lurch inside his chest. "Not exactly the wedding night I had envisioned," she said sheepishly. "Sorry 'bout that."

Picking her up, he plopped her into his lap. Her head fell to his chest. "We have an entire lifetime to have wedding nights. With you, with Zoe, that's where I want to be, that's all I need."

She yawned again and nuzzled into him more tightly. "I love you so much, Brock Hart. Thank you so much for our beautiful little girl, for coming into my life ... for saving me."

He waited until he heard the soft rumble of her snoring, his hand rhythmically stroking her hair, before he whispered, "I'm the one who was saved."

EPILOGUE

Two years later ...

"BY THE POWER vested in me by the province of British Columbia, I now pronounce you husband and wife. You may now kiss the bride."

Krista lunged at Brock before Chase even finished his speech. She wrapped her arms around his neck, letting her feet leave earth. Because when she was with Brock, she felt like she was floating. He kissed her in turn, ignoring the hoots and hollers from the peanut gallery.

When they finally came up for air, there was more clapping, the attention of all their loved ones making Krista's shy and quiet husband go bright red in the cheeks. But he was all smiles as he accepted Zoe from his mother's arms and the three of them made their way down the aisle, white rose petals being thrown over their heads by all the smiling guests.

"So now what?" he asked, planting a big smack of a smooch on Zoe's chubby little cheek. She giggled and then pulled on his ear.

"Whatever we want." Krista grinned. "We're the bride and groom. We can do whatever we like."

He pulled her hard against his chest, shifting Zoe to one hip while she continued to explore his ear with her tiny fingers. "Well, if I had my way, I'd send everyone home, leave Zo-Zo with the grandparents and go *consummate* this *union* of ours." The caterpillars bobbed furiously along his forehead. "In the back of the limo!"

Krista tossed her head back and let out a *whoop* of a laugh. But Brock just took that as an invitation, and his teeth found her neck.

"Zoe needs a sibling," he said with a growl, his lips traveling along her jaw.

A crowd began to gather, and the wedding planner scurried around trying to get everyone in the wedding party organized.

Krista leaned into his ear, the other ear, not the one Zoe was trying to find buried treasure in. "I'm glad you think that, because I'm pregnant."

His eyes flashed wide, and she smiled.

"Really?"

She nodded. "About six weeks or so."

He scooped her up around the waist, Zoe still perched firmly on his hip, and he spun them all around. "Well, now this really is cause for a celebration! Back to light duty, woman!"

She laughed and kissed him on the lips when he finally put her down. "Oh, Mr. Hart, every day with you is a cause for a celebration."

Zoe squirmed her way between them, and they both planted a kiss on each of her cheeks. The photographer was right in front of them and ready to catch the cutesy pic.

"Oh, Mrs. Hart," Brock murmured against Zoe's face, so only Krista could hear, "the kind of celebration I'm talking about involves just the two of us, in the bedroom, wearing nothing but handcuffs and smiles."

Krista smirked at him, the flash from the photographer's camera blinding her temporarily. "And a wooden spatula?"

They both turned to face the camera, his enormous grin visible even in her peripheral vision. "But of course."

IF YOU'VE ENJOYED THIS BOOK

If you've enjoyed this book, please consider leaving a review. It
really does make a difference.
Thank you again.
Xoxo
Whitley Cox

ALSO BY WHITLEY COX

Quick & Dirty

Book 1, A Quick Billionaires Novel

Quick & Easy

Book 2, A Quick Billionaires Novella

Quick & Reckless

Book 3, A Quick Billionaires Novel

Hot Dad

Lust Abroad

Snowed In & Set Up

UPCOMING BOOKS

Quick & Dangerous
Book 4, A Quick Billionaires Novel

Hired by the Single Dad
The Single Dads of Seattle, Book 1

Dancing with the Single Dad
The Single Dads of Seattle, Book 2

Saved by the Single Dad
The Single Dads of Seattle, Book 3

Living with the Single Dad
The Single Dads of Seattle, Book 4

Lost Hart
The Harty Boys Book 2

ACKNOWLEDGMENTS

There are so many people to thank who help along the way. Publishing a book is definitely not a solo mission, that's for sure. First and foremost, my friend and editor Chris Kridler, you lady are a blessing, a gem and an all-around amazing human being. Thank you for your honesty and hard work.

Author Jeanne St. James for doing the first alpha-read for me, your notes, brutal honesty, insight and ideas were so helpful. You really are my sister from another mister.

Thank you, Laura Malo for all your firsthand knowledge about the RCMP, it was invaluable.

Thank you, Andi Babcock for your truthful, thorough beta-read. It means so much when I find such loyal readers who want to go that extra step in helping me produce something I can be proud of.

Thank you, Justine and Krista for your beta-reads as well. I love that I can hand you the rough, unedited stuff and you'll read it and give me your feedback.

Tara at Fantasia Frog Designs, your patience with my indecisions when it comes to covers is appreciated. You never disappoint.

My Naughty Room Readers Crew, authors Jeanne, Erica and Cailin, I love being part of such a tremendous set of inspiring, talented and supportive women. Thank you for letting me learn, lean on and join the team.

My street team, Whitley Cox's Curiously Kinky Reviewers, you are all awesome and I feel so blessed to have found such wonderful fans.

The ladies in Vancouver Island Romance Authors, your support and insight have been incredibly helpful, and I'm so honored to be a part of a group of such talented writers.

And lastly, of course, the husband. You are my forever. I love you.

JOIN MY STREET TEAM

WHITLEY COX'S CURIOUSLY KINKY REVIEWERS

Hear about giveaways, games, ARC opportunities, new releases, teasers, author news, character and plot development and more!

Facebook Street Team
Join NOW!

DON'T FORGET TO SUBSCRIBE TO MY NEWSLETTER

Be the first to hear about pre-orders, new releases, giveaways, 99 cent deals, and freebies!

Click here to Subscribe
http://eepurl.com/ckh5yT

ABOUT THE AUTHOR

A Canadian West Coast baby born and raised, Whitley is married to her high school sweetheart, and together they have two beautiful daughters and a fluffy dog. She spends her days making food that gets thrown on the floor, vacuuming Cheerios out from under the couch and making sure that the dog food doesn't end up in the air conditioner. But when nap time comes, and it's not quite wine o'clock, Whitley sits down, avoids the pile of laundry on the couch, and writes.

A lover of all things decadent; wine, cheese, chocolate and spicy erotic romance, Whitley brings the humorous side of sex, the ridiculous side of relationships and the suspense of everyday life into her stories. With mommy wars, body issues, threesomes, bondage and role playing, these books have everything we need to satisfy the curious kink in all of us.

YOU CAN ALSO FIND ME HERE

Website: WhitleyCox.com
Twitter: @WhitleyCoxBooks
Instagram: @CoxWhitley
Facebook Page: https://www.facebook.com/CoxWhitley/
Blog: https://whitleycox.blogspot.ca/
Multi-Author Blog:
https://romancewritersbehavingbadly.blogspot.com
Exclusive Facebook Reader Group:
https://www.facebook.com/groups/234716323653592/
Booksprout: https://booksprout.co/author/994/whitley-cox
Bookbub: https://www.bookbub.com/authors/whitley-cox

SNEAK PEEK - LOST HART

Read on for a sneak peek of Chapter 1 from
Lost Hart
Book 2 in The Harty Boys series

CHAPTER 1 - LOST HART

Friend or foe?

Stacey Saunders peered out the window of her two-story, Edmonton townhouse. A big black SUV had pulled up two minutes ago but so far no one had gotten out. Fear ratcheted up her spine as she held her sleeping newborn baby, Thea, tight against her chest.

Ever since she'd found out that her late husband had been in bed with a crime family and owed them money, she'd been on high alert. It didn't matter that Ted was dead, he owed them money, and the Petralia family always got paid.

Had they finally come to make good on their threat? Or was this the bodyguard her husband's other wife had arranged for her?

Yes, her husband's *other* wife.

Not ex-wife. *Other* wife.

Yes, in addition to being a new mother of two, a widow and now the target of a crime family, Stacey had recently discovered that Ted had been married to two women at the same time. She was a sister-wife without her knowledge and against her will. Because never in a million years would Stacey have agreed to share a man with someone.

No wonder Ted had been gone two weeks a month. Here Stacey thought he was busy working as a safety inspector for hospitals, while lo and behold he was actually working for the Petralia crime family based out of Victoria and helping traffic drugs, launder money and God only knows what else. Then after a long day of crime, he'd go home to his first wife and lie to her face about where he'd been all day.

But thankfully, as shitty a husband as Ted turned out to be, his choice in women was above par, and Freya, wife number one, was a wonderful human being. She'd flown out just a few weeks ago to meet Stacey and Connor, and they'd hit it off immediately. Then when Stacey went into labor with Thea, Freya had flown back to Edmonton to be with Stacey for the birth as she had no one.

She shook her head and kissed the top of Thea's head, marvelling at the downy softness of her peach fuzz hair. Without Ted she wouldn't have her children. Without Ted she never would have met Freya. Without Ted she wouldn't be caught up in this mess with a crime family and waiting for either an enforcer or a bodyguard to step out of that vehicle parked on her curb.

Yeah, Ted was a treasure.

She was happy to have children. Happy to know Freya. But also happy he was gone.

"Mama?"

Stacey jumped nearly a foot in the air, jostling Thea and making the baby squawk out in protest. She spun around, releasing the drapes to find her son, Connor, staring at her with the kind of wide-eyed curiosity only toddlers could have.

"Honey, don't sneak up on me like that." She ran her hand over the back of his head and pulled him close against her thigh.

He blinked up at her with those big baby blues of his. "I'm hungry."

Stacey swallowed, followed by a nod. "Where's Daniella?"

He shrugged.

Since Thea was born Daniella, the nanny, had been a lifesaver. Stacey wasn't sure how'd she be able to handle both kids, particularly the colicky Thea, without Daniella's help. Connor hadn't been nearly as challenging, and at that time she had the on-off help of her husband. At least when he was in town he was helpful.

But two kids was a whole new ball game, and she was grateful for Daniella. The woman was also a fantastic cook, which was great considering how hungry Stacey constantly felt now that she was nursing again.

"I'm hungry," Connor said again, this time with more of a whine to his tone. Stacey shut her eyes and counted to five in her head. He was three. He was three. He was three. Three-year-olds whined. He was being normal. Normal, but irritating. And she was sleep deprived. She couldn't forget that.

Opening her eyes, she ruffled his head with her hand and smiled down at her precocious son. "All right, let's find you something to eat. Would you like a PB and J sandwich?"

He nodded.

Thank goodness he wasn't a picky eater.

She crossed her fingers his love of food would stick around and that eventually Thea would love food too. Ted had been a picky eater and Stacey was terrified the kids would be too.

No red sauce. No legumes. No pepper. No garlic. No onion. No fruit with seeds.

She shook her head and encouraged Connor to make his way downstairs.

Fucking Ted.

Now that he was gone they could eat normal food again. When he wasn't home she ate spaghetti and stir-fries, beans and fruit. A real melee of flavors and dishes. When he was home they ate meat, potatoes and broccoli in various *non*-red sauces. The only thing she couldn't eat was strawberries and that was because of a deathly allergy. And of course, that was the only fruit Ted *did* like.

Fucking Ted.

They were halfway down the stairs when the undeniable sound of a truck door slamming outside made her body stiffen.

She wanted to run back upstairs and watch the person approach. Though if it was a member of the Petralia family what could she do? Lock the doors and cross her fingers?

They made it to the bottom of the stairs and Stacey's heart was in her throat. She clutched a still snoozing Thea tighter against her as she and Connor entered the kitchen. Daniella was standing over the stove stirring a pot which appeared to have soup in it.

"I know it's the summer," she said with a smile, grabbing the salt shaker off the back of the stove and adding a pinch to the dish, "but it just seemed like a soup day. The clouds were low and gray this morning, felt like rain."

Stacey forced a smile.

"PB and J, please," Connor said, sidling up to the kitchen table.

Daniella nodded at Connor before letting her dark brown eyes drift back to Stacey. The woman was old enough to be Stacey's mother and had wisdom and patience in spades. Stacey was so thankful for her. Concerned colored Daniella's face, her lips dipping down into a pensive frown. "Everything all right, dear?"

Stacey was about to open her mouth when the door bell chimed.

Did thugs ring the bell?

She'd been waiting for a heavy fist to pound, followed by a shout to "open the door, or else."

"I'll get it!" Connor cheered, leaping up from the table and beelining it for the door.

"NO!" Stacey hollered, jostling Thea as she rushed after Connor toward the door. Thea let out another wail, squirmed and then started to cry.

Crap.

Connor's little fist was around the door latch just as Stacey got there. Her hand fell on his and she looked down at her son. Confusion stole across his features with a wrinkled nose and cocked eyebrow. Oh, how he looked like his father at that moment.

"Mama, I want to open it," Connor said, trying to bat her hand away.

Thea was now doing what Stacey called her "newborn lamb cry" and was bashing her face into Stacey's chest and collarbone in search of sustenance.

"I'll answer it," Daniella offered, wandering in, wiping her hands on her frilly white apron. She must have brought that with her, Stacey certainly didn't have anything that girly in the house.

"NO!" Stacey barked, making both Daniella and Connor jump. Thea was still screaming her head off. She passed the baby to Daniella. "I'll get it. Please go feed her. I pumped last night, there should be a bottle warming in the sink."

Eyeing her up suspiciously, Daniella accepted the furious infant and retreated to the other room.

"Go with her, honey," Stacey said to Connor.

Connor stomped his foot. "I want to get the door."

"You can have an extra episode of Paw Patrol after snack if you go see Daniella right now."

His face lit up and without another word he was off to the kitchen singing that insidious Paw Patrol theme song.

Lifting up on her tiptoes, she peered through the peephole. All she saw was a big, thick chest in a black t-shirt. "Who is it?" she called through the door.

"Miss Saunders?" came a deep, gravelly voice.

"Who are you? What do you want?"

"Name's Chase Hart, Miss, I'm here to protect you. Escort you and your family to Victoria where you'll be safe."

"Step back so I can see you in the peephole." She wasn't taking any chances. Sure thugs probably looked like average Joes most of the time, until you put brass knuckles on their fist and a sawed-off shot gun in the trunk of their car. But at one time in her life Stacey had considered herself a good judge of character.

Ted proved you wrong there.

He took a couple of steps back, but it wasn't enough. Now all she saw was a thick neck with corded muscle and broad shoulders that lead to tree truck biceps.

"Further back," she ordered.

His broad chest expanded on what she could only assume was a huff of impatience before he took another step back. She let her gaze travel up from his neck to a chiseled jaw, strong chin, slightly crooked nose and directly into blazing green eyes. They stared straight ahead at her as if he could see past the door and right into her soul. He was also bald, but he owned it. Pulled it off. If anything, it just made him seem all the tougher. He was too cool, too tough, too *sexy* for hair.

Did she just call him sexy?

Yes, yes she had.

Thick bushy eyebrow ascended slightly up his forehead and his plump lips pursed in irritation. "Seen what you need to see?"

"How do I know you are who you say you are?" she asked.

"Call Freya. She knows what I look like," he said blandly, appearing almost bored.

Quickly, Stacy grabbed her phone out of the back pocket of her shorts and dialed Freya.

"Hey!" Freya answered on the second ring.

"Hey. What does Chase look like? You know, the guy coming to help us move to Victoria."

"Big. Bald. Beefy. Green eyes."

Stacey peered back out through the peephole again. "Okay. But a Petralia thug would probably be big bald and beefy too, no?"

Freya chuckled on the other end. "Hold on." Stacey heard

murmuring in the background for a moment or two before Freya came back on. "Ask him what his baby brother's middle name is."

"Okay. What's your baby brother's middle name?" she called out through the door.

His lip twitched, but he didn't manage a smile. "Leppard."

"Leppard," she said to Freya.

"That's right. It's him. Let him in and I'll see you in a few days, okay?"

Stacey nodded, her hand on the door knob. "Fine."

"It's going to be okay, Stace. Once we have you and the kids here, we'll all be able to help you. Safety in numbers, right?"

"Right."

"I gotta go. I'm in the middle of teaching a class."

"Shit, sorry."

"Don't apologize. I told you to call me no matter what or when, and I meant it. It's going to be okay."

"Okay, bye." Stacey unclenched her jaw and massaged it with her finger. She hadn't even realized she'd been grinding her molars until a dull ache wormed its way through her neck and temples.

"Can I come in?" Chase asked again.

She unlocked the door and opened it. He was even bigger than he seemed through the peephole. Taller too. Sexier too.

His eyes softened as he slowly raked her body from tip to toe. She fought the urge to squirm under his intense scrutiny. She was only a few weeks postpartum and was certain it was going to be a lot tougher to lose the baby belly this time around. When he finally met her gaze one corner of his mouth lifted up and he took a step forward, his arm outstretched. "Miss Saunders, I'm Chase Hart of Harty Boys Security. I'm hear to keep you safe and escort you and your children to Victoria."

Stacey squinted at him before extending her hand forward. "You said that already."

His lip twitched again, but no smile. "Yes, well, now there's no door between us and I figured I should say it again."

They clasped hands and shook. His hand was huge in comparison to hers, and warm, but not sweaty. Ted had always had sweaty hands. "Why were you sitting in your SUV out in front of my building for so long?"

"I was on a call."

Oh.

His head cocked to the side and he extended his neck out as if trying to see around the corner into her home. "Can I come in please, ma'am?"

"Mama!"

Connor came barreling down the hallway toward the door, the corners of his mouth caked in peanut butter and raspberry jam. Stacey caught her wild child and hoisted him up onto her hip before taking a step back and allowing the bigger than life man with incredible green eyes to step over her threshold and into her home. Into her life.

Made in the USA
Coppell, TX
01 December 2022

87503660R00196